THE LEVELING

THE LEVELING

DAN MAYLAND

Text copyright © 2013 Dan Mayland

Published by Thomas & Mercer
P.O. Box 400818
Las Vegas, NV 89140

ISBN-13: 9781612183367
ISBN-10: 1612183360
Library of Congress Control Number: 2013903561

WITHDRAWN

For Corinne

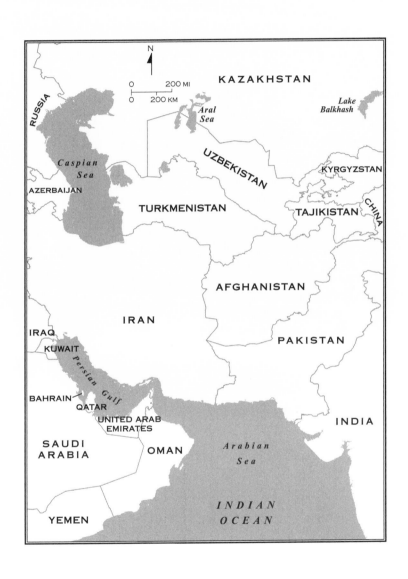

Prologue
Kish Island, Iran

———————○———————

*T*HE YOUNG WOMAN LOWERED HER BIKE TO THE GROUND AT *the edge of a grove of palm trees and looked left, then right. Seeing no one, she slipped off her shoes and ventured onto the beach. It was two in the morning. The moonless sky was clear, the stars bright. Whitecaps twinkled in the Persian Gulf.*

Near the water she sat in the sand and pulled her knees up to her chest. A black cotton chador covered her head and body and was clasped tight underneath her chin. The exposed part of her face glowed with reflected starlight.

She bit her bottom lip and looked both ways down the beach. After a minute she tapped her fingers against her knees and smiled nervously.

She removed her chador and the tightly bound headscarf underneath, revealing straight brown hair that fell to the center of her back. Her yellow T-shirt was printed with a fancy pink butterfly pattern. Her jeans had bell-bottom flares.

She folded the chador carefully, hid it in the crevice of a coral formation that had washed up on the sand, stripped off the rest of her clothes, and hid those too.

It was windy, and the water was colder than she'd anticipated. She walked out until the waves reached the tops of her thighs. An involuntary shiver ran through her, and she wrapped her strong arms around her chest. Then she counted to three and dove in.

The cold shocked her at first, but she stayed underwater for a long time. When she surfaced she was breathing quickly—because

1

of the cold but also because she was worried about skinny-dipping on a forbidden beach.

She swam out farther, past where the waves were breaking. Her feet made little splashes as they broke the water with each kick. She looked back at the faintly luminescent beach but didn't notice the two men staring at her from the dark grove of palm trees.

When the wind ebbed, she flipped over on her back and spread her arms wide. By now she was used to the water. Her neck was arched. Sea swells lifted her up and down with gentle regularity. The bright strip of the Milky Way was visible, and she spotted the Big Dipper. Directly above her, the night was as black as the water, and for a moment the two became one. As she imagined herself floating free in the void of space, a look of deep contentment appeared on her face.

PART I

1
Baku, Azerbaijan

───────○───────

H EYDAR GAMBAR FURROWED HIS OVERSIZED BROW AS HE studied his SAT practice book.

The farmer _____ the beaver dam in order to drain the pond.
> A. *constructed*
> B. *examined*
> C. *dismantled*
> D. *climbed*
> E. *revealed*

He sighed. "What is meaning of *farmer?*"

"*Fermaçı,*" replied former CIA station chief Mark Sava, translating the word to Azeri.

Mark and Heydar were seated next to each other in a reading room in the national library of Azerbaijan. The room's soothing cream-colored walls had been decorated with tasteful handwoven carpets. Natural light spilled in through a tall row of soundproof windows, each of which was framed by thick beige drapes.

Beyond the windows, daily life in the city of Baku played like a silent film. A dirty minibus belching diesel fumes and packed with people lurched by. An old man in a three-piece suit slowly painted the trunk of a sidewalk tree white. A lady in high heels and a miniskirt chatted on a cell phone while a withered Gypsy woman in bright clothes swept the street.

Heydar put his thick index finger on the book and stared blankly at the question in front of him.

"Are there any words you can rule out?" asked Mark.

The boy made a fist in frustration and stared hard at the question for a few more seconds. Then he cocked his head and flashed Mark a conspiratorial smirk. "I know the beaver." When Mark didn't respond, Heydar added, "You know the beaver?"

"It's an animal—*qunduz*." Mark had downed one cup of Turkish coffee before meeting Heydar at the library but was now wishing he'd ordered a second one to go. "It builds dams. And it's not one of the answers offered. Focus on prefixes if you don't understand the words."

They'd been working for a full half hour already and were only on question five.

"I take you to Turan, I show you the beaver."

The Turan was a dive bar in Baku known for its weak drinks, sticky floors, and remarkable prostitute-to-customer ratio. Mark hadn't been there for years.

"No thanks."

"Serious, I take you."

Mark ran a hand through his hair. "Focus on the question. Guess if you have to."

Heydar made a show of concentrating.

"What does *constructed* mean?" pressed Mark. "You should know that word. It was on last week's vocabulary list."

Heydar stuck out his chin, which was covered with thick black stubble. "When someone has built something."

"That's right." As Mark nodded with as much feigned encouragement as he could muster, he noted the sound of footsteps behind him—someone was entering the room. "And *examined*?"

Heydar's jaw muscles went slack and his mouth dropped open as he stared at the SAT book. He breathed loudly through his mouth.

"To look at closely," said Mark eventually. "Like if you look at the cover of this book for a long time, you have examined it. Understand?"

Because Heydar's father was the powerful Azeri minister of national security, the kid had a bodyguard assigned to him at all times. Out of the corner of his eye, Mark saw the bodyguard currently on duty slowly lower a natural gas industry magazine he'd been pretending to read.

"At the Turan you can examine the beaver," said Heydar.

"You're not funny. And if you don't study the vocabulary lists, I can't help you."

"I think I am funny."

"You're not."

The boy shrugged and looked up at the ceiling. "I have too much hunger."

"I don't care."

"We buy two chicken *donors*, one for me one for you. Then we study in the park."

It was eight thirty in the morning. Mark had just eaten breakfast. Besides, he'd tried the studying-in-the-park routine before; Heydar had spent far more time ogling women than he had studying.

"If you don't want to do this, fine. Personally, I don't give a shit. That's between you and your dad. We both know I'm just doing him a favor."

"They do not like your big speech, I see. This is why you have such a bad mood. This is why you think nothing is funny."

Mark cradled his head in his hands. "My speech went fine."

"OK. If you say so."

"I do say so."

But that was a lie.

Yesterday afternoon, at an academic conference in Tbilisi, Georgia, Mark had given a speech about Russian influence in Azerbaijan during the 1920s. Two of the paltry ten people in the audience, including a fellow professor from Western University—a colleague!—had nodded off. Mark had spent two weeks preparing for that presentation. He should have just passed out packets of Ambien right at the start and not bothered.

Also, he was a little hungover. The kid was right. He was in a foul mood.

Mark stood up. Heydar's bodyguard stood up as well.

"Wait. I try, I try," said Heydar.

That Mark began to think of his own death at this point was pure coincidence. It was a technique he used, whenever he got annoyed at something or someone, to put things in perspective. He reasoned that in forty years or so, maybe a lot sooner, he'd be a rotting corpse. So why let an eighteen-year-old kid get under his skin? And so what if his presentation had flopped? Would that matter when he was on his deathbed? Let it go already.

"Then tell me what *dismantled* means, or what you think it might mean. Focus on the prefix, *dis*. Come on, Heydar, you can do this."

Heydar's jaw went slack again as he looked at the word. Twice he almost began to speak, as though he hoped the answer would come to him if he just opened his mouth and let the words form on their own. Finally he said, "Screw up the University of Texas. I don't care if I go."

"Well, your father does."

Just then, three shots rang out in quick succession.

2

———o———

JOHN DECKER OPENED HIS EYES SLOWLY, FORCED INTO CON-sciousness by the excruciating throbbing in his head. Walls pressed around him on all four sides, as if he were in a coffin. Each time his heart beat, he felt as though his skull were going to split open.

He blinked a few times and brought his fingers up to his eyelids, to confirm that nothing was impeding his vision. His eyes were clear; it was simply that the darkness was absolute. He wondered whether he was dead, but the pain in his head—and his leg, what was wrong with his leg?—suggested otherwise.

He touched his massive left thigh, but instead of hard muscle, he felt something spongy and warm and wet.

You've been shot.

Decker grabbed at his chest, intending to break the rubber band that held his emergency tourniquet in place on his gear vest, worried that his femoral artery had been hit. But there was nothing. No vest. No tourniquet.

His mind flashed back to the disaster at the mansion, and he remembered that he'd already used his tourniquet, but only as a pressure dressing. Someone had removed it. He felt his leg again. It was wet, but the bleeding had stopped.

Calm down, you're not going to bleed out.

It all came back to him in a rush. A little swell of panic began to rise up in his throat. He had a sudden urge to kick out at the darkness.

Keep your shit together, buddy. Manage your emotions. Remember your training.

3
Baku, Azerbaijan

————————o————————

THE MINISTRY OF NATIONAL SECURITY OCCUPIED A MONO-
lithic limestone building on Parlament Prospekti. It was the
same building that had housed the KGB back in the Soviet era,
which Mark thought appropriate, given what he knew about the
Azeri national security ministry. He was taken to an interrogation room in the basement. To be questioned about the incident.

"But I've already been questioned. I've already told you
everything I know."

It didn't matter. He was a witness. There were forms that
needed to be filled out, procedures that needed to be followed.

"Does Orkhan Gambar know I'm here?" he asked, just as the
door was closing shut.

It was a cheerless room, with just a table, a few metal chairs,
bare concrete walls that leaned in a little bit, and a stopped clock
that hung above the door. As he sat down, he replayed the scene
from the library in his head: Heydar struggling with the SAT
practice questions, the sound of gunfire, the would-be assassin
shot through the head and crumbling into an untidy heap of
flesh, Heydar panicking, and the bodyguard blocking the door
and calling in reinforcements with ruthless, unflappable effi-
ciency.

Mark had just stood there until the Azeri security forces had
escorted him away.

He should have noticed the gunman sooner, been more
attentive to the bodyguard's reaction, sat at a table that would

have allowed him an easy exit, used a book or a chair or a pen as a weapon...

Not that it really mattered. He didn't need to be sharp anymore. Heydar's father had survived two assassination attempts within the past year. This latest spasm of violence was undoubtedly just a way to try to get at the father by coming after the son.

It didn't have anything to do with him. Security on Heydar would be redoubled. Life in Baku would go on.

Mark fished his cell phone out of his pocket and checked the time—it was a little after eleven. He was starting to get hungry.

He'd cooperate with the Azeris as best he could today, but by evening he planned to be drinking a bottle of wine on the balcony of his eighth-floor apartment, figuring out a lesson plan for the senior seminar he was teaching at Western University the next day. He'd go to sleep just after the sun went down, and by morning the memory of his lousy presentation and the incident at the library would be behind him.

Heydar's father showed up around noon, wearing a dark tailored suit and a showy gold watch that matched the gold fillings that gleamed in the back of his mouth. Although he wasn't much taller than Mark, he was much heavier and built in a powerful, bear-like way. His nose was thick, long, and hawk-like. He smelled of aftershave.

"Get out," said Orkhan to the guards who'd accompanied him.

The door clicked shut. To break the ice, Mark leaned back in his metal chair and said in Azeri, "I spent last night with a Russian."

Orkhan grunted as he considered this information for a moment. His eyes, usually dead in a KGB sort of way, showed a brief flicker of interest, as Mark had known they would.

11

Mark had been declared to the Azeris, both when he'd run the CIA's Azerbaijan station and when he'd served as an operations officer. As a result, he'd known Orkhan for the better part of a decade. Early on in their relationship, he'd learned that there were few things Orkhan liked better than hearing the Russians insulted.

"It was on the train back from Tbilisi," said Mark. "I was unlucky. He was assigned to my sleeping compartment."

"This is why you should drive."

"He was drunk."

"Of course he is drunk, you already told me he was a Russian."

"He had a bottle of vodka. Dovgan. Kept me up all night." Mark intentionally didn't mention that he and the Russian had hit it off well and talked late into the night about Russian politics, a conversation partly fueled by the many toasts the Russian had offered and Mark had accepted. To their collective health! To love! To friendship between the United States and Russia! To the men who made the train! To blow jobs! To...

Orkhan exhaled loudly through his nose. "The drink is their religion! You should have asked for a different compartment the minute you see he is a Russian. They are as bad as the Armenians. Filthy, drunk, and not to be trusted. You should know this."

"I never learn." A moment of silence passed as Mark waited for Orkhan to begin questioning him about the shooting. Finally Mark said, "Heydar's bodyguard was quick."

"Of course." Orkhan sat down, plumping onto a metal seat and letting out a huff as he did so. "He is one of my men."

"Heydar is OK?"

"Ah yes, Heydar." Orkhan spoke with a tinge of weariness. "The problem with Heydar is that he is lazy, like his mother. It's his genes."

"English is a hard language to learn. And the SAT is a hard test."

Eight months ago, when the CIA station in Baku was under siege, Orkhan had done Mark a favor. To repay this favor, Mark was trying to help Heydar get into the University of Texas so that Heydar could become a petroleum engineer and help run Azerbaijan's oil industry. The SAT, however, was proving to be a nearly insurmountable obstacle for the boy.

"I am not speaking of the SAT. I am speaking of his performance after the shooting."

After first running away in a panic, Heydar had returned with false bravado and piss-stained pants to try to belatedly kick at the corpse. His bodyguard had held him back.

"Don't be too hard on him," said Mark. "He's still young."

"It is not his age, of course. Did you act this way at his age?"

"I don't know."

As if Mark hadn't spoken, Orkhan said, "Did I act this way at his age? Of course not. It is the person, not the age."

"He'll learn from it. He's a good kid."

Orkhan waved his hand dismissively, paused, then said, "There was no identification on the body of the assassin."

"Tattoos? Any items we can trace?"

"Possibly. But..." Orkhan shifted in his seat. "But we must first speak of other matters."

Mark waited for Orkhan to elaborate, but instead Orkhan just sat there looking as if he'd detected an embarrassing smell. "What other matters?" asked Mark.

"Heydar's bodyguard has informed me that the assassin was aiming at you, not Heydar."

Mark took a moment to let that bit of information sink in.

"Of course you realized this," said Orkhan.

Mark hadn't.

"And you were wise not to try to run," said Orkhan. "Heydar's bodyguard had a clear shot, and you did nothing to interfere with that. Allowing professionals to do their job is often the best course of action in cases such as this. Few can resist the temptation to panic, however. You have my respect."

It was interesting, Mark thought, how a person could live off their résumé long after whatever skills they might have once possessed had atrophied. "The shooter probably thought I was the one guarding Heydar. And wanted to take me out first."

"You do not look like a bodyguard."

Mark couldn't argue with that. His height was average, as was his build. Good qualities for a spy, not for a bodyguard.

Orkhan added, "I must also tell you that the only thing the assassin was carrying, besides his gun, was a photo of you. You will not take offense, I hope, when I tell you that I was relieved. Evidently Heydar was not the target. You were."

4

Kazakhstan, a Slum Outside Almaty

———————o———————

FORMER CIA OPERATIONS OFFICER DARIA BUCKINGHAM strode quickly past a ramshackle street stand packed with cheap liter bottles of soda and rotgut vodka, past a stinking heap of trash—old coffee grounds and dirty diapers and apple cores and greasy auto parts—and past a cluster of small children playing in the dirt road. But she didn't notice any of it; all she could think of was money.

How much would she need? The number kept growing. Whatever it was, she'd find a way to get it. She'd made a lot of mistakes in her life, but she wasn't going to screw this up.

She turned down an alley framed by mud-brick walls and stepped over a wet trench that reeked of sewage. Though she was only a few kilometers from the modern, tree-lined center of Almaty, she was deep in the slums, in another world entirely.

At a metal door, where kids' plastic riding toys had been piled up in two unruly heaps on either side, she knocked.

An old man wearing a blue flannel shirt and traditional brown *tubeteika* skullcap answered.

"I'm here to see the director," she said in Kazakh, a language she could get by in because of her fluency with Azeri, which, like Kazakh, was a Turkic language.

Daria saw the old man fixate for a moment on her face. She wondered whether he could see the scars.

"He's expecting me," she added.

The old man stepped back, gesturing that she should follow. He led her to a small foyer. The concrete floor was pitted and stained. An open door led to a much larger room, which looked equally dreary. In the distance Daria heard a child crying and a woman's voice rising in anger. The blue plaster walls were cracked and soiled from the waist down with grime from the hands of young children. She thought of all the little hands, and then forced herself not to. Sympathy wouldn't help them, or her.

"Wait here." The old man gestured to a rickety wood school chair. "I will bring tea."

Forget the tea, just bring me to the director, Daria wanted to say, but she held her tongue and took a seat.

Patience was needed in these situations, she knew. The director would be suspicious of her intentions. It would take time. She would need to sit and listen for hours for even a modicum of trust to be established.

Her cell phone vibrated, interrupting her thoughts. A new e-mail had just come in. She glanced at the time stamp; the message had actually been sent eleven hours earlier, but with the lousy cell reception it had only just come through.

She didn't recognize the sender's address, so she clicked off her phone. Whatever it was, it could wait.

5
Baku, Azerbaijan

———————o———————

S INCE QUITTING THE CIA AND TAKING A TEACHING POSI-
tion at Western University, he'd done a pretty good job of
shutting out the chaos and confusion of the world around him—
the bitter political fights, the brutal all-consuming intelligence
wars, the rank corruption...he'd put all that behind him. He'd
beaten that cancer.

But now it was back.

After a while, he asked, "May I see the photo?"

"No," said Orkhan. "It is with our forensic department."

"Was it a recent one?"

"No. You are younger. Not so much gray."

"File photo or—"

"You are walking on the street, I think. Not looking at the
camera. I would guess the photo was taken by an opposition
intelligence agency."

"The paper?"

"Printed off a computer printer, low quality. It tells us nothing."

"How would an assassin have even known that I was going
to be at the library this morning? I didn't tell anyone I was going
to be there."

"I don't know. But it doesn't matter. Nor will it matter if
we find out who tried to kill you and why—whether it was the
Iranians or the Chinese or the Russians or some person you
fought with years ago, the result is the same."

Mark waited for Orkhan to explain, but Orkhan just stared at him, so Mark asked, "What result?"

With some discomfort, Orkhan said, "Clearly you have become a source of disturbance."

"I was shot at. I would say whoever shot at me was the source of the disturbance."

Mark recalled that the would-be assassin had been a man of about thirty, with short-cropped black hair, dark skin, and a mix of Caucasian and Asian features. The pistol the bodyguard had kicked out of the assassin's lifeless hand was a Russian-made Makarov, but that told Mark nothing—Makarovs were a dime a dozen in the region.

Who would want him dead? He was out of the intelligence game.

"The incident at the library will be widely reported on. It makes it seem as if Azerbaijan is out of control."

"So do what you always do—pull the report from the news."

"Yes, of course we will do this."

"So?"

"So we will do this, but Aliyev will still be unhappy."

"I'll try not to let it happen again."

Ignoring Mark's sarcasm, Orkhan said, "My friend…"

Mark always got worried when Orkhan started addressing him as *my friend*. After all the years he'd collaborated with Orkhan—on oil deals, on ways to curtail Russian and Iranian influence in the region, on creative ways for the Americans to arm the Azeris—he'd come to realize that *my friend* usually meant something unpleasant was coming.

"My friend," repeated Orkhan, "I'm saying you need to leave."

"Leave where? Baku?"

"No. Azerbaijan."

"For how long?" Mark figured he could lay low and do some book research in Russia for a few months. Western University wouldn't like him taking off on such short notice—he had classes to teach, one tomorrow in fact—but there was a dearth of English-speaking professors in Baku, and he knew they'd take him back whenever they could get him.

Orkhan got up and began to pace. Without making eye contact with Mark, he said, "Permanently."

"I have a valid work permit. It's good for another six months. And the Agency likes having me here as backup. You can't just toss me out."

"Your work permit has been revoked."

"By whom?"

"The minister of labor."

Mark leaned back in his chair and stared briefly at the ceiling. "You've got to be kidding me."

For eleven years Baku had been his home. *Eleven years.* As a young man, he'd bounced around the Caucasus and Central Asia as a part of the CIA's Special Activities Division. But then he'd been posted to Baku, and the place had quickly grown on him. The Agency had let him stay.

His whole life—everything he had—was in Baku.

Besides, this wasn't exactly the first time he'd been associated with violence in Azerbaijan. And he hadn't gotten kicked out of the country in those previous cases. Instead, he'd worked with the Azeris to resolve the problem.

He pointed that out to Orkhan.

"Yes, but back then you were working for your government. There would have been diplomatic consequences if we had expelled you."

"There may be consequences now as well."

"I don't think so."

"I still have ties to the Agency."

"They will not be enough."

"What kind of time frame are we talking about here?"

"Immediately."

"As in I'm notified immediately, but have a reasonable period of time to get my things together?"

"In a few minutes you will be escorted back to your apartment to gather what you can carry, and then you will be escorted to the airport. Once the paperwork goes through, probably by later today, you will officially be a persona non grata."

"Jesus, Orkhan. You couldn't give me a couple days? To fucking pack?"

"I could not. Your furniture and other belongings will be packed for you."

"That's over the top and you know it."

"This was my decision, but if I hadn't made it, it would have been made for me. You understand?"

Mark was an intensely private person. He didn't like the thought of Orkhan's goons rummaging through his things.

"I'll need to know where you want me to send your belongings. As a courtesy from my country to yours, we will pay to have them shipped wherever you like."

"I can't believe this."

"Perhaps you have a relative, back in the United States?" asked Orkhan.

Mark's mother was dead, and his father wasn't an option because the guy was a prick. His one living grandmother had been battling senility for years in a cheerless nursing home in Elizabeth, New Jersey.

He thought briefly of his older sister and two younger brothers. Any one of them would probably be too polite to decline a request, but the conversation would be awkward. The last time he'd talked with any of his siblings was fifteen years ago.

Baku was his home, his family.

"Or a friend?" pressed Orkhan.

Mark had plenty of colleagues from Western University with whom he was friendly. But they weren't friends, in the true sense of the word. He was kind of on friendly terms with this young guy named John Decker, a private security contractor, and an old guy named Larry Bowlan, his first boss at the CIA, but not on such friendly terms that he felt like asking either of them to store his stuff. He briefly considered Daria Buckingham, a former lover. As far as he knew, she was still back in the States.

"Or I could store your things here for now," said Orkhan. "And when you are settled in your new home, you can call me and I can send them to you."

No, he *couldn't* call Daria.

It occurred to Mark that it was a poor reflection on his social skills for it to have come to the point where the only person he could turn to in a time of desperate need was the corrupt minister of national security from an oil-rich kleptocracy—the same person, in fact, who was throwing him out on his ass.

"I would appreciate that."

6

J OHN DECKER WOKE UP IN DARKNESS AGAIN.
He was in motion. That realization, coupled with the sound of an engine and the high-pitched squeaking of rear shocks pounding up and down right underneath his head, led him to conclude he was locked inside the trunk of a car.

In front of him, he detected the muffled voices of several men.

Every time the car went over a large bump or pothole, the shocks bottomed out and sent a punch-like jolt through his body.

Assess your wounds.

He felt his fingers, then his forearms, then his shoulders. After working his way over his entire body, he concluded that he had a massive bruise on the top of his head—and probably a concussion, given the throbbing pain and the fact that he felt like puking. His arm had small puncture wounds in it from a dog bite, and he'd been shot twice in his left leg—once up in his thigh and again just behind his shinbone.

The bullet to his thigh had entered about six inches above his knee. Because of the placement of the exit and entry wounds, and the fact that he was alive and could still move his leg, he knew it hadn't struck bone. The bullet to his shin had grazed the bone but hadn't shattered it. He didn't remember taking that hit. Someone must have tagged him just as he was jumping off the roof of the mansion. That would explain why he'd screwed up the landing.

He also determined that he must have been knocked out for quite a while, because both wounds had stopped bleeding on their own. His thigh muscle had tightened up into a rock-hard knot that ached like hell.

The pounding in his head made it hard to think. His training told him that he should be trying to notice details, trying to figure out where he was being taken.

You're going up. The road is bumpy. Lots of turns.

He remembered the e-mail he'd sent to Mark and Daria. He'd only managed to attach three photos to it. There hadn't been time for more.

Decker briefly thought of Daria with a sense of longing, then stopped himself.

He thought again of the e-mail he'd sent. If he'd been on the receiving end of it, he'd have sent it right to the trash with the rest of his spam. After all, he'd sent it from an address neither Mark nor Daria would recognize. But Mark had been one of the CIA's best spies and Daria was no slouch either. They were trained to notice things that most people didn't.

But even if they looked at the photos, what then?

Mark will use people, like he once used you. He knows how to leverage his power. God knows, he can be a mean son of a bitch when he needs to be.

Decker closed his eyes.

But even if Mark makes sense of the photos, you'll still be screwed.

Decker had sent Mark and Daria those photos so that the evidence he'd collected wouldn't be lost forever. Not to save his own ass. He'd gotten himself into this mess, and it was up to him to get himself out. He had no overwatch looking out for him, no tracker telling backup where he was.

The car was climbing a moderate incline, straining the engine.

Decker thought back to Hell Week at Coronado, when he'd trained to be a SEAL. He'd punished his body beyond what he thought was possible, swimming for hours in freezing salt water, staying awake for the better part of five days…He'd cracked four ribs falling off an obstacle course, but he'd kept going because the only thing worse than soldiering on was the thought of quitting. One hundred and three guys in kick-ass shape had started off in his BUDS class that week, but only twenty-two had made it to the end. And of those twenty-two, only fifteen had made it through the rest of the training to become full-fledged SEALs.

Even after getting tossed from the teams—he'd disobeyed a direct order, a bullshit order that he was pretty sure had been issued because he'd screwed his squad leader's wife without knowing who she was—he'd always been proud that he'd been part of that group of fifteen, had worn it like a badge of honor.

His thoughts turned back to the present, and what would happen next. His captors would question him, which was probably the only reason he was still alive.

Probe for weakness. Remember your training.

Code of Conduct. Article III. If I am captured, I will continue to resist by all means available. I will make every effort to escape…

Decker ran his hands inch by inch over the entire interior of the trunk, searching for, but not finding, a cable that might release the lock. He did, however, locate the back sides of the rear seats. On one of them, he felt the imprint of a body. The springs on that seat squeaked whenever the car went over a bump. That squeak, combined with the loud banging of the rear shocks, wasn't doing anything to help his splitting headache.

Be patient. But don't wait for the perfect moment to make your move because the perfect moment may never come.

Decker adjusted his six-foot-four frame so that one shoulder was lightly touching the back side of the occupied rear seat and his feet were planted on the opposite wall of the trunk. The pain in his wounded thigh was searing. His neck was crimped and he wished he were a foot shorter.

His first explosive push blasted the seat forward a foot. On his second push, Decker threw the rear passenger halfway into the front seat.

The car swerved, and the driver and everyone else in the car started shouting at each other. Decker kept ramming forward until he'd flattened the rear seat. Then he pistoned his shoulder into the small of a skinny man's back. The car skidded to a stop. Decker lunged for the skinny man's neck and twisted until he heard a crack.

It was bright outside, possibly early morning. Through the windshield Decker caught a glimpse of craggy, barren hills and a roadside bakery where flatbread was stacked high in baskets out front.

A big man in the front passenger seat rolled out of the car. The driver was in a panic, trying to unlock the safety on his gun. Decker pulled himself completely out of the trunk and into the backseat of the car, then lunged for the throat of the man with the gun.

Someone grabbed his legs from the back of the trunk just as a bearded guy yanked open the car's rear doors and started smashing Decker's face with the butt of an AK-47. Decker felt a second set of hands on his legs—this time, right on his bullet wound.

A young guy in a white shirt ran out of the bakery and into the road, yelling something that Decker couldn't understand. The guy with the AK-47 fired a few shots in the air and the man in the white shirt stopped short.

Decker was dragged out of the car. Once on the ground, four men who'd evidently been traveling close behind in a backup car began to kick him. He grabbed hold of the leg of the tallest of his assailants, threaded an arm around the man's knee, twisted until he heard a snap, used his thumb to gouge the man's eye as he fell, and then crushed the man's esophagus with a fist to the throat. Someone kicked road gravel into Decker's face, temporarily blinding him, but he grabbed another assailant's leg and threw a fist up into the guy's balls.

Decker heard one of his own ribs snap and felt a kick to his head. The last thing he heard before experiencing the strange sensation that his head was being knocked off his neck was a swish of something—a rifle butt?—traveling fast through the air.

7

Almaty, Kazakhstan

———o———

D ARIA BUCKINGHAM SAT DOWN ON A BENCH IN A LITTLE park near her apartment, took a sip of the coffee she'd just bought, and closed her eyes. It was only two in the afternoon, but she was tired. In just over three hours, she needed to show up for her third day at her new job—concierge at the plush InterContinental Hotel in downtown Almaty. These side trips outside the city were taking their toll on her. Physically and emotionally.

She tried to block the image of the slum from her mind and allowed herself to rest for a moment, enjoying the feel of the spring sun on her face. The oak trees in the park had just leafed out. In the distance, the rugged mountains of the Tian Shan poked through the white clouds that hugged their steep sides. A flower vendor sat nearby, beneath a rainbow-colored sun umbrella, and little kids swung back and forth on an orange-and-green-painted swing set.

Almaty was a beautiful city, she thought, telling herself she should notice that beauty more often than she did. In the years since the fall of the Soviet Union, it had gone from a dismal backwater dump to a wealthy center of commerce.

On a bench adjacent to her own, an old woman with dirty swollen fingers was tossing bread crumbs to pigeons. She wore old army boots, some soldier's castoffs that she'd laced up with rough twine.

That made Daria think of the slums again.

The meeting with the director had gone well. She hadn't made any promises, but she had seen the hope in his eyes when she'd asked what—if money *was* available—would be most useful to him. Even with the trace of scarring on her face, she knew she looked like someone who had lived a privileged life, someone who might actually be able to deliver such funds. Her teeth were white and straight. She dressed well, and she knew how to carry herself like a rich foreigner when she found it advantageous to be perceived that way.

Daria thought about the meeting for a moment longer, jotted down a few notes to herself on her phone, and then checked her e-mail.

The new message had a blank subject line.

She didn't recognize the sender's address—Alty8@online. tm—and was about to delete it, thinking it was spam. But the .tm domain indicated that the e-mail had come from a server in Turkmenistan, which struck her as odd.

Turkmenistan was one of the most insular and technologically backward countries in the world. All Internet traffic was closely monitored, so the country generated far less spam than some of the other former Soviet republics in Central Asia. Daria knew the country fairly well. Until just three weeks ago, she'd been working there.

The e-mail came with three attachments.

Another reason not to open it, thought Daria. An e-mail from an unknown sender, from a backwater country, with attachments that were probably viruses.

On the other hand, most viruses out there weren't designed to hit smartphones. And she did know someone who was probably in Turkmenistan right now. This wasn't his e-mail address, but...

Daria opened the e-mail. There was nothing in the text box. Which left the attachments, all JPEG photo files.

She looked around to see if anyone was behind her, anticipating that porn ads would pop up when she clicked on them.

The first photo was of two men—one tall with Asian features, the other olive skinned and wearing a black turban—exchanging a briefcase; the second was of a three-story brick mansion with a tile roof, high balconies, and a large portico; and the third was a strange blurry nighttime photo that Daria had trouble deciphering at first.

She stared at the last photo for a long time, trying to make sense of it.

The center was dominated by a vertical swath of white. But it was the blurry form on the edge of the photo that really captured her attention. A hand and muscular arm were held high in the air. A single finger extended up from the hand. Affixed to the wrist was a bulky black watch trimmed in blue.

She enlarged the photo, focusing on the watch. The lousy quality of the photo made it impossible for Daria to be sure, but she could have sworn the watch was a Timex Ironman. And that the same arm, wearing that same watch, had been around her shoulders just a few weeks ago.

Decker, she thought.

Daria stared at her phone. The faceplate of the watch glowed green, as if the nightlight button had just been pushed—maybe with the hope that the day and time would be visible? It wasn't.

John Decker was a former Navy SEAL, a freak of nature when it came to physical ability—one of those guys who Daria was sure, by the age of ten, had been able to run faster, climb higher, and lift more weight than 90 percent of guys twice his age—and an unlikely friend. Until two weeks ago, she and Deck had been working for the same private intelligence contractor in Turkmenistan. Decker had gotten her the job, pulling her away from a lousy situation back in the States. She'd been grateful that he'd thought of her.

You're weirding me out, Deck.

Daria hit Reply and sent Alty8@online.tm a message: *wtf?*

She tried calling Decker's cell phone. No one answered. When she tried to leave a message, an automated voice told her

Decker's voice mail account was full. Which was also odd, she thought. You'd have to have an awful lot of unopened or saved voice mail messages to fill up an account.

Or maybe someone had just butt dialed Decker and left an hour-long message by mistake. That could fill up a mailbox. Or maybe Decker had just butt dialed himself. *That* she could see happening.

She sent him a text message—*Hey John, what can you tell me about 3 photos from Alty8?*

Then she called the Hotel President in Ashgabat, Turkmenistan, where, last she knew, Decker had been staying.

No one named John Decker was currently a guest, the receptionist told her.

"He'd be registered under CAIN, or Central Asian Information Networks. A group of us had a block of rooms."

"Everyone from CAIN checked out three days ago."

As Daria considered that bit of information, she thought to click on Details at the top of the e-mail from Alty8. It turned out that Alty8 had CC'd one other person: Mark.Sava@wu.edu.az.

She drew in a quick breath.

What the hell is going on, Deck? And what could *Mark* possibly have to do with it?

---○---

Mark's apartment in Baku, eight months earlier...

"I didn't know you were up," said Mark.

It was seven in the morning. Daria had heard him making coffee in the kitchen but hadn't wanted to ask for his help.

She was slumped on the hardwood floor in the spare bedroom—a room that had been his office until two weeks ago—trying to tie a plastic garbage bag around the fiberglass cast on her broken arm. Her teeth marks were all over the ripped black plastic. Mark stood in the doorway, his brow furrowed with concern.

The intelligence war that had decimated the CIA's Baku station was over. That bloody conflict, fought over a proposed oil pipeline from China to Iran, had left her deeply wounded, physically and emotionally. The only reason she was still alive was because of Mark. But she couldn't stay in his apartment forever. She had to learn to care for herself.

"I want to take a shower."

Daria tried to speak calmly, but found it impossible to mask her anger. She was breathing heavily and trembling, partly from frustration, partly from the exertion of having attempted to tie the plastic bag around her arm with only one hand and her teeth. She wanted to rip the bag apart and throw it out the window.

"OK," said Mark.

"I'm not supposed to get the cast wet. I need help tying the bag around my arm. Please."

She glanced at her bicep, where the cast ended, and was struck by how waiflike it looked. She knew the bruises and cuts on her face still looked angry and raw. She turned her face away from Mark.

"I didn't know you were up," he said again. "I would have helped you."

Daria was embarrassed by the sweat on her forehead. Mark noticed the smallest details when it came to other people; he was always sizing people up. The sweat would tell him how hard she'd been trying to tie the bag herself, how utterly dependent she was on him for even the smallest things.

"Just get it around my arm, above the cast."

"Yeah, sure."

As he approached her, she looked at the crow's-feet around his deep-set, heavy-lidded eyes. Feeling his fingers on her arm filled her with a sense of well-being, and for a second it didn't bother her that he could see the sheen of sweat on her forehead. He cinched a knot tight above her bicep. She stood up.

"You want help getting to the shower?" he asked.

"I'll be OK."

But she wasn't OK.

She could feel his eyes on her as she made her way from the bedroom to the bathroom. He was sizing her up, she was sure. He was so damn calculating.

Part of her hated him for what he saw. But part of her wanted him to touch her again. To put his hand lightly on her forehead or her shoulders.

She managed to turn on the water and adjust the heat, but a minute into her shower—as she was trying to shampoo her hair— her legs gave way and she fell.

"Daria?" called Mark from the bathroom door.

The deep bruises in her thigh muscles were spasming. Water from the shower sprayed into her nose. She felt as though she were drowning. She wasn't sure she could pick herself up without falling again.

The bathroom door opened and a little stream of cool air blew over her face.

"Daria?"

"I slipped."

Her good arm grasped the lip of the bathtub, poking out a bit from behind the dark blue shower curtain.

"Can you stand?"

"I think so."

She tried to push herself up, but her legs spasmed again.

Mark reached around the curtain, grabbed her wet arm, and lifted her up. Her hand trembled as she struggled to stay upright.

"I'll stay here," said Mark from the other side of the curtain.

You've wasted over thirty years of your life. Promise yourself that, if you live through this, you won't waste any more.

I promise.

"Just hold on when you need to," Mark added.

"I'll be OK." But she continued to grip his arm tightly, afraid she would fall again if she let go.

She wished she could see Mark's face.

8
Baku, Azerbaijan

———————o———————

"THE AZERIS ARE TRYING TO GIVE ME THE BOOT."
Mark spoke into his cell phone as two plainclothes agents from the Ministry of National Security—protection, to ensure Mark's safety, Orkhan had explained diplomatically—escorted him across town in a black Mercedes. Mark was seated in the back.

"I know," said the new CIA chief of station/Azerbaijan, a woman who'd been transferred from Turkey six months ago. "I've been in touch with the Az interior minister. Where are you?"

"Almost at my apartment." The tree-lined promenade between Neftchilar Avenue and the Caspian Sea was crowded with pedestrians, and a knot of people had gathered at the base of a nearby carnival ride. In the distance, rusted shipping cranes and oil derricks poked out of the shallow waters of the sea. After the violence at the library, Mark found the normalcy of the city—even the stink of diesel exhaust and petroleum—to be comforting. There had to be a way for him to resolve this in a way that allowed him to remain in Baku, he thought. There was always a workaround, always an angle. "Listen, I want to stay on."

The CIA hadn't been thrilled about his staying in Baku after he'd quit the Agency. Such an unorthodox move had only confirmed his superiors' fears that he'd been abroad too long and had gone a little too native. But in exchange for being given the green light to stay on in Baku, he'd agreed to provide the Agency with a monthly report on the state of Azeri politics. And then eight months ago, he'd bailed the Agency out when a bloody intelligence war over an oil pipeline had erupted.

So they owed him. Just how much he was about to find out.

"Not a chance."

"Get me six months to wrap things up on my own terms. I'll make it worth the Agency's while."

"It's not my decision."

One of Mark's minders from the Ministry of National Security glanced back at him from the front seat.

"Besides," added the new station chief, "Kaufman wants you back for a full debriefing."

Ted Kaufman was the division chief for the CIA's Central Eurasia Division. Mark had reported to him for years.

"Kaufman can screw himself. He owes me."

"I wouldn't get on the bad side of the seventh floor if I were you," she said, referring to the upper management of the CIA. "They're your reference for the twenty-five years of work you put in."

"Twenty-three years."

Mark had been twenty-one years old when the Agency recruited him.

"Whatever."

"No, not whatever. I helped build this station. And I bailed Kaufman's ass out eight months ago. I'm calling in my chits."

"Listen, even if Washington was inclined to let you stay on, which they're not, I don't think we'd get far with the Azeris anyway. You've got too much history with them, not all of it good."

"Not all of it bad, either. Orkhan and I are tight."

"The interior minister was adamant, and he was speaking for Aliyev."

Aliyev was the guy who ran the country.

"Great."

"Go back to the States, get debriefed, let the dust settle. Meanwhile the station will start digging. After what happened at the library, we're all on alert, I can guarantee you that. You're still one of our own."

9
Almaty, Kazakhstan

———○———

D ARIA CONSIDERED THE THREE PHOTOS AGAIN. EVEN AFTER she'd studied them for the better part of a half hour, the first two meant nothing to her. Nor did the e-mail address of the sender—Alty8@online.tm. She couldn't remember having met anyone named Alty when she'd been in Turkmenistan.

The only thing she was reasonably sure of was that the third photo showed Decker's arm.

Which meant what?

Had someone captured him, and the photo of the arm was there to prove it? Would demands for cash follow?

Or had Decker himself sent the e-mails to her?

Was he in trouble?

One person who might be able to answer those questions was Bruce Holtz, Decker's boss. Holtz owned Central Asian Information Networks—CAIN for short—a spies-for-hire firm. Although Daria had worked for Holtz too, she and Holtz hadn't left on good terms. On top of that, she was now competing against him in the intelligence business. No, Holtz wouldn't tell her anything.

But he might talk to Mark.

Mark. Her stomach turned over.

She checked her watch. She should start getting ready for work soon. If she was going to call him, she should do it now. But was she overreacting? Just looking for an excuse to call? Or was she looking for an excuse *not* to call him, when it was obvious she should?

She thought about the first of the three photos. Two men had been exchanging a briefcase. A briefcase full of what?

Daria had a bad feeling about that briefcase.

Call him.

She checked her phone, confirmed that Mark's contact info was still in it, and hit Dial. His cell number was no longer good—which didn't surprise her. When he'd been her boss at the CIA, he'd been religious about regularly swapping the SIM card out in his phone; he'd rarely kept the same number for more than a few days. Old habits die hard, she thought. She tried his home phone. The answering machine picked up.

"Mark, this is Daria. Call me back, please, as soon as you get this message. I need you to call Bruce Holtz for me. I'm hoping he knows where I can find John Decker. Something weird's come up. I wouldn't bother you if I didn't think it might be important." Then she left her number.

She'd sounded professional, she thought. Nothing more.

10
Baku, Azerbaijan

———○———

M ARK TOOK ONE STEP INTO HIS APARTMENT AND STOPPED short.

The bookshelves in the living room had been torn apart, and the hand-knotted Azeri carpets he'd hung on the wall had been ripped down. The kitchen cabinets had been pulled open, and glass jars of red pasta sauce lay shattered on the tile floor. All the furniture cushions had been slit; white stuffing protruded from them like entrails.

In the center of his living room, three twentysomething uniformed officers from the Ministry of National Security sat on his mutilated leather couch, smoking cigarettes and using one of his kitchen plates as an ashtray. One of them stopped mid-laugh when he saw Mark and his escorts.

"What the hell?" said Mark.

The security officers stood as one. The tallest demanded to know who Mark was.

Mark stood there in shock for a moment, taking it all in. His easy chair, where he liked to read in the early evening, when natural light spilled in from the balcony, had been flattened. The tomato plants he'd kept outside had been overturned. The little American flag he'd stuck in one of the planters lay on the floor half-covered with potting soil. "I live here."

One of his plainclothes minders from the Ministry of National Security nodded in confirmation.

Mark's apartment building was a gleaming modern construction, completed just two years ago as part of the oil-fueled gentrification that was sweeping the city, but he'd always loved the literal window into history his balcony had afforded him—the end of the Cold War, the ruins of an empire he'd helped, in a very small way, to bring down…Past the sliding glass doors leading onto his balcony, he could see the top of the old Dom Soviet, a government building that had been built during the Stalin era. Next to the Dom Soviet sat the Absheron, an enormous, bulky Soviet-era hotel that had recently been turned into a high-priced Marriott.

"It was like this when we got here," said one of the officers. He placed his cigarette on Mark's plate and stood up. "Now we just wait for instructions. The movers are outside. You can gather the things you wish to take with you."

"You and your men didn't do this?"

"Of course not."

Mark wasn't sure whether to believe him or not.

He walked slowly through his kitchen, stepping over the remnants of a takeout Chinese dinner from the week before. In a way, he thought, it didn't matter that his place was trashed. What would he have done with his stuff anyway? All it meant was that Orkhan would have less to store.

One question that had been eating away at him—how an assassin had known to find him at the library—was answered by the wall calendar hanging in his kitchen. On today's date, he'd written *8:30, Heydar, library reading room.* He'd bought the calendar after taking the job at Western University, to keep track of his classes. Stupid, he told himself. There were some habits he'd developed while working for the Agency—like an obsession with never keeping a set schedule, and certainly never posting his appointments where people could read them—that, evidently, he should have held on to.

In his bedroom, his dresser drawers had been ripped all the way out, his clothes scattered around the floor, and his mattress slashed. More importantly, his laptop was gone.

He looked around, then back at his desk again, then under it, and then in the closet.

The book-length manuscript he'd been working on, *Soviet Intelligence Operations in the Azerbaijan Democratic Republic, 1918-1922*, had been saved on that computer. Nearly two years of intense research, two hundred thousand words of text. He was only a few months away from finishing it. It was going to be the book that established his academic credentials, his gateway to landing a university job in the States or Europe.

He'd backed it up, though. In several places, just in case.

He wasn't an idiot; he'd be OK.

Mark rifled through the jumble of papers and pens and scholarly books that were still on his desk. Where was the damn thumb drive? It was neon yellow, and he'd left it to the right of the computer, next to the coffee mug he'd been using as a penholder.

But it wasn't there now.

"You motherfuckers," he muttered.

It's probably somewhere on the floor, he told himself. Besides, he had a third backup, one that he'd made on a CD a couple of months ago. He'd lose a lot of work, but losing two months was better than losing two years. He'd stored the CD in his bedroom closet, in an old shoebox.

The shoebox was upended on the floor of his closet. Scattered around it were old computer cords, spare rolls of Scotch tape, extra pens, envelopes, and Post-it notes—but no CD.

Beginning to panic now, Mark dropped to the floor and searched through everything in the room. The security guards eventually took pity on him, asked what he was looking for, and joined in the hunt. Together they scoured every inch of the apartment.

Eventually Mark's minders said it was time to leave for the airport. Then the phone rang.

11
Washington, DC

———o———

THE CONFERENCE ROOM ON THE GROUND FLOOR OF THE West Wing had an unnatural smell to it, the result of the ozone from constantly running air filters.

"This meeting is called to order," said the president. "We're here to discuss how to respond to recent intelligence reports coming out of Iran. I'll cede the floor to Jim."

A bald former four-star admiral, currently the director of national intelligence, produced a sheaf of papers from his briefcase and began to pass them out. "The president's daily brief. The president has already reviewed it and approved its distribution to the Security Council. It provides a summary of all that we know to date."

The room fell silent, except for the sound of papers rustling, as the vice president, the secretary of defense, the secretary of state, the chairman of the joint chiefs of staff, and the national security advisor all read the two-page document.

After a minute, the secretary of state smacked her palm on the table. "Good God. Do we have any independent confirmation that this really happened to Khorasani's daughter?"

"The CIA station in Dubai runs a couple agents on Kish Island," said the DNI. "They're telling us local police responded to an incident around the time that we believe the attack occurred. No charges were filed and the police incident log makes reference to a robbery, but evidently that wouldn't be unusual for a case like this, especially given that she is, in fact, the youngest daughter of the supreme leader of Iran. CIA and DIA think she was targeted by Sunni extremists hoping to inflame the whole situation in the Middle East and goad Khorasani into doing something crazy. Hence the Star of David marks carved on her body."

"Jesus," said the secretary of defense. He shook his head, evidently dumbfounded by the report. "When is this transfer supposed to take place?"

"Three days."

"Has anyone tried to reach out to Khorasani directly?"

"Our back channel through the Turks got shut down two months ago."

"Is the Mossad report all we have to go on? The Israelis aren't exactly objective observers here."

"Persia House," said the DNI, referring to the CIA group that had split from the Near East Division to focus exclusively on Iran, "reports that two hours ago the Iranian resistance group the MEK confirmed with their CIA liaison key elements of what you just read. The question now is, what do we do about it?"

"Or rather, what are the Israelis going to do about it?" said the president, tapping an arthritic finger on the table. "Because I can tell you all with certainty that the Israelis are going to act soon to stop Khorasani, regardless of what we do. I know they've thrown out threats to Iran before and haven't acted on them. But this is the real deal. There's no way in hell they're going to let the Iranians throw a punch like that."

"How soon is soon?" asked the secretary of state.

"Forty-eight hours tops. The only question is whether we get ahead of the shit storm by joining them, or whether we sit on our asses and take our lumps as they come."

12
Baku, Azerbaijan

———o———

THE CALLER ID THAT POPPED UP ON MARK'S LANDLINE phone just said *International*. Probably Langley, he thought, wanting to make sure he was clearing out. He was tempted to just let it ring.

He picked up.

"Sava here."

"Is this Mark Sava?" It was a man, and he sounded slightly out of breath.

"Ah, yeah, that's what I said."

"Did you get my messages?"

Mark glanced down to the rapidly blinking light on his answering machine. "No."

"I tried calling yesterday, and earlier today."

"I'm sorry, I didn't get your name."

Mark's minders looked at him impatiently.

"John. I'm John Junior's dad."

"I think you have the wrong number."

"You said you were Mark Sava. John gave me this number. He said he sometimes stayed here, that you were his friend."

A lightbulb clicked on in Mark's head.

"Are you talking about John Decker?"

Eight months ago, when the CIA was under siege in Baku, Mark had worked with Decker. They'd gotten along well enough professionally, and Decker had proved his worth many times over. Then three months ago, Decker had shown up uninvited

42

at Mark's apartment and asked whether he could crash there for a week or so, seeing as he was between contractor jobs. Mark hadn't been thrilled with the arrangement, but he'd said OK.

"I'm trying to reach him."

"He's not here," said Mark. "Honestly, this isn't a good time."

"I haven't heard from him in two weeks, no phone calls, no e-mails, nothing. I've left a million messages for him, he just doesn't answer."

Mark heard a couple of dogs barking. Speaking in a thick New England accent, a woman said, "Tell him about my birthday."

Mark recalled that Decker had grown up in the north woods of New Hampshire. Born into a military family. That female voice in the background reminded Mark of Decker.

"I don't know what to tell you," said Mark. "I haven't heard from him in months, so if you were in touch with him two weeks ago, then your contact information would be a lot more up-to-date than mine."

"We're just a little bit worried here. It was his mother's birthday yesterday. He always remembers to call."

"You know, Mr. Decker…I can tell you're worried, but really there's nothing I can do."

"If you hear from him, will you tell him to call home?"

"Absolutely. Now, I'm sorry, but you've caught me at a rough time. I have to go."

Mark tried to call Orkhan on the way to the airport.

Orkhan's secretary claimed not to know where her boss was or when he'd be back, so Mark explained the situation with his computer and backup disks and said he expected the Azeri government to help recover his stolen belongings.

Orkhan needs to look into it personally, he said. *Personally!*

The receptionist said she'd relay the message.

Mark figured Orkhan was probably listening in on the conversation, blowing him off.

He took stock of what he had—a change of clothes, a black diplomatic passport that he was supposed to have turned in when he left the CIA, a credit card, and $456 in cash because the Azeris had let him stop at his bank in downtown Baku to close out his checking account.

He still hadn't decided where to go. He thought back to that morning, drinking a cup of thick Turkish coffee at an outdoor café in Molokan Gardens in downtown Baku. That was just before meeting Heydar—what?—five hours ago? Everything had been so pleasantly normal.

He used to thrive on chaos when he was younger, but now… now he was getting too old for this crap.

The Ministry of National Security agent driving the car weaved in and out of the heavy traffic, stopping and starting with sudden, aggressive jerks.

Mark turned in his seat to look back at the city. Several green-domed mosques were sandwiched in among gleaming new skyscrapers. In the distance, bleak desert hills—dotted with oil derricks—marked the southern edge of the city. He'd always liked thinking of Baku as an exotic oasis in the desert, secluded from the wider world. He loved the medieval walls of the old city, the long promenade along the Caspian with its carnival rides and tea shops, the views from the heights at the southern end of the city, the fourteenth-century caravansary restaurant where he'd often met with visiting diplomats in smoke-blackened private rooms.

He was romanticizing the place, he knew. Much of Baku was just a dump. But it had been his dump.

He told himself to let it go. Moving on might be better for him in the long run anyway.

What would anybody want with his damn book, though? What good would it be to them? What was the point, just mindless destruction?

He thought about how Buddhist monks would spend days constructing an intricate sand painting, only to destroy it right after they'd finished. The exercise allegedly helped them embrace impermanence. Which was exactly what he needed to do.

Let it go.

Embrace impermanence.

Those fucking Russians. I bet it was the fucking Russians.

They were obsessive about their history; they'd probably been monitoring him and decided they didn't like what he was writing. Maybe instead of embracing impermanence he'd just hunt down the Russian dickwads who'd stolen his book and rip their damn throats out.

He started to think through the logistics of how he would launch such a hunt, and the money and time and risk involved, and the odds of it turning out successfully, and then he sighed.

Orkhan pulled up to the airport in his armored black Jeep Commander as Mark was being escorted to the international terminal.

Mark's minder led him to the back of Orkhan's car. Orkhan opened the door and Mark climbed in.

"I've been speaking to Heydar." Orkhan frowned deeply.

The back of the car was sealed off from the chauffeur in front by a plate of soundproof glass.

"And?"

"And I have concluded I was too quick to judge the boy. Heydar found out that you were leaving and he was gravely disappointed. He considers you his best teacher." Orkhan paused, as if preparing to reveal some important bit of information. "He now tells me he thinks he can pass this SAT if he studies harder."

Given the look of stoic pride on Orkhan's face, Mark decided not to mention that the test wasn't pass-fail.

"I sometimes get frustrated with him, and forget that he is just a boy," said Orkhan. "I was not interested in my studies at that age either." He shook his head.

"I'm sure you'll be able to find another tutor," offered Mark.

"Heydar doesn't want another tutor. He wants you."

For a brief moment, Mark though Orkhan might be saying that he could stay in Azerbaijan. Maybe this whole mess could be put to rest right now. Maybe—

"He asks that when you get to America, will it be possible to do a videoconference once a week?"

A long moment passed. Mark reminded himself that one should never burn one's bridges unless the enemy was directly upon you. Orkhan wasn't the enemy. But still.

Orkhan added, "I will pay, of course, for all the equipment, and for all the charges. If you require a charge yourself, that will be no problem provided it is reasonable. You have already repaid your debt."

He looked outside to the airport. In the distance, at the end of one of the runways, he could see the top of a mound of twisted, weed-strewn metal, the remains of previous plane crashes that had been swept off the runway and left to rust. He was going to miss this place.

"I'll call you," Mark said. "When I'm settled."

"Heydar will be grateful."

That resolved, Orkhan unlocked the door of the Commander, a sign that it was time for Mark to leave.

"What about my computer?"

"What computer?"

Mark explained about his apartment, and his missing laptop and files. "Didn't your secretary mention it?"

Orkhan said, "Of course I will have my men look for it. Anything they find will be stored with the rest of your belongings."

"My book was on that computer. It means a lot to me."

As Mark was stepping out onto the sidewalk, Orkhan said, "Next time you should back up off-site."

"What?"

"Back up off-site, you know, through the Internet. Heydar tells me about this—he is not always as stupid as he seems. The young, they know these things."

"I'm only forty-four. That's not old."

Orkhan shrugged. "Have a good trip, my friend."

13
Baku, Azerbaijan

————————o————————

THE PERKY TWENTYSOMETHING WOMAN AT THE AZERBAIJAN Airlines ticketing window informed Mark that there were no direct flights to the States, but that a red-eye was leaving for London in three hours. From there he could catch a flight back to Washington.

If that was where he wanted to go.

It had been nearly three years since Mark had been stateside. The thought of going back now felt to him a little like going back to imperial Rome after a long stint manning a lonely outpost in the German hinterlands. It wasn't that he'd gone native, as some in the CIA had feared. But it was true that being abroad for so long had changed him. He suspected he knew how to navigate the intricacies of Azeri culture better than his own.

Back home, things were more complicated, more personal. There was too much lingering rancor.

"Sir?" prodded the woman.

Mark pictured the sterile halls of CIA headquarters in Langley. He imagined being hooked up to a polygraph when he first showed up, and then being debriefed by a bunch of young, well-intentioned analysts who'd never been to Azerbaijan. Did he really want to go back to that?

But Baku had changed since he'd first arrived. The airport terminal was modern and clean, having been recently reno-vated. At his local grocery store, the Russian checkout lady was no longer reflexively rude. There were giant malls, 3-D cinemas, and wireless hot spots all over the city. Armani and Tiffany had invaded years ago.

With all the oil money sloshing around, the idea that Baku was still the hinterlands was a fiction. Christ, he could see the sign for the airport Holiday Inn from where he was standing. He'd been hiding in a remote corner of the world, but the world had found him.

Langley, he thought. It would only be for a few days. Inevitably he'd run into people he knew, but that too could be minimized. But then what?

"Yeah, get me on the flight to London," he told the ticketing agent. "But route me all the way to Washington, DC, if you can."

"What class will you be flying, sir?"

Mark glanced back at his minders from the Ministry of National Security. One of them shrugged. Orkhan had approved payment for the flight home but evidently hadn't been more specific than that.

"Make it first."

While waiting for his flight, Mark ate a plate of bad lamb kebabs and downed a half-liter bottle of extra-strong Xirdalan beer—the local favorite—at the Holiday Inn bar.

As he watched BBC News on a flat-screen television and nursed a second beer, he remembered that he was scheduled to teach a senior seminar on American foreign policy during the Cold War the next morning.

At a computer station in the Holiday Inn, he composed his resignation—effective immediately—to the chairman of the International Relations Department, added a vague apology for the abruptness of his departure, CC'd half a dozen colleagues, and clicked Send. That done, he turned to the long list of unopened e-mails in his account.

He deleted the solicitations to visit porn sites or buy Viagra that had slipped past his spam filter. There were a few notices from Western University concerning changes to the spring schedule, which he deleted as well.

Then he came to an e-mail with a blank subject line. It had been sent from Alty8@online.tm. Someone with the e-mail address of 75351@ulradns.sc had been CC'd.

If he'd been on his own computer, he might not have opened the e-mail for fear of downloading a virus. But at the Holiday Inn, what did he care?

"What are you doing?" demanded one of his minders, jogging to keep up with Mark.

"I need to back up some files."

"Slow down."

"No."

Mark bought two thumb drives at a little hotel store just off the main atrium. Back at the Holiday Inn business center, he made two copies of the photo files. Then he deleted all the e-mails in his online account and changed his password.

"Change in plans," he told his minders. "I'm not going to London."

"There is no choice, sir. Minister Gambar has insisted that we witness you leaving the country."

Mark recalled with photographic precision the departure list he'd seen in the airport terminal, comforted by the fact that he was naturally reverting back to his hypervigilant self. He considered about ten flights that were departing soon before deciding, "Flight nine eighty to Bishkek takes off in fifteen minutes."

"Why there?"

"Personal business."

That e-mail had been sent just ten hours before someone had tried to kill him. If he hadn't been at the conference in

Tbilisi, he would have downloaded all his e-mails to his laptop first thing in the morning, just like he always did.

That's why someone had stolen his laptop.

Nobody gives a shit about your book.

Whoever had tried to kill him, whoever had ransacked his apartment, had done so because of something to do with those photos.

But why take the backup files too? Maybe they'd been looking for passwords. Like passwords to his e-mail account, so they'd be able to get the photos.

He might never get his old life back, but he wasn't going to be driven out of town with his tail between his legs. At least not until he figured out who was doing the driving, and what could be done to stop them.

Running to catch up, Mark's minder said, "The flight to Bishkek will already have boarded."

Mark thought about the assassin in the library, and his conversation with Orkhan, and his stolen book, and the indignity of his ruined tomato plants, and the rushed and unprofessional resignation letter he'd just written to Western University. He thought about the view from his apartment that he would never see again and the casual way the Azeri security forces had been ashing their cigarettes on one of his plates.

Then he thought about the picture with the arm in it, an arm that he was now virtually certain he recognized.

"Then insist that they hold the plane until I'm on it. Airport security will listen to you."

"You don't have a visa."

There was a reason why Mark had kept his black diplomatic passport. "I don't need one."

14
Washington, DC

———————◦———————

"**C**ENTCOM IS REQUESTING THAT THE *USS STENNIS* DIVERT to the Arabian Gulf."

The president steepled his hands and waited for his chief of staff to continue.

"So that when you come to a decision, whatever course you choose won't be limited by a lack of assets in the region. If you approve the request, the Iranians are sure to protest. You can expect a complaint to be filed with the Swiss embassy in Tehran."

If the *USS Stennis* was ordered to the Arabian Gulf, three aircraft carriers would be patrolling just off the coast of Iran. The *Eisenhower* was already in the Persian Gulf, and the *Nimitz* was in the Arabian Sea.

Two aircraft carriers was normal. But three? That was an anomaly.

"If the Iranians protest, tell them the *Stennis* will be replacing the *Nimitz*," said the president.

"They'll know that the *Nimitz* has only been on patrol for one month and isn't due for replacement."

"Then we'll tell them the *Nimitz* is experiencing mechanical problems and needs to be recalled early."

"They won't believe it."

"I don't expect them to. Parliamentary elections in Afghanistan are going to be held five days from now, on the seventeenth. We'll tell them the *Nimitz* will be fully repaired and leaving the Arabian Sea by the eighteenth. They'll think we're trying to tell them not to meddle with the elections."

"That might fly."

15

Manas Air Base, Kyrgyzstan

———————o———————

B RUCE HOLTZ WAS A SQUARE-JAWED THIRTY-TWO-YEAR-OLD former football player for Texas A&M who towered over Mark as they faced each other at the entrance to Manas Air Base, the main transit station for NATO supplies bound for Afghanistan. On his hip he wore a smartphone as if it were a sidearm.

"Mark Sava. I gotta say, this is definitely a surprise."

Holtz flashed a big smile that appeared genuine, extended his hand, and did the squeeze-too-hard thing.

It was early evening. The air was cold, the sky an angry gray that promised rain. In the distance, a few US Air Force C-130 planes were lined up near the main runway, ready to fly arms and rations to Bagram. The flight from Baku to Manas International Airport—Kyrgyzstan's biggest airport, located just outside the leafy capital city of Bishkek—had taken four hours. After landing, Mark had caught a cab to the section of the airport leased by the US military, the part known as Manas Air Base.

He and Holtz exchanged a few lies disguised as pleasantries. Eventually Mark got around to saying that he'd gotten sick of teaching college kids, so he'd quit his university job in Baku and left for good.

"That mean you're looking for work?"

"Maybe…"

"CAIN could use you."

"I'll give it some thought. Right now I'm working on another project."

"You've been giving it some thought for a year now."

"I'll think harder."

Over the course of his career, Mark had served in Azerbaijan, Georgia, Abkhazia, Tajikistan, Nagorno-Karabakh Kazakhstan, Uzbekistan, and even briefly in Kyrgyzstan when the Americans were building Manas Air Base in the run-up to the war in Afghanistan. All that experience had earned him the kind of reputation that was worth something. Especially to someone like Holtz, who had only served with the CIA as an operations officer for five years before starting up CAIN.

Mark added, "I'm actually trying to track down one of your employees. Was hoping you might have some contact info."

"I got a lot of employees. We're up to twenty now."

"John Decker."

"What do you want with him?"

"He's kind of a friend."

"Friend?" Holtz crossed his arms and stared down at Mark. Mark noted that Holtz's eyes were small and mouse-like.

"I didn't think you had friends, Sava."

"Well, acquaintance might be closer to the mark. We worked together last year. Can you help me?"

"Come on, we'll talk inside."

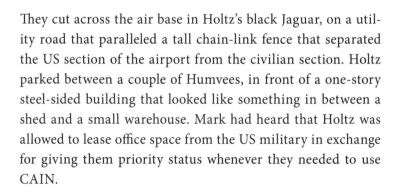

They cut across the air base in Holtz's black Jaguar, on a utility road that paralleled a tall chain-link fence that separated the US section of the airport from the civilian section. Holtz parked between a couple of Humvees, in front of a one-story steel-sided building that looked like something in between a shed and a small warehouse. Mark had heard that Holtz was allowed to lease office space from the US military in exchange for giving them priority status whenever they needed to use CAIN.

"So, yeah, we're up to twenty employees now," Holtz repeated as they entered his office. On his desk were a couple of manila folders, a few loose papers, and a laptop.

Mark took a step toward the desk. One of the papers showed a diagram that looked like the sketch of a subway system. On the back wall, a Dallas Cowboys pennant was pinned to imitation-wood paneling, just above a watercooler. The whole place had a temporary, slapped-together feel to it.

"That so?"

Holtz gathered the papers on his desk and placed them inside his top drawer. "We're in five countries; business is good. Decent client base, some industry gigs, some government."

Mark had heard that Holtz, though considered more brash than bright by CIA insiders, had landed quite a few DoD and State Department jobs simply because the United States had no one else to turn to in Central Asia. After all the cutbacks at the CIA, Holtz was one of the few players in the region.

"Heard you were in Turkmenistan," said Mark.

"Who told you that? Decker?"

Decker had indeed been the one to tell him, over beers in Baku, three months ago. He'd said that Holtz had approached him about a security job in Turkmenistan and that he planned to take it.

"No, but word gets around, you know."

"That's confidential information. Deck shouldn't have been running his mouth."

"You're making quite a name for yourself. I've been impressed."

Holtz nodded, as if this didn't surprise him. "What I can tell you is that we're well positioned in most of Central Asia, Turkmenistan included. You come to CAIN and you can run your own minidivision if you like, pick your country. Hire your own guys. I wouldn't be in your hair. And I'll tell you something else—I'm looking at selling in a couple years. A few of the big military contractors want to get into the private intelligence game, and it might be easier for them to buy CAIN than build from scratch and compete against us. You could make out like a bandit. We both could. I can show you some figures if you like."

Mark didn't much care for the idea of working for, or even with, Holtz. But he certainly wasn't opposed to making out like a bandit. "I'm not saying no, but I'd rather focus on Decker first."

Holtz sat down in his leather executive chair, popped open his laptop, tapped and dragged his finger on the touch pad for a while, and then grabbed a piece of paper and a pen.

"Here," he said to Mark. "E-mail, cell phone, address on record in Baku. You're welcome."

Mark studied the information. "This is my address in Baku."

"That's the address he gave me."

"Because he didn't have one of his own at the time, so he used mine. I need a current address."

"Then call or e-mail him."

"I already tried. He's either not answering or not getting his e-mails. And his cell phone number has changed. I need his real contact info, Bruce. As in, a way to reach him now."

"Unfortunately I can't help you in that department, buddy."

"Doesn't he work for you?"

Holtz moved his tongue around in his mouth before finally saying, "Not no more."

"What happened?"

"Well, I don't want to shit talk the guy behind his back."

"What's that supposed to mean?"

"Means I don't want to shit talk the guy behind his back."

Mark just stared at him.

Finally Holtz said, "A few days ago, John Decker pretty much went AWOL on me. I don't know where he is."

"Went AWOL or disappeared?"

Holtz just leaned back in his seat.

Mark said, "What was Decker doing in Turkmenistan?"

"What CAIN was doing in Turkmenistan is classified information. I've signed confidentiality agreements with my clients, which means I can't tell you jack and you know it. I will say this—whatever Decker was doing, he was doing it with full knowledge of all the occupational hazards involved."

"Occupational hazards? I thought you said he went AWOL?"

"This conversation is over."

"Bruce, I'm here because there's been blowback. And I think it might have something to do with whatever Decker was up to."

Holtz stared at him. "What kind of blowback?"

"Someone came after me. In Baku."

"When you say came after you…"

"As in tried to kill me. Yesterday."

Holtz took a moment to run a hand through his short-cropped hair, then said, "What makes you think it had anything to do with Decker?"

Mark studied Holtz, wondering whether he was the person who'd been CC'd on the photos and was just playing dumb. No, he didn't think Holtz was playing. "Call it intuition."

Holtz leaned back in his chair. "Intuition's not going to cut it. I'm sorry, but I can't help you. And that's final."

Mark stared at the Dallas Cowboys pennant behind Holtz's desk. "So I see you're gathering intel on the Atyrau oil collection station. The one the Chinese are putting in for the Kazakhs, if I'm not mistaken?"

Holtz glanced down at his desk, to where the sketch of the oil collection station, the one resembling a subway map, had been.

"You already put it away." Mark's vision wasn't so great anymore when it came to focusing on small print—he knew he should wear reading glasses more than he did. But the map had been far enough away for him to see it just fine.

"That's classified information."

"Then you should be more careful with it."

"Up yours, Mark. You know, I don't think you have a base pass. I think maybe it's time for you to leave."

Mark made eye contact with Holtz. "Bet the Kazakhs would be interested to know what you're up to. Of course, if they ever found out, you could kiss the idea of ever setting foot in Kazakhstan again good-bye."

Holtz crossed his arms in a way that made his biceps bulge and assumed an expression that Mark interpreted as an attempt to appear intimidating.

"Don't go there, brother. I don't respond well to bribes. Remember, we're on the same team."

"It's actually called blackmail. And if I don't get help with Decker, I guarantee you I'll be on the phone selling this info to the Kazakhs within the hour. Whether you respond well or not."

Holtz pointed a long finger at Mark. "I'm warning you. Don't. Go. There. I will find a way to fuck you over, and that is a promise."

Mark stood and began walking to the door. "You're embarrassing yourself, Bruce. I'm outta here."

Holtz caught up with Mark outside.

"Hold on, buddy. Jesus, don't be such a dickhead. I had a contract with the State Department. That's why I was in Turkmenistan. I hired your guy Decker to protect State diplomats and stand around and look tough."

"A contract to do what?"

Sounding ruffled, Holtz said, "Help State get some leverage with the Turkmen before the ChiComs sign deals that'll guarantee they, and they alone, get to spend the next hundred years sucking every last drop of gas and oil out of the region."

That bit of news didn't surprise Mark.

The Americans, Russians, and Chinese—or to Holtz, ChiComs, short for Chinese communists—had long been waging diplomatic and intelligence wars on multiple fronts as they fought over Central Asia's resources. It was the New Great Game, and it had kept Mark employed for years.

As for the specific case of Turkmenistan, that country happened to be sitting on top of huge natural gas reserves. A lot of that gas currently went north through aging Russian pipelines, and the Turkmen had recently inked a deal to send some of it to the Arabian Sea via Afghanistan and Pakistan. But the Chinese were pressing hard to get the Turkmen to send the bulk of their natural gas east, to China.

At the same time, Mark knew that the Chinese had signed a secret deal to build a huge oil pipeline from Iran to China, which would cross through both Turkmenistan and Kazakhstan. That's what the eruption of violence in Baku eight months ago had been about. State would be doing everything they could to get the Turkmen to deny or delay extending transit rights.

"How'd it go?" Mark asked.

"Shitty. Negotiations broke down two days ago and we got kicked out of the country. Decker never showed up for the plane home. I've asked the Turkmen to try to figure out where the hell he is, but so far I haven't gotten a response. Needless to say, this is a bit of a clusterfuck for me."

"That's it?"

"That's it. That's what I know."

"Where was Decker staying in Turkmenistan?"

"President Hotel, big place in Ashgabat. I will say this—not long after I hired him, he gave me the name of this half-Iranian ex-CIA girl who speaks Turkmen and half a dozen other languages. Daria Buckingham. You know her?"

"You could say that."

"Yeah, she worked in Azerbaijan for a while, so I figured."

"I was under the impression she'd gone back to the States."

What the hell was Daria doing working for Holtz?

"Guess she came back. Anyway, there's only a handful of people out there who can translate Turkmen so I hired her, and for the next two weeks Decker was like a tick on her ass. It was embarrassing. He really had a thing for her, always following her around, which I don't get because if you ask me, she's a first-class bitch. But if you want to find out about Decker, you might start by talking to her. Don't fucking look at me like that, I'm just telling you what I know."

"What did Daria say when *you* talked to her?"

"I haven't."

"You're really leaving no stone unturned here, aren't you? Mounting a real manhunt."

"I had to fire her a couple weeks ago, long before we got kicked out of the country. I'm the last person she'd talk to."

"Fire her for what?"

"It's confidential."

"Where is she now?"

"Almaty, I think. I heard she was trying to run private intelligence ops against the ChiComs."

Almaty was only 150 or so miles northwest of where they were now, in Kazakhstan. Mark figured he could be there in a few hours.

"Try the InterContinental," said Holtz. "I heard she's working there as a concierge, probably just to gain access to the ChiComs who hang out there, but who knows, maybe she's just hard up for money."

16

DECKER WOKE UP TO SOMEONE PUNCHING HIS SOLAR PLEXUS. When he tried to fight back, he found that he couldn't because his arms had been immobilized.

Someone yanked him up to a sitting position and then onto a metal chair. He wondered how long he had been unconscious. Minutes? Days? His head was still throbbing, and his left leg was excruciatingly stiff and swollen.

"I wanted you to see this."

Metal bit into his wrists. Old-style handcuffs, he determined. He turned toward the voice, but someone shone a bright light in his eyes. He blinked and squinted.

Absorb the pain, don't fight it.

"Turn down the light for our guest, please."

As Decker's eyes adjusted, a form slowly took shape in front of him—it was a man, he realized, slumped in a wooden chair. A small man. Perhaps just a boy.

"Do you recognize your friend?"

It took Decker another moment to get a grip on his pain, to understand it and accept it and probe its limits. When he did, he was able to recognize the figure in front of him.

Alty.

Eighteen hours earlier...

Decker marveled for a moment at the absurdity of what he was witnessing.

Get the hell out of here, you jackass.

Alty, a twenty-one-year-old Turkmen bartender that Decker had been using as a guide, was headed his way.

Decker just hoped to God the security guards were looking elsewhere. He watched in horror as Alty risked a fifty-foot run across open grass. The moonlight made the kid an easy target.

He could guess at Alty's game plan. Sneak up to the ayatollah's mansion, find a lighted window, start snapping photos or short video clips, hoping to get lucky, maybe even hear something. All for the glory of Turkmenistan or some such nonsense. But Alty didn't have the equipment to do any of that right, much less the training. That was Decker's job. That was why Decker had approached the mansion in the shadows cast on the lawn by trees and hedges, why he'd staked out the place for hours before scaling the fence and establishing a surveillance post on the roof of the ayatollah's mansion, why he'd camouflaged himself to blend in with the rust-colored tile roof. The night vision goggles he was wearing kind of sucked, but they were better than nothing. Alty was as good as blind in the dark.

He'd warned the kid to stay away. Getting just one of them inside the grounds had been risky enough.

Ten minutes passed and nothing bad happened. Decker remained perfectly still, his body aligned in the moon shadow of a tall chimney, rendering him nearly invisible. He couldn't see where Alty had ended up once the kid got close to the building. He got to hoping that Alty had just snapped a few photos with his iPhone and then hightailed it back over the fence that encircled the estate. It was possible. Decker couldn't see every potential exit route, even from the roof. He might have missed Alty's departure.

But then a bark came from one of the well-lit outbuildings. Decker flipped up his night vision goggles, slowly raised his camera to his right eye, focused the telephoto lens on the building, and watched as a guard released two German shepherds. He checked his watch—it was exactly midnight. Probably the time the dogs were let out every night.

He remembered the conversation he'd had with Alty a few hours earlier, when they were casing the estate. He'd specifically asked Alty about dogs.

"No dogs."

"How can you be sure?"

"The mullahs think dogs are dirty."

"I'm not talking about people's pets, I'm talking about guard dogs."

"Is against Islam."

"But I saw dogs in Turkmenistan."

"No dogs."

But evidently there were.

And if Alty was still on the property, at ground level, he was screwed.

On the front lawn of the mansion, two dim swaths of light spilled out from ground-floor windows. Alty had run toward the light on the left. Decker flipped his night vision goggles back down, stuffed his equipment into his waterproof gear bag, strapped the bag tight to his back, and then crawled on all fours, spiderlike, silently down the gentle pitch of the roof. When he reached the section directly above where he suspected Alty was, he extended his head past the copper gutter and scanned the area below him.

Alty was wedged between a hedge and a Greek column that marked the edge of the raised portico in front of the mansion. His iPhone was held up to the window.

"Alty!" Decker called down in a loud whisper.

Alty's head snapped around.

"Look up. It's Deck!"

"Deck?"

"Get the hell out of here. There are dogs."

"No dogs."

"Yes, dogs! I saw them; they're loose. Run!"

"You see dogs?"

"Two of them. Big ones. Run!"

Alty finally got it, because now he stood up, pocketed his iPhone, took a quick look at the lawn in front of him, and began to sprint toward the distant perimeter fence. But he'd only gone maybe twenty feet when the frantic barking started. A second later, one of the German shepherds rounded the corner at full speed.

When Alty saw the dog, he spun around and headed back toward the house.

That fucking idiot is going to try to climb one of the columns, Decker guessed. Which might save him temporarily from the dogs but will ensure that he'll be captured.

Ditch him. You can make it out on your own.

Alty reached the column and tried to shimmy up it, but the dog was right there. It sank its teeth into Alty's calf and didn't let go. Decker eyed the perimeter fence.

I can be over that fence in less than thirty seconds, dogs or no dogs...

Alty screamed.

Shit.

Decker unsheathed his SOG SEAL Team knife, swung his body off the roof, dropped twenty feet, and landed directly on the back of the dog. A second later he slit the dog's throat.

Alty was still frantic, trying to shimmy up the column. Decker grabbed his belt and yanked him to the ground. "Run for the fence!"

Alty tried to run, but his wounded leg kept giving out on him, so Decker half dragged him across the lawn. When the second dog tore up, crazed and barking wildly, Decker offered his left arm, which the German shepherd took in its jaws. With his right arm, Decker plunged his knife deep into the dog's chest, twisting it as he heaved up. He threw the dog several feet up in the air and left it writhing on the ground.

A guard ran out, gun drawn, from a grove of limbed-up plane trees not far from the main entrance gate. The perimeter fence was still a good hundred feet away. Decker hadn't wanted to escalate matters by using his gun, but as the guard took aim at them, he pulled a Sig Sauer P226 from his nylon thigh holster and shot the guy in the chest. He grabbed Alty around the waist just as a volley of shots rang out.

Alty's body jumped. Decker returned fire, but he didn't have a good sense of where the new threat was coming from. A quick glance at Alty's neck told him the kid was either dead or would be within seconds.

More shots rang out. Decker felt a bee-sting-like prick as a bullet grazed his left shoulder.

Time to get the hell out of here, buddy.

Using Alty's body as a shield, Decker tried to advance toward the border fence. By now, he'd figured out that whoever was shooting at him was doing so from behind a low stone wall near the front of the mansion. Then someone started shooting at him from another angle.

One of the shots hit the slide of Decker's Sig.

Decker didn't drop the gun, but when he went to fire it, nothing happened.

Goddamn motherfucking sonofabitch…

He started pulling Alty back toward the house, still using the kid as a shield. No way he could make the front fence, not unarmed with two guys taking potshots at him.

He'd try for the back fence instead. It was farther away, but the forest of trees in the rear of the estate would provide cover. He got to a row of hedges in front of the mansion, ripped Alty's iPhone out of the kid's back pocket, let the boy drop, and sprinted on all fours, behind the hedges, toward the back of the mansion.

Decker was remarkably fast for such a big man, and the wild shots into the hedges all missed their mark. But then a third security guard ran out from the rear of the property. And then a fourth, blocking yet another avenue of escape.

With a working pistol, it wouldn't have mattered. Without one, he was trapped.

Or maybe not.

Earlier that night he'd scaled the roof from a secluded alcove on the side of the mansion. Using the hedges in front of the mansion for cover, Decker sprinted to that alcove now, grabbed a vertical copper gutter with both hands—pulling it partially out of its wall anchors—and began to climb. Near the top, someone shot him in the thigh. For a moment he thought he might fall, but with one last Herculean burst of strength he lifted himself over the lip of the roof.

He scrambled as fast as he could up the tiles, dove into a wedge between the roof and one of the five chimneys, and pulled a tourniquet off of his stripped-down chest rig, snapping the rubber band that had held it in place. After determining that the bullet hadn't hit his femoral artery, he used the tourniquet to hold a pressure dressing in place, being sure not to completely cut off the flow of blood above the wound.

What he wouldn't give for a link to a Predator feed right now, he thought, working as fast as he could on the dressing. He had no eyes above and no weapon; the enemy had the advantage.

When he finished the dressing, he pulled out his Sig and inspected the slide. No time to fieldstrip, no time to fix.

Fuck, you are in a bad place, buddy. Gotta face reality.

He pulled out Alty's iPhone. He was breathing heavily. The tiles underneath him became slick from the blood dripping from his thigh.

A couple of bullets ricocheted off the chimney. Decker had positioned himself so that the guards couldn't get a good shot off at him from the ground, but he knew they'd be on the roof itself any minute.

He used his thick finger to tap Alty's iPhone to life.

What was Holtz's e-mail address?

He closed his eyes for a moment.

Pull yourself together.

You're not going to make it.

Not Holtz. Sava. And Daria.

He opened the e-mail app, typed Mark.Sava@wu.edu.az, CC'd Daria, and attached a photo Alty had taken with his phone, and then another. The pictures were lousy, but they'd have to do—there was no way he had time to transfer all the high-res photos and voice data he'd collected.

He couldn't risk writing anything in the e-mail—all e-mail traffic here was monitored—so he raised his arm straight up and twirled his index finger in a circle as he used the iPhone to snap a photo of his arm. Mark would understand.

He hit Send, took the gear bag off his back, snaked his arm quickly up over the top of the chimney, found a protruding screw he'd noticed earlier in the night while lowering microphone wires into the house, and used the microphone wires to hang his bag on the screw.

Had the guards on the ground seen him? He'd been quick, no more than two seconds. And since the top of the chimney rose six feet above the highest point of the roof, his bag would stay hidden unless someone shimmied up the chimney and looked down it.

A ladder clanged, first as it was raised, then as it fell onto the side of the house.

Shit, you forgot the iPhone.

Decker took a step toward the chimney, intending to hide the iPhone in his gear bag, just as one of the security guards crested the roof. They looked at each other for a moment and then the guard raised his gun. Decker pivoted and ran, stumbling across the roof as he tried to block out the pain in his thigh, his wet soles slipping on the tiles, taking fire from several angles because he was now exposed to guards on the ground.

On the back side of the mansion, a ten-foot wall marked the perimeter of an inner courtyard. Decker ran toward where he thought this wall intersected with the house. Just before he hit the end of the roof, he dropped the iPhone into the gutter, hoping that's where it would stay.

Shots rang out as he took a giant leap off the roof, but he was moving fast and none connected. For a brief moment he was weightless under the bright moon, at peace and unafraid, his legs scissored apart in midstride.

17

Almaty, Kazakhstan

A LMATY HAD CHANGED IN THE YEARS SINCE MARK HAD been there last—the skyscrapers were taller, the expensive foreign cars more plentiful, and there were more fancy shops on the tree-lined streets, all lit up and still packed with shoppers even at nine at night. Like Baku, it had been a dumpy backwater for the better part of a century while under Soviet rule—an old Silk Road town that had been completely bypassed by modernity—but now it was overflowing with oil money.

The InterContinental sat on the heights on the south side of town. Mark found Daria working behind the marble-topped concierge desk, speaking Russian to a guest who had inquired about nearby restaurants. Beyond the desk lay a spacious lobby full of palm trees, a tropical curiosity that seemed absurdly luxurious against the backdrop of the rugged, snowcapped Tian Shan Mountains surrounding the city.

Daria wore a charcoal-gray skirt suit with a white blouse and a name tag that read *Maira*.

At first, Mark tried not to stare, but then he just let himself take her in. She was still striking, still the Daria he knew, but slightly fuller in her face, arms, and breasts than she'd been when they'd parted six months ago. When she'd first come to Baku to work for him as one of his operations officers, she'd been so slender and young looking that she could have passed for a senior in high school. Now she looked like a woman in her early thirties, which is what she was.

The Russian guest left and Mark stepped forward.

Daria's eyes registered a hint of alarm, then she quickly looked down at the desk. "You are looking for a restaurant too?"

"Sure. I guess I'd like to get a late dinner at the hotel." Mark spoke Azeri.

A long pause followed. Another guest, a bald man in a suit, got in line behind Mark.

"That won't be possible," replied Daria in Azeri. "The hotel doesn't serve dinner."

Mark could see a half-full dining room from where he was standing, one of several restaurants in the hotel serving dinner. "It's urgent."

"I can recommend other restaurants."

The scarring that had been evident on her face the last time he'd seen her wasn't noticeable, both because it had healed well and because she was wearing more makeup than she used to. Mark wasn't crazy about the makeup—it dulled her absolutely smooth olive-skinned complexion, a feature that had been a powerful lure when, as a CIA officer, she'd been trying to recruit people to spy for the United States. She'd cut her dark hair shorter, so that it just grazed the tops of her shoulders. Her high cheekbones, however, remained unchanged—and made her look more refined than any of the rich guests mingling in the lobby.

"OK."

She took out a map and pen, and with the certainty of a professional concierge who knew the city well, circled an area at the far northern end of Abylay Khan, a wide thoroughfare that bisected the city. "The Glasnost," she said. It was near the train section, in a poorer section of the city.

"I could use some company."

"I'll see what I can do."

Mark had a sudden urge to say that he'd missed her, but from the way she'd addressed him from the start as a stranger, he assumed that she didn't want to advertise that they knew each other. So instead he just thanked her and walked away, his mind distracted by the past.

———○———

Mark's apartment in Baku, eight months earlier...

For the second night in a row, Daria made dinner.

For the first two weeks after arriving at his apartment to convalesce, all she had done was lie on her side in bed, with the window shades drawn and the door closed, agonizing in the semidarkness of his spare bedroom. Most of the food he'd brought to her bedside had gone uneaten. He'd tried to talk to her, to bring her back from the darkness, but his attempts had been clumsy and ineffective.

Yesterday morning, though, after falling in the shower, Daria had seemed to turn a corner.

"I've been too useless for too long," she'd said.

Last night, instead of huddling in the darkness, she'd made an Iranian pomegranate-walnut stew. Tonight, she cooked a small roast chicken, rice and vegetable plov, and dovga yogurt soup. It had taken her most of the day, given her injuries, but she hadn't complained or accepted help when Mark had offered.

They ate it all slowly, out on the balcony, with the sounds of Baku drifting up from the streets eight stories below them. The rumble of old Russian trucks mingled with the distant thuds of pile drivers pounding foundation supports for new skyscrapers deep into the ground. They drank a bottle of wine with dinner, then started in on another. As darkness fell, obscuring her scars, she grew cheerier, even elated at times.

"I've been thinking," she said, after finishing the last of her plov.

"Of?"

Daria got up from the little dinner table and sat down on a bench near the edge of the balcony.

"Of getting a master's in international affairs."

Daria already had a law degree from Georgetown but had joined the CIA before taking the bar.

"Oh?"

"I need to think about a career. With a master's in international affairs, and a JD, and my language skills, I could get a job practicing international law at, like, the UN, or Amnesty International. I need to do something decent with my life."

"You'd be good at that." Those weren't career options that appealed to Mark—he wasn't much of a do-gooder—but he could see Daria enjoying that kind of work.

"If I don't I'll just go back to..."

Daria didn't finish her sentence, but she didn't have to—Mark knew what she meant.

She'd been born in Tehran some thirty years ago, as the Islamic revolution was raging. Her Iranian mother had been slaughtered by revolutionaries. Her American father had refused to care for her. Despite being raised in a wealthy Virginia suburb by well-intentioned adoptive parents, her inauspicious start in life, coupled with her own inclinations, had led her to a backstabbing underworld populated by spies and thieves. That underworld was what she didn't want to go back to.

"I'd have to finish a master's program in the States or Europe," said Daria, "but I was thinking of taking some courses here at Western first. It'd be cheaper and the credits should transfer."

"Sounds like a plan."

"Maybe I could take one of your courses."

Mark got up and sat next to her on the bench. "You wouldn't learn much."

She leaned into him. "Easy A, though."

"Not necessarily. I am, however, receptive to bribes."

The Glasnost restaurant was popular with retired Kazakh men who liked to sit at the plastic tables covered with plastic table-cloths, sip Derbes beer, and play *toguz kumalaki*, a popular board game. It was located on a potholed street lined with shops that sold little more than the bare necessities of life, reminding Mark of the neighborhood in Elizabeth, New Jersey, where he'd grown up.

Daria appeared just after he'd started in on a Derbes. She was still wearing her InterContinental uniform, though she'd removed the name tag. Mark had meant to offer a brief explanation of why he was here, but instead he thought back to the last time he'd seen her naked, on his bed, after sex.

He wondered what the state of affairs was between her and Decker. None of his business, he knew. But he still wondered.

"Let's go," she said.

Mark pointed to his beer, and the one he'd bought for her. "Thought we could catch up over dinner."

"I'm assuming you're here about Deck?"

"Yeah."

"Follow me. I don't want to talk here."

Daria started walking.

Mark left a twenty-dollar American bill on the table—the smallest he had—to cover what was only four dollars' worth of beer, and followed her out the back of the restaurant. She led him down an alley that smelled of cat piss, then through the rear door of a two-story apartment building. After turning down a flight of steps, she stopped in front of a metal door and fished an over-sized key out of her jacket pocket.

The door opened onto a small room. A streetlamp cast dim light through the basement windows near the ceiling. The dirty white walls were bare, and a single uncovered lightbulb dangled from the ceiling. Daria turned it on. A brown mini-refrigerator with a dented door sat in the corner next to a utility sink. The faded green plastic table in the center of the room looked as though it had spent many years aging in the sunshine. There was one fold-up chair, on which Daria now sat down.

She pointed to a couple of wooden milk crates in the corner. "Grab a few."

Mark stacked them on top of one another and sat across the table from her. They looked at each other for a while.

"It's good to see you," said Mark.

"Stop staring at my face."

"I wasn't staring."

"Yes you were."

"I was just staring at you, not at—"

"You were staring at the scars." She put a hand to her temple and turned away from him.

"I can't even notice them. You look great, Daria."

Mark's apartment in Baku, seven months earlier...

Mark had slept around plenty, and had even had some decent long-term relationships over the years, but the only other time he'd woken up in the morning with a woman actually in his arms was when he'd had sex for the first time, back when he'd been a sophomore in high school.

Ordinarily he preferred a certain distance when he slept. He didn't like people breathing on him, no matter how good they looked or how nice they smelled, and he got hot if he felt crowded in bed. Even a light hand on his chest could lead to insomnia.

So even though he and Daria had started having sex weeks ago, not long after she'd started making good dinners and he'd started buying good wine, he'd always moved over to his side of the bed afterward. Until last night, that is, when they'd fallen asleep in each other's arms.

Now it was morning, and since he'd woken up before her, he just lay there for a while, thinking. Her breathing was light, and her bare skin was cool where it touched his own. On the end table next to the bed, the wilted stargazer lilies that he'd bought two weeks ago hung limp in a vase. After fifteen minutes of just lying there, he started getting antsy, remembering why he liked his space in bed. He considered getting up. It was already late.

Then the phone on his end table rang.

"What time is it?" Daria stretched her arms up toward the headboard.

"Eight."

Mark leaned out of bed and checked the caller ID. It just registered as an international number. "Shit," he said.

"Are you going to answer it?"

Mark picked up the phone and listened silently as Daria curled up into the covers. He said "Yeah" a couple of times, and then, "Is that subject to discussion?" and finally, just before hanging up, "I'll tell her."

"Tell me what?"

Mark sat up in bed and ran his hand through his hair. "That was Kaufman."

"And?"

"He's calling you in. Back to Washington, to debrief you."

"You mean fire me."

"We knew it was coming." The fight over the pipeline had exposed Daria's divided loyalties between the CIA and an Iranian resistance group. It had just been a matter of time until the CIA fired her. They'd just been waiting until she recovered enough to go through the exit interviews.

Daria curled into him. "Can't I do the debrief at the embassy?"

"No."

"Fine, then I'll go back to the States for a few weeks. What's wrong? You're tense."

Mark didn't answer right away. "Kaufman also told me the Azeris have filed a PNG on you."

Daria froze up. PNG stood for persona non grata. It meant the Azeris were kicking her out of Azerbaijan.

"*It sucks, I know,*" *said Mark.*

They lay in silence for a minute as they both considered the full implications of what that meant.

"*Did you know this was coming?*" *asked Daria.*

Ordinarily Mark considered himself to be an adept liar. As a CIA officer, he'd had plenty of practice. But even before he spoke, he was afraid that his timing and intonation would be subtly off. A normal person would never notice, but Daria wasn't normal. She'd been his best operations officer. "*No.*"

"*You did know. Didn't you?*" *She pulled her hand off his chest.*

"*I suspected, that's all.*"

"*You didn't talk to Orkhan about it? He didn't tell you?*"

"*He didn't tell me anything.*"

"*So all that talk about my taking courses here—*"

"*I didn't know this was going to happen, Daria. I just know the system. I knew it was a possibility.*"

She took a while to let that settle. "*Did you try to stop it from happening?*"

The last time Mark had spoken to Orkhan, Daria had still been holed up in his spare bedroom, driving herself crazy with her dark thoughts and recriminations. And while he and Orkhan hadn't talked about Daria being served with a PNG, if they had, Mark might not have pushed back on the idea. At the time, he certainly hadn't thought that her hanging out with an introverted washed-up spy who used to be her boss, in the very city where her life had gone to hell, in a country famous for corruption, was a recipe for long-term happiness. Now he wasn't so sure.

"*Maybe I should have,*" *said Mark.*

"*Can you get the Azeris to reconsider?*"

"*No. They're responding to Washington, Kaufman was adamant, and the PNG has already been filed.*"

A long silence passed between them.

"*And you're staying here.*"

When Mark didn't answer, Daria sat up in bed. "Well...I guess that's it then." She sounded angry, but it was a hurt, sad kind of anger.

"Daria."

"Don't worry, I won't make this hard."

"I work here."

"I understand."

"My whole life is here. I can't just—"

"I wouldn't want to take you away from that. It's no big deal. I'll pack today,"

They kept talking, but it soon became clear there really wasn't much more to say. Daria had to leave, and Mark wasn't willing to go with her.

"What is this place?" Mark figured maybe it was a safe house she kept for meetings like this, when she wanted to be away from prying eyes.

"I live here."

He took a closer look around him. There was no bed, but there was a door—he'd assumed it was a closet—in the far corner. Maybe that was the bedroom. A glass was perched on the side of the utility sink. Inside the glass was a toothbrush. "I like it."

He hated it. He hated to think that this was what Daria's life had come to.

Mark looked around the room again. "How do you cook?"

"I don't."

Daria had been raised by upper-crust diplomats, so her voice had a sophisticated lilt to it. It sounded completely out of place in a shit hole like this.

"What are you doing here, Daria?"

"What I'm doing here is none of your business. The question is what are you doing here?"

"You even go back to the States?"

He knew she had, because he'd kept tabs on her without her knowing it. She'd been staying with her adoptive parents, doing pro bono work for a charity that was trying to help orphans in Iran. Mark had been touched, given that Daria was an orphan of sorts herself. Knowing that she'd started to build a new life for herself had put his mind at ease.

"For a bit."

"How was it?"

"Not so great. The CIA wouldn't lift my cover, so my résumé's got a six-year blank on it. People would let me work for them for free, but that's about it. And I got sick of living with my parents."

"You said you would call me when you got settled. You never did."

"I know," she said. "What do you want?"

18

ALTY HAD BEEN PROPPED UP IN THE CHAIR, BUT HIS HEAD
sagged at an unnatural angle.

"We must bury him soon."

Decker turned toward the voice. The man who'd spoken had
distinctive dark circles under his eyes and wore a black turban.
But it was the cauliflower wrestler ears, bulbous and ugly, that
Decker—a former heavyweight wrestler himself—really noticed.
This was the man he'd been tracking.

He was in what he guessed was a basement, seated in the
center of a threadbare carpet that had been rolled out over a rough
concrete floor. The concrete foundation walls were mottled with
water stains. A workbench whose top was cluttered with assorted
tools stood in one corner. There was a strong smell of mold.

Decker glanced behind him. Two men with automatic rifles
slouched beside a utilitarian staircase leading up to the floor
above. Above him ran exposed floor joists.

"And your friend," said the man in the black turban. "What
is his religion?"

Decker didn't really know. The subject had never come up.
"Muslim." Decker hardly recognized his own voice. It sounded
parched and scratchy.

"Then we will arrange for a proper burial. And your religion?"

Decker remembered Mark Sava once giving him advice. If
you're ever captured by Islamists, Mark had said, don't try to
get them to sympathize with you by saying you're a Muslim,

or that you've read the Qur'an. If you get a genuine religious nut as an interrogator, things will be worse for you if he thinks you've been exposed to the word of Allah and have rejected it, or haven't properly followed it. If he thinks you're a Christian or Buddhist or Jew or whatever, he might just feel sorry for you.

"Christian." That was even kind of true.

"You have read the Qur'an?"

"No, never."

The man in the black turban asked why Decker had been at the ayatollah's house.

"I'm under orders not to say."

"Under whose orders?"

"I can't tell you." Decker hoped they would think some government was actually issuing him orders—that someone would actually care if he disappeared.

"You wish the same fate as your friend?"

Confuse them. Buy time. They won't kill you until they think they've learned everything they can from you.

"In two weeks you'll figure it all out for yourself."

"Two weeks? Why two weeks?"

"In two weeks you'll find out."

"You lie."

"Whatever, dude."

"You speak like an American."

"I am an American."

"What is your name?"

"John Decker." Decker hoped that they'd find out about his Navy SEAL experience and mistakenly assume that he was still a SEAL, and think that he was a high-value capture.

The man produced Alty's iPhone and placed it on a stool a few feet in front of Decker.

Decker tried not to stare at it, tried not to show his distress.

"You sent an e-mail from this phone just before you were captured. Why?"

"That's not my phone."

"One of the people you sent the e-mail to is a CIA agent named Mark Sava. Are you working for him?"

So they knew about the photos he'd e-mailed to Mark and Daria. It was so stupid of him, forgetting to put the damn iPhone in his gear bag inside the chimney.

"I said that's not my phone. I didn't send any e-mails from it." Decker gestured to Alty with his chin. "It's his phone."

"Then why wasn't it with him?"

"I don't know. Maybe he dropped it."

"It was recovered from the roof."

"So maybe he dropped it when he was on the roof with me."

"When was he on the roof with you?"

"Before you shot him. We were both up there."

"If this isn't your phone, then surely you have a cell phone of your own. Or a camera?"

"They're with my partner." *In two weeks something happens. You have a partner. Keep track of your lies. Believe your lies.*

"Your partner is dead. You can see this for yourself." The man wearing the black turban lifted Alty's chin and let the life-less head drop.

"Alty was our guide. My partner wasn't captured."

"You have no partner."

"I did."

"And you claim this partner now has your belongings, including your cell phone and camera?"

"He does."

"Where is this partner now?"

"I don't know."

"Is he also working for Sava?"

"I told you I'm not working for Sava. I can't tell you who I'm working for."

A second later, Decker absorbed a heavy blow to the head, which was followed by another, and another. Amateurs, he thought.

Beating someone was a lousy way to extract information. He began to think that maybe he could handle this.

You have a partner. Something happens in two weeks. Keep the lies simple. Wait for them to make a mistake.

19
Almaty, Kazakhstan

DARIA SAT WITH HER HANDS CROSSED OVER HER CHEST AS Mark told her about the assassination attempt, his expulsion from Azerbaijan, the e-mail from Decker, and finally, his meeting with Holtz.

She thought he looked about the same as the last time she'd seen him. The same brown eyes; still not visibly muscular, though she knew he was deceptively strong, in a lithe, sinewy way. Maybe a little more gray around the temples, but not much. He could have passed for an old thirty or a young fifty. Not the kind of guy most people would notice.

She'd once been fooled by his average-looking appearance, but now she saw past it. Now she noticed right away that his eyes were cold, and just a bit too wide set, making him look a little reptilian. Now she picked up immediately on the natural half sneer on his lips. Though she knew he was capable of great kindness, that expression reminded her that he was equally capable of apathy, even cruelty.

"It was Holtz who told me where to find you," said Mark.

"You didn't get my message?"

"What message?"

"I called you in Baku."

"Must have been after I left."

"I called because I got the e-mail too."

"So you were the CC on it. I wondered."

"I recognized Deck's arm too. I thought he might be in trouble, so I wanted you to contact Holtz. Which you did anyway."

"Why didn't someone come after you the way they did to me?"

"Maybe because my e-mail address doesn't have my name on it?"

"Clever."

"Maybe because all my e-mails are run through an account that encrypts them before forwarding them to a second account?"

His eyes fixed on her. "I wasn't thinking like a spy, Daria. I was thinking like a professor. Because that's what I am. Or rather, was."

"By the way. Holtz was lying. He didn't fire me. I quit."

"OK."

Daria stared at Mark for a second, trying to gauge whether he believed her. Then it hit her—he didn't care one way or the other. Because he didn't care about her. She had to get that through her head once and for all.

"Let's look at the pictures," she said.

Mark pulled the flash drive out of his coat pocket.

"Don't bother, I've got them on my laptop," said Daria. "They're in my bedroom."

20
Almaty, Kazakhstan

———————○———————

DARIA CRACKED HER BEDROOM DOOR OPEN JUST ENOUGH TO slip inside, but Mark was still able to get a glimpse of her setup. A hotel blanket covered a low cot, she'd stacked her clothes on an industrial metal shelf, and a postcard-sized reproduction of van Gogh's *Irises* had been affixed to the wall with a pink thumbtack. He thought of Daria going to sleep in there alone, staring up at those irises as the night closed in around her.

She emerged from the room with a new-looking laptop in hand.

"Jesus, Daria. This place depresses me."

Daria had always been a bit of a loner—the old-school boys at the CIA had never really trusted her, given the Iranian-American mixed-race thing—but not this much of a loner.

"I don't need your pity."

"I was just—"

"It's not as bad as it looks."

"OK."

"I'm spying on the Chinese. I've only been here a couple weeks. I'm still getting settled, and most of the time I'm at the hotel, which is where all the Chinese government types hang out. Don't be so quick to judge."

Mark wondered what it would have been like if, instead of saying good-bye when Daria had been kicked out of Azerbaijan, he'd gone with her to Washington and settled down. What would have happened if he'd taken a few consulting jobs, cashed in on his Agency experience, made some real money, bought a big house...

He had a sense that Daria would have been OK with that scenario. But a big part of him had genuinely thought that she'd have a better chance at a normal life without him. And though he'd fallen for her, and had longed for her after she'd left, he hadn't wanted to leave Baku.

It occurred to him, though, that just eight months later, she'd failed completely at living a normal life, and he'd had to leave Baku anyway.

Daria opened the photo files. "So we're talking lousy quality. Worse than even a cheap digital camera."

She pulled up information about the memory size of each photo, then clicked from one picture to the next, quickly highlighting one detail here and another there, using the laptop as a natural extension of her brain in a way that made Mark feel stupid. Back in the dark ages, when he'd actually spied on people, he'd used film. Since leaving the Agency, it had never occurred to him to take pictures for pleasure.

"The only digital cameras that take these kinds of low-res pictures are kids' cameras and older cell phones," she said.

"Focus on Deck's arm."

Daria navigated to that window. "I think he was taking a picture of himself—the arm in the photo looks like it's really close to the camera lens. And from the time stamp on this, I can tell it was e-mailed to us a minute after the photo was taken. So it's likely John sent the e-mail himself. Why would he—"

"Rally on me," said Mark.

"What?"

"That's what Deck's telling us. You're leading a squad or platoon or whatever. You want your men to rally around you, come to where you are, but you can't just yell out the order. Instead you raise your index finger up like Deck's doing and circle your hand around in the air. That's why his hand is blurry. He's circling it."

"Why not just come out and write that in the e-mail?"

Mark shrugged. "Maybe he was afraid someone would read the e-mail. If he sent this from Turkmenistan, that would have been a legitimate concern. They read everything. Instead, he sent a sign that he knew I would probably understand but that the Turkmen wouldn't."

Daria clicked on the next two photos and placed them side by side on her laptop screen. "These two are older—the one of the mansion was taken a day before the arm photo, the one of two guys exchanging a briefcase, two days before. We can assume the man in the black turban is a sayyid, probably a Shiite."

A sayyid was considered a direct descendant of Muhammad. Most wore black turbans.

"Which narrows it down to what, a few million people?" said Mark. "We could be talking Azerbaijan, Iraq, Iran, and Bahrain...and even if the sayyid in the photo was from one of those countries, it doesn't mean that's where the picture was taken."

They spent the next twenty minutes staring at that photo, enlarging it, cropping it, doing everything they could to try to get more information off of it. But the resolution was awful, the background dark, and other than the black turban, the clothes the men wore revealed nothing. They had no better luck with the photo of the mansion. It was adorned with Ionic Greek columns, surrounded by shrubbery, and didn't look like anything that belonged anywhere in Central Asia or the Middle East, much less Turkmenistan.

Eventually they ran out of things to scrutinize. The room went quiet for a moment, at which point Mark said, "Hey, Daria. You think now would be a good time for you to tell me what you guys were really doing in Turkmenistan?"

For the first time, Daria smiled. "I thought your buddy Holtz already told you."

"Give me a break. He didn't tell me shit. I'm not that stupid."

21

D ECKER LAY ON HIS BACK, NAKED AND CHAINED TO A RUSTED
metal bed frame.

Someone asked him another question, but the English was heavily accented and he couldn't concentrate well enough to follow it.

He didn't need to hear the question, though, because the questions were always the same. His captors knew from the photos on the iPhone that he'd followed a trail of money from Ashgabat, Turkmenistan, to the ayatollah's mansion. What they wanted to know was—why? Who had ordered him to do this? Who else knew that he had done this? Who was the second person he'd e-mailed just before being captured?

Decker figured that the only reason he was still alive was that he hadn't answered those questions yet. At least not to their satisfaction. What he'd told them was that his partner, the fictional man he still insisted was out there, had hired him to help watch the ayatollah's house, but that he didn't know why.

He heard the swish of the truncheon cutting through air. A new burst of pain spiked up through his feet like an electric shock—then coursed up his legs, side, and into his arms until finally it felt as though his brain might just short-circuit.

The bastinado, you know this. You've been trained to resist it.

No, not to resist it, to accept it. Don't fight the pain.

Beating a prisoner's bare feet, where there were clusters of sensitive nerves, was a common form of torture, Decker knew.

During training, he'd inflicted it on fellow SEALs and they'd done the same to him.

Time passed. There was more pain. Men left, men arrived. Decker heard voices whispering in his ear. He couldn't understand them, though he vaguely realized they were speaking in English.

Through the agony he thought, *amateurs.* He was beyond listening, beyond being able to respond. The pain racking his body was too great. They were wasting their breath.

After a while, someone unchained him and rolled him off the bed frame. He fell to the carpet, and someone dragged him into a corner. The concrete floor felt blissfully cold on the swelling around his eyes. He watched as the old carpet was pulled back, revealing a trapdoor that two men struggled to lift. When they'd gotten it open, they turned to him. He felt a hand under each of his armpits.

The hole smelled musty and wet. He was thrown in headfirst, unable to break his fall because his hands were still cuffed. He lifted his head up and looked around. The walls were made of brick. The floor was mostly dirt, though remnants of rotted wooden floor planks were visible around the perimeter. When he rolled onto his back, he saw the concrete ceiling was striped with rusted bars of steel rebar. The only object in the hole was an enormous safe.

The heavy trapdoor slammed shut. For a few seconds, rays of light seeped through the cracks where the edges of the trapdoor met the floor. Then he heard boots stomping above him and the carpet was pulled back over the door. Absolute darkness descended.

He crawled on his bare knees through the dirt until he felt the cold metal of the safe. With his cuffed hands, he gripped the handle of it, as though it were a door to another world. The Narnia movie flashed in his disjointed memory. He'd watched part of it with his SEAL buddies in a squad-sized can at a forward operating base in Afghanistan. They'd been waiting to leave on a night mission. Guys had been checking gear, charging spare batteries, going over maps, jacking steel, and taking turns using the freezing shitter next door to rub one out. It had been winter, in the Hindu Kush Mountains. He shivered, as if he were there now.

Pull open the door. It's a wardrobe that will lead to winter— no, to a beach.

An image of South Beach, Florida, flashed through his head, and he remembered a spring break trip when he was a military cadet at Norwich University. Downing shots, awesome sloppy sex in a bathroom with a girl from Baton Rouge with huge tits, nursing a brutal hangover on the beach...

My God, it had been so fantastically warm on that beach. The hot sand on his back, the hot sun on his face, healing him.

He pulled on the handle to the safe, but it didn't budge.

22
Almaty, Kazakhstan

———————◦———————

"**H**OLTZ WAS BEING HONEST WITH YOU—UP TO A POINT," said Daria. "He *was* trying to help the State Department build better relationships with the Turkmen, so the US won't get shut out of all the oil and gas deals."

"And helping State lobby the Turkmen on the pipeline from Iran to China."

"Of course. State was trying to get the Turkmen to deny transit rights."

"So that's why *you* were there. To help stop the pipeline."

"You don't know that."

"You couldn't just let that pipeline go? After all that happened?"

The scars on Daria's face were partially a result of a fight over that pipeline.

Personally, Mark didn't care whether that oil pipeline from Iran to China got built. Iran had oil that China wanted to buy. So what? Oil was a global commodity. If China bought more from Iran, then they'd buy less from the Saudis, or the Sudanese. There'd still be the same amount of oil on the planet for everyone to fight over. And fight they would. Nothing would ever change that.

Daria's eyes narrowed. "That thing gets built, the mullahs get a steady stream of cash for the next thirty years. Say good-bye to any dream of a free Iran."

Mark wanted to say something to the effect that maybe it wasn't her battle to fight, that maybe whether Iran ever became free was up to the people living inside the country, not her, but they'd already had that conversation, and it hadn't ended well.

"I admire your idealism," he said.

"Oh, please."

"So anyway, Holtz was in Turkmenistan helping State. I'm listening."

Daria stared him down for a moment, then said, "Having an opportunity to help stop that pipeline from getting built was a large part of why I took the job. But Holtz hadn't been hired just to get the Turkmen to deny transit rights on the pipeline. The bigger focus was stopping the Chinese from cutting deals to lock up Turkmenistan's natural gas reserves. The problem was the Chinese were playing dirty."

"I'm shocked."

"State had only been negotiating for two weeks when inflation in Turkmenistan started going crazy. Like, in a few days the price of everything doubled. Which meant all of a sudden Turkmenistan had a serious cash problem. The government needed money for subsidies, and quick, so people didn't starve or revolt because they couldn't buy food."

"So Turkmenistan starts looking around for a big pile of cash to solve their problems."

"Long-term you could say we were offering a better package deal—"

"But the Chinese were offering more up front. For the natural gas and transit rights for the pipeline."

Mark had seen this movie before. In Angola, Sudan, Myanmar…throwing money at sketchy third world governments was often the way China got deals done.

"Yeah," said Daria. "A lot more cash. And with everyone suddenly going crazy over inflation, Turkmenistan needed cash to keep people from rioting."

"So'd you figure out how China rigged the inflation spike?"

"By buying up massive amounts of black market US dollars with Turkmen manats."

Mark considered the implications of such a move. "That would only cause inflation if the manats being used to buy up dollars were new to the system—like if the government was printing money." You print a lot of money, you dilute your currency, the value of the currency goes down, inflation goes up.

"Or if someone else was printing counterfeit money."

Daria leaned toward Mark from across the table. Her face was animated now, in a way that reminded Mark of how she used to be, when she was just a young, overly enthusiastic operations officer.

"I didn't know it at the time," she said, "but it turns out that's exactly what was happening. Anyway, around three weeks ago, when inflation really started to run wild, I told Holtz that I suspected the Chinese were behind it. I didn't have any real evidence yet, but the fact that inflation was mysteriously spiking just as the Chinese were preparing their cash offer was too much of a coincidence. The thing is, Holtz had just seen some intel suggesting that it was the Russians."

"The currency scam is too sophisticated for the Russians," said Mark, trying to make sense of it all. "They go more for straight-up bullying. Send your damn gas and oil north through Russia or else."

"That's what I thought. Holtz didn't see it that way, though. Since we hadn't really been getting along anyway, I quit."

"Huh. Just like that."

"Well, I figured if Holtz wasn't going to look into it, I'd look into it on my own."

"Here? In Almaty?"

"Chinese intelligence uses this city as a hub—their diplomats are always flying back and forth between here and their Central Asia stations. They usually stay at the InterContinental."

"What's your end game, Daria?" Mark wasn't sure what Daria was up to, but he was certain she was up to something. "I mean, say you get incriminating intel on the Chinese and leak it to the Turkmen. Worst-case scenario, they just have to throw more money at the problem to smooth things over."

Between the Chinese and the Turkmen and the currency scam and now Daria, Mark's head was starting to spin.

"If I can come up with proof that the Chinese were screwing with Turkmenistan's currency, it would be worth something. It'd be intel I could sell."

"So you really are freelancing as a spy-for-hire. Competing against Holtz."

Mark hadn't believed it when he'd heard it from Holtz.

"Something like that. If I can find a way to slow down the China-Iran oil pipeline along the way, great. In the meantime, I have to eat. I need money to live."

"Fantastic. Sounds like a plan."

"Don't give me that."

"I'm just saying."

"You know, this might come as a shock to you, but I've actually put some thought into what I'm doing. I tried going home."

"For how long?"

"Long enough."

"Sometimes it takes a while to really change gears."

"Yeah. Like you'd know."

"So say you get the proof you want that the Chinese are screwing with Turkmenistan's currency. Who do you sell it to? The Americans?"

"Or the Turkmen, or the Russians. I'd even sell it back to the Chinese if they wanted to pay me to keep it quiet."

Everything that Mark knew about Daria suggested she was an idealist. To a fault.

A suicide mission to scuttle the Iran-China pipeline was right up her alley. Making money off the Chinese by selling them back incriminating intel, that was a stretch. He looked around at her dismal living quarters and reconsidered. Maybe she was telling the truth. Maybe she was desperate; maybe she just *really* needed the money.

"I've already found out enough to be worth plenty," she said.

Daria stood up, walked to her bedroom, and came back with a large black imitation-leather shoulder bag. From the way she was handling it, Mark could tell it was heavy. She dropped it on the table and pulled out a bound stack of brightly colored Turkmen manats. "If you add up everything in this bag, it comes to about twenty thousand dollars. All counterfeit. I have videotape of these bills being exchanged by Guoanbu agents at the InterContinental."

"You stole this from the Guoanbu?"

"It's not like it's real money."

Mark picked up the stack of manats. The Guoanbu was China's Ministry of State Security, their main overseas intelligence agency. They were like the CIA, only a lot meaner. Daria was playing with fire. "How can you tell they're counterfeit?"

"The little horse you see in the center of the Turkmen star—in the real bills it's screwed up, but in the counterfeit bills, it's perfect. North Korean work, I figure."

Mark squinted at the top bill for a bit but his eyesight wasn't what it once was. He handed the manats back to Daria. "You think Deck got involved in any of this?"

"He shouldn't have. He was just there to protect State Department negotiators."

"But you think he did."

"It's a possibility. When I think of what could have gone wrong over there, this is what comes to mind."

23

───────○───────

WHEN DECKER WOKE UP, HIS BARE BACK WAS PRESSED against the cold safe and he was shivering. He wondered when he'd last had anything to eat.

He thought back to when he was just a kid, eating pancakes in his mother's kitchen with his dad and older brother and sister. They'd had syrup from the sugar maples in the woods out back, and lots of butter. Sunny Delight orange drink. Bacon. My God, what he would give to be able to go back, maybe take Daria with him to meet—

Stop it.

No more Narnia, no more South Beach, no more Daria, no more pancakes. You're hungry. So what. Focus.

He slid his legs through his arms, so that his cuffed hands were in front of him. Dirt had accumulated in both the entry and exit gunshot wounds on his leg, so he lowered his head and cleaned the wounds with his mouth like a dog. He spit out the dirt and kept at it until the wounds bled a bit.

Now what?

Now you think about how to get your ass out of here. For starters, where is here?

Decker recalled the exposed ceiling joists, cinder-block walls, and smell of mold in the room above him. He'd been certain it was a basement. But he was below that room now, in a cellar below the basement.

He forced himself to stand. He couldn't see a thing, but he could feel that the wall he was bracing himself against was

97

made of brick. He ran his finger across the mortar joints. They felt solid. When he pounded the wall with his elbow, the bricks didn't move. He ran his hand over every inch of the wall. It was in decent shape all the way down to the rotted bits of floor planks that ringed the perimeter of the hole.

The rotted floor planks, and the dirt beneath them, felt damp on his bare feet. He could try to start tunneling down through the floor. But in what direction? And he was presumably deep underground. He'd be found out long before he made much progress. If that was his only option, he'd try to make a go of it, but he was almost certain the effort would be futile.

The floor is damp. Almost muddy. Water's getting in from somewhere.

Decker slowly made his way over to another wall, and here, up near where the brick wall met the concrete slab of the basement floor, he felt a damp, flaky substance on the brick and mortar. He put a finger to his mouth and tasted salt.

When Decker had patched up the leaky basement walls of his family home in New Hampshire, he'd tasted that same salt.

It came from disintegrating mortar, or from the soil behind the mortar. He knew it had to have leeched through the porous wall, pushed through by the water, before crystallizing. There was no leaky bathroom right above him. The only place that water could have come from was from rain or snow.

Which meant the salt patch on the wall had to be close to the exterior of whatever building he was in.

Decker felt the mortar joints. Behind the salt crystals, they were damp and soft. He hammered his elbow right into the center of the soft spot, and felt a little movement.

24

M ARK STOOD UP AND WALKED SLOWLY OVER TO THE BASE-
ment window. Outside lay a pile of yellow snow. He could
faintly smell the cat piss even though the window was closed.
With his back turned to Daria, he said, "Holtz said Deck had a
thing for you."

They'd all known each other back in Baku. Mark hadn't been
surprised by what Holtz had said. Daria, scarred or not, was the
kind of woman who attracted a lot of guys. Some were attracted
to her broad smile, some to her high cheekbones, some—he
counted himself in this group—to her quick wit and natural
intelligence.

Mark figured Deck—not exactly the most sophisticated
guy—had probably just fancied her ass.

Daria's chair creaked as she adjusted herself in it. Eventually
she said, "What's that got to do with anything?"

"Did you have any contact with Deck—conversations or
e-mails or whatever—after you left Turkmenistan?"

"He sent one e-mail right after I left."

"Saying what?"

"That he wanted to meet me here in Almaty after he got done
with the job in Turkmenistan."

"How'd you respond?"

"I didn't. I mean, I like John well enough, but…anyway, I
didn't want him around when I was working here."

"So you two weren't—"

"No."

Mark decided Decker was actually a pretty good guy. And a lot more sophisticated than people gave him credit for.

"And nothing since then?"

"I don't think so."

"Meaning?"

Daria pulled out a new-looking smartphone from the pocket of her hotel-uniform blazer, tapped the touch pad a few times, stared at the screen for a moment, and then handed the phone to Mark.

"What do you think?" she said.

Meet me in front of Turkmenbashi Ruhy Mosque, Tuesday noon. If not Tuesday, Wednesday, noon. Sincerely, John Decker.

Below that e-mail was another consisting of just three letters.

"What does *W-T-F* mean?" asked Mark, reading the second e-mail. "Is that a code or something?"

Daria gave him a funny look. "That's how I responded to the e-mail with the photos attached to it."

"With a code?"

"No not a code." Her mouth formed a big, broad, pretty smile. "It just means, you know, 'what's up with this?' I was asking whoever sent the photos why they sent them."

Mark didn't get it, but he didn't feel like pressing the point. He studied the e-mail that had allegedly been sent by Decker.

Located on the outskirts of Ashgabat, the capital of Turkmenistan, the Turkmenbashi Ruhy Mosque was, he knew, the largest mosque in Central Asia. But it was also a bit of a joke—few Muslims actually worshipped there because the Soviet bureaucrat-turned-dictator who'd ordered it built had inscribed his personal words of wisdom all over it, right next to verses from the Qur'an. Attendance at prayers was more likely to consist of ten worshippers than the ten thousand the mosque could hold. Mark doubted that Decker had even heard of the place.

"He would never sign off on an e-mail with *sincerely*," Mark also noted.

"With me he always signed off as *D* or *Deck*."

"And he wouldn't use any capital letters," said Mark. "Worth a trip to Ashgabat, though."

"Yeah, if we show up at the mosque tomorrow and act polite—"

"You know the kind of operation I'm talking about."

"It's Monday night. How are you going to get a visa for Turkmenistan by tomorrow? It takes them a week just to open a piece of mail, much less process a visa."

Mark knew Daria was right. The Turkmen government was vigilant about keeping foreigners out of their country. Even his black diplomatic passport wouldn't let him cut any corners. But someone would be at the Turkmen embassy at this hour, and bribes to rush through visas weren't exactly unheard of. He eyed the sack of counterfeit money.

"That's evidence," said Daria.

"One or two bills would be enough to prove your point about Chinese meddling. You can take a picture of the rest."

"I'm not giving you twenty thousand dollars."

"It's not twenty thousand dollars. It's a bag full of paper made to look like twenty thousand dollars' worth of Turkmen manats. Besides, this is my life we're talking about."

"Your life?"

"Yeah. My job, my book, my home. My life. All that got trashed. I want to know why, and what I can do to fix it."

"The only reason you *had* a life to get trashed was because of Decker. You'd be dead if it weren't for him."

"Are you talking about what happened in Baku?"

"What else?"

"I was paying him a boatload to provide protection then, Daria. He was doing his job. I don't owe him anything." Although, as Mark spoke, he realized that wasn't quite true. The first time

Decker had saved his life, Decker had been under contract with the US embassy in Baku. It was only later, because of that incident, that Mark had hired him. "Besides, we don't even know that he's in trouble."

Daria stood up, shouldered the bag of money, flipped a lock of hair out of her face, and began walking toward the door. Then she turned to face Mark.

"Did you ever consider that whoever came after you might also be after me? I might not have been stupid enough to use an e-mail address that sent them straight to my door, like you did, but encryption software isn't perfect. There's a digital trail that they can use to track me down if whoever came after you has enough money and expertise. I'm not safe here any more than you were safe in Baku. Did you ever think about that?"

"I didn't even know you were involved until now. Where are you going?"

"First the Turkmen embassy on Abay Street to get myself a five-day transit visa, then the President Hotel in Ashgabat, which is where Decker and I and everyone else involved in the negotiations stayed while we were over there. I'll see if I can pick up any leads at the hotel. Then I'll go to the meeting at the mosque."

Mark doubted that the few hundred dollars in US cash he had on hand would be enough for the bribes that would be needed to secure a visa. Prior experience suggested it would cost several thousand. Maybe more, given that it was after-hours.

"You know I can help, Daria."

"Yeah, but help at what? I'm going over there to help Decker. That's my main objective. I have to know you're OK with that. If you can get your life back in the process and I can get some peace of mind, that's great too, but…"

"If I can help Deck, I will. You have my word."

Daria let out a genuine, spontaneous laugh.

"That wasn't meant to be a joke," said Mark.

"Are you forgetting I know you?"

"Come on, Daria. I bullshit people when I need to bullshit them, but I'm not bullshitting you now."

After a long time she gave a slight nod.

"Thank you," said Mark.

25

D ECKER ALMOST PASSED OUT FROM THE PAIN WHEN HE FIRST sank his swollen hands into the dirt behind the two-layer-thick portion of the brick wall he'd removed. But after a couple of minutes, his injured fingers numbed up and he began to use them like little spades. Each shovelful of dirt he placed quietly on the ground.

He focused on his training. Even when things seem hopeless, keep pushing, keep probing any way you can. Make every effort to escape.

Knock this out.

Above him, he heard voices arguing, but he couldn't tell what about.

When light appeared in the cracks around the trapdoor, he spread out the bricks and pile of dirt on the ground and tamped it down, slipped his legs back through his arms so that his hands were behind him, limped to a spot beneath the trapdoor, and carefully positioned his body so that it hid his handiwork. He couldn't let anyone come down to get him.

"I'm hungry!" Decker called out, his voice barely a whisper. The trapdoor creaked and the guard lifting it groaned. "Please."

The man with the black turban appeared from above.

"Don't shut the door," said Decker. "I can't stand it down here."

"If you agree to help us, you may eat as much as you like."

"I'll help you," said Decker.

"You may breathe fresh air. Why should you live like an animal?"

"I'll tell you where my partner is, and why I was sent here."

"Then climb up."

Decker struggled to ascend the rickety wooden ladder they lowered down. When he'd almost reached the top, two guards hooked their hands under his armpits and pulled him out the rest of the way.

"Now what was it you wanted to tell me?" asked the man in the black turban.

Decker didn't say anything. When the question was repeated, he turned his head and waited for the blow.

PART II

26
Ashgabat, Turkmenistan

———————○———————

"WHAT THE HELL IS *HE* DOING HERE?" ASKED DARIA.

She and Mark had landed at Saparmurat Turkmenbashi International Airport at dawn. Even with approved visas, purchased for the Turkmen equivalent of five thousand dollars apiece, they'd spent an hour in airport limbo before an officious luggage inspector was assigned to search their bags. Then they'd spent another half hour waiting for an aging nurse to inspect them, as if they were livestock, for communicable diseases. Then they'd spent another half hour answering routine questions posed by grim-faced bureaucrats who wore hats with comical upturned brims and who wrote painfully slowly in giant ledger books.

It was nearly nine before they were able to catch a cab to the President Hotel.

And now, when they stepped into the cavernous front lobby, intending to start questioning the staff about Decker, they instead ran into Bruce Holtz.

"You got me," said Mark.

"You didn't tell him we were coming?"

"Nope."

Holtz was slumped in a green-and-gold easy chair. Above him hung an enormous crystal chandelier. Two other men in business suits sat at tables nearby. Other than that, the place was empty, which didn't surprise Mark. He'd stayed at the President a few years back, while visiting the CIA station in Ashgabat. It was like a lot of things in Ashgabat: superficially fancy, but pretty crappy when you actually got to know it. Its main draw was that it was located right next to the Oil and Gas Ministry.

Holtz looked up when Daria and Mark approached.

"Hello, Bruce," said Mark.

Holtz took a sip of coffee and motioned to the small table in front of him, upon which sat a basket filled with breakfast pastries. "Join me, please. They brought too much."

He wore a dark custom-made suit with Gucci wingtip shoes, a gold tie, and gold, diamond-studded cufflinks. His hair was slicked back; a pair of sunglasses, with the Prada logo displayed prominently in gold on the frame, were folded on the table. Mark thought he looked ridiculous, like a Russian gangster on holiday, but he couldn't fault Holtz for it. That kind of look commanded respect in these parts.

"I take it this is not a coincidence," said Mark.

"I figured you'd show up here eventually."

Mark sat down in an adjacent easy chair.

Daria seemed to prefer standing to sitting next to Holtz. "What do you want, Bruce?" she asked.

Holtz turned, as if noticing Daria for the first time. "I see you found her," he said to Mark, and then he raised his finger for the lounge waitress. "Coffee?"

Mark grabbed a raspberry danish from the basket in middle of the table. "Don't bother. Cut to the chase, Bruce."

"You know, Sava, sometimes you can come off as rude."

"I've been told."

"It occurred to me that we might be in a position to help each other."

Mark said nothing.

Holtz added, "And that maybe I could have been a little more helpful when you first came to me. Like about where you should start your search for Decker. In fact, I'll give you a hint right now—not here."

"If you know where we should be looking, why haven't you started looking for him yourself?" Daria asked.

Mark could guess at the answer to that question.

Turkmenistan was one of the strangest countries on earth. It had been ruled for years by a megalomaniac who called himself Turkmenbashi, and was now ruled by the late dictator's dentist. Burdened with an ungodly bureaucracy and obsessed with secrecy, it was as though the Cold War had never ended. Holtz spoke some Russian, which evidently had been enough for him to help the State Department connect with higher-level government types in Ashgabat—Russian was the common language of Central Asia—but he couldn't navigate the absurdities of Turkmenistan without speaking Turkmen himself. Which he didn't.

Mark and Daria could speak passable Turkmen, though, because the language was closely related to Azeri, as were many of the other Turkic languages of Central Asia. On top of that, Mark spoke fluent Russian, and Daria spoke fluent Farsi.

"For the same reason that the owner of this hotel doesn't clean the bathrooms himself," said Holtz, looking at Daria. "That's where you come in."

Mark said, "Enough. What have you got?"

From the inner pocket of his suit coat, Holtz produced a sheet of paper. "This is a contract my attorney drafted last night. I'd like you to sign it."

Mark picked it up.

The contract said that, for the next five years, Mark agreed to serve as executive vice president of intelligence for CAIN, Incorporated.

"Let me break it down for you," said Mark. "I don't really like you, Bruce. Which makes me not want to work for you. And if I sign this, I'm still not going to want to work for you. And that means I'm not going to produce for you, regardless of any contract I may or may not have signed."

"Relax. I just want to be able to use your name and your résumé to help bring in business."

Mark didn't respond.

"You may have to sit in on a few conference calls," said Holtz. "That's all. And before you start threatening to tell the Kazakhs about CAIN's surveillance op up at Atyrau, you might want to think about who hired me to gather that information. Go on, take a guess."

Mark still didn't respond.

"Try the US military," said Holtz. "I fell for your BS blackmail the first time, but then I got to thinking, and I'm not falling for it again. You want to expose your own government? Because that's what you'd be doing."

Holtz pushed the contract toward Mark. "I didn't think so. You get one dollar a year for each of the five years. But if you actually want to go to work and bring in any new business, I'll give you twenty-five percent of the profits from it. It's a fair deal. The contract is clear. If you want to do jack squat, you get jack squat but I still get to say you're part of CAIN. If you want to do more—"

"Hundred thousand yearly retainer for the use of my name, fifty percent of profits from business I bring in."

"Fuck you."

Mark glanced at Daria. She looked appalled by the whole exchange.

"I'm also gonna need a little preview on what you have on Decker."

"I can tell you who he was with when he disappeared, what he was doing, and where he was going. I can't tell you where he is."

"Is he alive?"

"I have no idea."

"Hundred thousand, fifty percent. Keep in mind, I've got a good sense of what you're raking in by bilking State and DoD. I know you can afford it."

"Fine," said Holtz. "I accept your terms."

"I guess that means I should have asked for more."

"You're making a mistake, dealing with this asshole," Daria said to Mark.

Holtz pulled another set of papers out of his inner coat pocket. "One more thing. Noncompete agreements." To Mark he said, "When you're working for CAIN, you're not two-timing me on the side." To Daria he said, "Yours is the noncompete I should have had you sign when you were working for me. Translator, my ass. I did a little asking around. You were a fucking CIA NOC that went bad. The only reason you were working for me was to gather intel from my operation so that you could start up your own operation and cash in."

"You can't enforce a noncompete over here," said Mark. "What's the point?"

"Step one foot in the States and they're enforceable. You guys won't be hanging out over here forever. Eventually you'll go back."

Mark sighed. He figured that, if he put his mind to it, he could find a way to get Holtz to back down. But that would take effort. And besides, he was pretty psyched about the hundred-thousand-dollars-a-year-for-sitting-on-his-butt deal.

Daria said, "This is a joke."

"Those are *my* terms if you want to know what I know about Decker. Take them or leave them."

Mark looked at Daria.

"I don't care," she said, clearly disgusted. "Let's just get it done."

27
Washington, DC

———————○———————

"I TALKED TO THE ISRAELI DEFENSE MINISTER AN HOUR AGO. At minimum they're talking about targeting the reactor at Bushehr, the uranium enrichment sites at Natanz and Fordo, and the nuclear-related sites in Arak, Tehran, Ardakan, Darkovin, and Esfahan," said the secretary of defense.

It was well after midnight. The president was seated in his cramped study just off the Oval Office, cradling his head in his hand. On his desk was a crystal tumbler that held his nightly two fingers of single-malt Scotch—Lagavulin, his favorite. But tonight the Scotch had gone untouched for hours.

The Iranians had pushed too far this time. While the attack on Khorasani's daughter was appalling, the Israelis probably didn't even have anything to do with it. And even if they had, what Khorasani planned to do in retaliation was insane. He had to be stopped. It was just a question of whether the Israelis stopped him on their own, or with the help of the United States.

"They should be able to hit those targets on their own," continued the secretary of defense. "Whether they can actually destroy them all—"

"They can't."

"—is another matter."

"Can we?"

"You've read the latest assessment from CENTCOM."

"I'm asking you."

"Assuming our targeting intel is good, I agree with CIA and DIA that the odds would be in our favor. But destroying Fordo and confirming that the two nukes we believe are there have been taken out will require a ground team."

"And your personal view on whether the Israelis can pull off that kind of insertion on their own?" asked the president.

"I'm skeptical. Very skeptical. At the minimum we'd have to allow their helicopters to refuel on one of our carriers, or piss off the Iraqis and find a way to set up a refueling station in western Iraq. They're close to being able to pull it off, but they're not there yet."

Dammit all, thought the president, thinking not of what his secretary of defense had just said—he'd already known the answers, he'd just wanted to hear them one more time—but of the overall predicament. The Iranians had it coming, nobody disputed that, but an attack would come with a cost. He imagined the Iranians mining the bejesus out of the Strait of Hormuz, causing the price of oil to go through the roof and triggering a worldwide depression, while every living Iranian rallied around their idiotic government because they loved their country more than they hated the mullahs who ran it.

Knowing what his friend was thinking, the secretary of defense said, "Don't forget about a possible invasion or uprising in Bahrain. Sixty-five percent Shiite, and the Iranians would love to get rid of our Fifth Fleet."

The best-case scenario? The attack successfully wiped out the Iranian nuclear program, oil prices spiked temporarily but the market absorbed it, Iran made a stink and lobbed a few missiles at Israel but backed down because it didn't want to provoke a land invasion from the United States, and the Saudis and other Sunni dictators cheered silently while their people decided they hated the United States a bit more than they already did.

The president shook his head. It galled him that whatever happened, best case or worst case, the United States would bear all the costs while China and Russia and even the Europeans would probably reap all the benefits. All because of what had happened to one woman.

"I'll talk to CENTCOM one more time and then sleep on it," said the president. "You'll have my decision by morning."

28

Ashgabat, Turkmenistan

M ARK SIGNED ALL THE FORMS HOLTZ PUT IN FRONT OF HIM. Daria did too.

"There's just one other thing," said Holtz.

"No, there isn't," said Daria.

"Actually, there is. I just got the call an hour ago. Apparently Langley's been looking all over for Mark, calling everyone. We're talking a brief detour to the embassy, that's all."

"Tell us about Decker first," said Mark.

Holtz gestured with his finger, prompting Mark to look behind him. Across the lobby, standing in front of an interior waterfall that ran between two enormous plates of clear glass, stood the CIA's chief of station, Turkmenistan.

"You're a dickhead, Bruce."

"Relax, Sava. Langley just wants to debrief you on whatever went down in Baku, that's all. I couldn't say no, not if I want to stay in business over here. Shouldn't be more than an hour. Then I'll tell you everything I know about Deck, just like we agreed."

Mark recognized William Thompson, the lanky gray-haired guy who walked over to greet him; they'd worked together on a couple of occasions over the years. Mark remembered him as cautious and competent. Nearing retirement age.

They shook hands and exchanged a few greetings.

"You've been recalled," said Thompson. He settled his long frame into an easy chair next to Mark. He had a patrician, but not pretentious, air to him. "I suspect that's not what you want to hear, but there it is. I've been ordered to see to it that you're on the next flight back to Washington."

"Way to go, Bruce," said Mark.

"That wasn't the deal," said Holtz to Thompson. "You were going to debrief him at the embassy."

"I was OK with that," said Thompson. "Turns out Langley wasn't. I'm sorry, it wasn't my intention to mislead anyone."

"Sorry?" Holtz looked from Thompson to Mark and then back at Thompson again. "Sorry? We had a deal."

"I can't be recalled," said Mark. "I'm not on duty, I'm a private citizen."

"Langley says you're not," said Thompson. "Something about a contract to write political reports?"

"It was a once-a-month deal. I did it for them for free."

"I apologize if this comes as an unwelcome surprise, Mark. Everyone knows the Baku station was one of the best in the division when you ran it. But my orders from Langley are explicit."

Thompson picked up a secure cable printout and handed it to Mark. Mark studied it for a moment, then stared at Holtz.

"I was kind of in the middle of something here, William."

Thompson sighed. He looked tired and unwilling to argue. Mark wondered how long he'd been posted in Ashgabat.

"Well regardless, at this point it's out of my hands," said Thompson. "I don't know why Langley wants you back, but they do. If you want to call the seventh floor and duke it out with them, be my guest."

"What's your sense of it?"

Thompson shrugged. "Waste of time. The decision's already been made. I understand there was an incident in Baku—"

"Someone came after me. I'm trying to figure out who."

"So they mentioned. The whole Central Eurasia Division's been on heightened alert ever since. I'm sorry, there isn't a thing I can do about it. You know the drill."

Mark took a moment to think before saying, "Well, then that's it. I've been recalled, I'll go to Washington."

"Thank you for your understanding."

"The only thing I would ask is that you extend me the courtesy of allowing me to retrieve my belongings prior to departure."

Thompson smiled weakly. "I'm sure I can arrange to have them picked up. You're not staying here?"

"I flew in this morning and hoped to catch a flight back to Almaty this evening."

"Hmm..."

"I left my bags with a German expat who manages an Internet café downtown. He did some work for me in Baku a few years back. I stopped in to see him."

"Are you talking about the Matrix?" asked Thompson.

"That's the place. My man won't release my bags to anyone but me. I have some sensitive documents with them."

"Wouldn't you carry sensitive documents with you?"

"No."

Thompson waited for Mark to elaborate. When it became clear that Mark had no intention of doing so, Thompson scratched his temple and said, "Well, why don't we pick up your bags on the way to the airport."

"When do we need to leave?"

"Now. Langley was clear on that point. Find you, deliver the message, bring you to the airport, and watch you get on the plane. I've got to call in the flight info. They'll probably have an escort waiting for you at your first connection."

"Such trust," said Mark.

"It's not about trust—"

Mark checked his cell phone. "I just need to make a few calls first. To cancel the appointments I'd made for the day. Daria, I don't have much of a signal here. What about you?"

Daria checked her phone. "I'm good." She tapped a code into the touch screen, unlocking it. "Here."

Mark took it from her. Then he looked at Thompson and Holtz and Daria. "If you don't mind? A little privacy would be nice."

Thompson looked as if he did mind.

"Don't worry, William. I won't run."

"I'll wait for you right there." Thompson gestured to the entrance doors, which were just across the lobby. "Please, don't take too long."

After Holtz and Daria left with Thompson, Mark took Daria's phone and checked the time—it was a little after ten in the morning. He e-mailed Alty8@online.tm a message: *Dear John, noon at the mosque won't work. Instead meet me in twenty minutes at the Arch of Neutrality.*

Then Mark dialed the number for Daria's cell phone—the one in his hand—and left her a voice message telling her what the new plan was and what he wanted her to do.

As he was exiting the hotel, he handed Daria her phone. "Someone tried to call when I was using it. I think they left a message."

29

JOHN DECKER'S HALLUCINATIONS INCLUDED VISIONS OF THE vast north woods of New Hampshire, of swimming through the air and then floating over the trees, of finally being able to realize his boyhood dream of flying. Below him he saw the house where he grew up, his dad splitting firewood by the woodshed, his brother cranking up the ATV for a Saturday ride. He was soaring with the turkey vultures, circling and tipping his wings. A breeze started to blow, which gradually turned into a gale.

The winds blew him off his house. Soon he lost the ability to steer and struggled even to stay aloft. He was blown over the state line, northeast into the vast stretches of forest in Maine. There were no more houses below him, and as he was pushed farther north, he began to see patches of snow. The air was cold. He began to shiver.

You are a Navy SEAL. Navy SEALs don't give up.

And you are not in New Hampshire.

The gale was pushing him toward Canada with phenomenal velocity. The Arctic would soon be below him. He should have dropped to the ground in the forest. At least there he would have had a chance.

You are cold because you are in shock. Control your body. Control your emotions.

The brief glimpse Decker had caught of the mountains when he'd fought his way out of the trunk of the car had hurt him as much as the beatings he was taking. They were so steep and so bare. There'd been nothing out there—no color, no comfort. Those were mountains where you went to die.

He needed trees and streams and moss-covered rocks. He needed laughter at the kitchen table with his mom and dad and brother and sister.

Don't give up on yourself, asshole.

Decker woke up choking on mud. He felt the damp ground beneath his naked body. When he tried to push himself up, a pain like needles being stabbed into his fingers caused his whole body to seize up. He moaned and rolled to his side. Everything smelled rotten and damp.

He teetered for a moment, and swallowed a scream as he dug out a new handful of dirt from the wall.

A small hole eventually became a two-foot-long tunnel. At three feet he hit something that felt depressingly solid. He held his breath, preparing himself for the disappointment of encountering a concrete footing wall that he guessed extended below the basement slab. With the few good fingers that he had left, he brushed the dirt off the wall and felt for cracks in it.

He found lots of them.

The footing for the slab, he realized, had been made of crushed stone—which is why water had been able to run right through it. When he pulled on the rock directly in front of him, it moved. With the first rock gone, the next three were easy to dislodge. Soon he had a hole big enough to squeeze through.

He flipped onto his back and redoubled his efforts, digging up now that he was past the foundation. How many feet was it to the surface, he wondered. Six? Eight?

The darkness and the dank air pressed in on him. His huge frame wasn't doing him any favors. Most SEALs were just normal size—and more agile, which meant they could squeeze into tight places without much trouble. He'd been an anomaly. A clump of dirt fell into his mouth and he began to choke, suddenly overwhelmed by claustrophobia.

He coughed up the dirt and squeezed his eyes shut and bit his lip. Every fiber in his body was screaming out for him to back out of his little tunnel, run up the steps, heave open the trapdoor, and run like hell in the hopes of seeing the open sky, even it was for just a second before they shot him.

Manage your emotions. They underestimated you. They underestimated what it was possible for you to do.

He listened to himself breathe for a moment. Then he felt the dirt in his mouth and forced himself to think of what it tasted like.

It tastes like dirt, you moron. Calm down. Keep digging.

Decker closed his eyes and mouth, drove his wounded hand into the dirt above his head, and was confused when his arm kept going up. He wondered whether he'd stumbled upon some underground chamber.

Then he opened his eyes and saw light. Sunlight, filtering through wooden deck boards. He blinked as his eyes struggled to focus.

30
Ashgabat, Turkmenistan

————————o————————

STANDING IN THE CENTER OF DOWNTOWN ASHGABAT, THE 230-foot Arch of Neutrality had been built in the shape of a gigantic three-pronged Turkmen cooking trivet, from which a pot might be hung. At the peak of the arch was a gigantic gold-plated statue of the dead dictator Turkmenbashi, which rotated throughout the day so that it always faced the sun. Mark peered at it from the backseat of Thompson's black government-issued Ford sedan.

The arch was a couple of hundred feet away. Thompson had pulled over closer to it than Mark had wanted him to.

Beyond the arch, a vast empty parade ground sprawled before a blindingly white, gold-domed government palace. Scores of other buildings surrounded the palace, all of them white-marble confections that had sprung up in the years after the Soviet Union had collapsed, built with money from natural gas sales. Most were largely empty inside.

Turkmenbashi's idea had been build it and they will come, but so far no one had. The whole place had an apocalyptic, neutron-bomb feeling to it.

There were a few soldiers lingering nearby, though. Two of them, wearing oversized peaked caps and dressed in green cer-emonial uniforms adorned with an excess of gold trim, stood stiffly at attention in little glass-walled guard shelters near the arch. A cheerful bed of marigolds lay between the guard shelters. Another soldier directed light street traffic, and a group of six air force guys, dressed in comically bright blue-and-white camou-flage, strolled by the World Trade Complex.

The World Trade Complex, despite its name, was really just an uninspired mall with a few tired shops inside, one of which was an Internet café known as the Matrix.

As Thompson unbuckled his seat belt, Mark said, "I think you should wait with the car."

"In sight at all times until you get on the plane. Those are my orders."

"Listen, William. It's not safe."

Thompson stared at Mark for a long moment. They were seated in the front seat, close enough to each other so that Mark could see the deep wrinkles and liver spots on Thompson's fore-head. Gray hairs sprouted out of Thompson's ears.

Thompson cleared his throat. "I thought you were just pick-ing up your bags."

"The people who tried to kill me in Baku may be close."

"You tell me this now?"

"I lied to you earlier. I can't go back to Washington. Not yet."

Thompson gripped the steering wheel with both hands and looked out the windshield. "Don't do this to me, Sava."

Thompson had a deep voice. For the first time, Mark detected a hard edge to it.

"You ever run into a guy named John Decker? Big guy, former SEAL. Did protection work."

Thompson turned back to Mark.

"He was working for Holtz, here in Turkmenistan," Mark added. "A few days ago he disappeared. I think his disappearance may have something to do with why I was targeted in Baku."

Thompson exhaled and tapped the steering wheel. "We kept a few tabs on Holtz's team. If this Decker guy's the same person I'm thinking of, I can tell you two things about him—he used to go drinking at the expat pubs, and he'd jog practically a half marathon nearly every morning. That's about all I remember from the reports. He wasn't a focus."

Mark smiled, reminded of why he'd liked Decker. No native Turkmen ever went jogging. If you wanted to stand out in Ashgabat, jogging was a good way to do it. But it sounded like just the kind of thing Deck might do. The guy was a fitness nut, in better shape—despite his nighttime activities—than anyone Mark had ever known.

Thompson said, "I can ask around about him. That much I'm willing to do. But you're still going to the airport."

Mark opened the car door and stepped out. "Just tell the Agency I screwed you over. Believe me, they'll buy it. I'll deal with the consequences when this is over. Not your fault."

"I'm warning you, Sava. Don't do this."

Mark took one last look around, inspecting the surrounding buildings. It was a hazy day, the sun was bright, and the air felt thick in his lungs. Benches lined the perimeter of the square surrounding the arch, but only a few of them were occupied. All told, even though it was the middle of the day, he could see no more than ten people, half of whom were soldiers.

He hoped Daria was out there somewhere, though. The original plan had been to wait until noon, e-mail Alty8 instructions to come to the base of the Arch of Neutrality instead of the mosque, and then go just close enough to the arch to flush out whoever showed up. Mark had figured that whoever did would be thrown off by the sudden change of venue and that the soldiers guarding the arch would provide some protection. He also knew that the square was always empty, so it would be easy for Daria to watch the situation unfold from a distance. Finally, since the arch was in the center of the city, there would be plenty of places to run to after giving it a quick brush-by.

Mark still hoped to execute a version of that plan, so he turned to Thompson and said, "I'm sorry."

31

―――――○―――――

ECKER LAY ON HIS BACK IN A LOW CRAWL SPACE, NAKED, blinking, nearly blinded by the light that filtered through the interstices of the deck planks above him, and hyperventilating from the pain engulfing his body. After a moment he forced himself to crawl out to the edge of the deck. As far as he could tell, he was on the side of a modest split-level house that had been built into the side of a hill. He'd gotten lucky, because he'd popped out in a spot where the basement floor was nearly at ground level.

The sun hit his face, and for a moment he just lay there, hypnotized by the warmth, not caring that someone might see him.

Eventually he looked around.

The house was situated near the bottom edge of a bowl-shaped ravine, beyond which rose jagged snowcapped peaks. Juniper and tall narrow aspen trees ringed the lower parts of the ravine and lined the banks of a small stream that cut through its center. Looking up, he could see that the top of the ravine consisted of an uneven line of jagged broken rocks, so unforgiving, exposed, and lonely that Decker's spirits sank. Climbing up unnoticed would be out of the question.

From underneath the house, he heard the distinctive creak of the trapdoor being opened.

What he needed was water. Water and a car.

Two cars sat parked on a long dirt driveway—a green Peugeot and a black Khodro—but they were a hundred feet away and completely exposed.

From inside the pit, Decker heard voices and then cries of alarm. He had to move quickly, but deliberately. No mistakes.

A detached garage stood in back of the house. Decker limped up to it and yanked open the side door. No car, just a large oil stain on the floor where one had been. A pair of baggy, grease-stained work pants, a collection of gardening tools, and a brown jacket hung on one wall.

He put on the work pants as best he could with his cuffed hands. They only came down to the middle of his shins, but the waist was OK. He grabbed the jacket and a pair of sharp pruning shears, wishing he'd also been able to steal shoes.

As he limped out the back of the garage, a door smacked against the side of the main house. He heard boots pounding on the deck, then more cries of alarm. He plunged into a dense cluster of juniper trees at the base of the ravine and watched the panic unfold. One of his captors raced down the dirt driveway. Another appeared on the deck and started shouting orders. Yet another ran off toward the floor of the ravine, head low like a bloodhound trying to pick up a scent.

32
Ashgabat, Turkmenistan

M ARK HEADED AWAY FROM THE ARCH, TOWARD THE TWO-story World Trade Complex—though his real destination was the old section of town, where he knew he could get lost in the crowded Russian tenements.

Several tall fountains, each layered like a wedding cake, stood anchored in the vast square that surrounded the arch. Soon after Mark left Thompson's car, a man wearing blue jeans and a black jacket emerged from behind one of them. A camera hung from his neck, as though he were a tourist. He was a good hundred feet away, but walking slowly toward Mark as he read what appeared to be a map. Mark took a closer look and thought he detected Chinese features in the man's face.

Mark bore off a bit toward the northern edge of the square, in the direction of a traffic cop. He had everything under control, he thought. The older Soviet tenements weren't far away. He'd be fine as long as he moved fast and kept anyone who might be on his tail guessing. Daria should be photographing the whole dance routine from wherever she was hidden; he hoped she'd gotten a good shot of the Chinese tourist.

Then he saw Thompson jogging behind him.

Come on, buddy. Give it a rest.

Mark sped up, but Thompson sped up as well. So Mark let him catch up but kept walking at a fast clip. "Eleven o'clock, the guy with the map and camera. Watch him."

"You're going to the airport."

Mark saw another man approaching. "Shit. More incoming at three o'clock."

Mark was forced to veer off toward the center of the square.

"He's one of mine," said Thompson, struggling to keep up. "I told you all embassies in the region are on alert. I can't leave the building without a guard tailing behind me. He's armed and he's coming for you. You're going with me to the airport."

A Caucasian guy with huge forearms and a neck like a tree trunk closed in. An embassy rent-a-soldier, Mark figured.

"Get us back to the car," Thompson said to his guard.

Mark observed yet another man approaching from the side. He wore a coat that was heavier than the mild weather called for, and looked Chinese. Until a moment ago, he'd been seated on one of the benches on the perimeter of the square.

Mark began to think he'd miscalculated by pushing forward with the plan in spite of the Thompson complication.

"Move!" Thompson's guard flashed a pistol he was holding underneath his jacket and grabbed Mark's arm. "The Mercedes on the edge of the square."

"William, we have to bail. Now!" Mark pointed to an alley that he knew led to the Russian quarter. "Don't be stupid!"

A gray BMW screeched to an abrupt stop on a street a hundred yards directly in front of them. A man climbed out of the back of the car.

"They yours too?" Mark said to Thompson. "Because if they're not, we could be screwed."

"Just get us to your car," Thompson said to his rent-a-soldier.

In the distance, Mark saw the two Turkmen army soldiers still standing at attention in their glass-walled shelters by the arch.

Thompson's interference had allowed the Chinese—they were Chinese, Mark was certain of it now—to close in on all sides. The closest was only ten feet away.

"*Ogry!*" Mark called out in Turkmen. *Thief!*

"Shut the hell up!" said Thompson's guard.

"*Ogry!*" Mark called out again. This time one of the soldiers by the arch turned. After taking a second to assess the situation, he started running awkwardly toward them, struggling to gain speed in his dress shoes and stiff slacks. Mark waved his arms.

The Chinese were upon them in seconds, each one positioning himself at a different point on an invisible triangle. They weren't big men, but they all looked like professionals. Each of them wore a radio earpiece.

"Get the fuck away from us," said Thompson's guard. He stuck out his elbows and pushed forward like a bull.

"If any of you lay a hand on me, there'll be hell to pay!" said Thompson.

Mark felt a sharp stab in his side. When he looked down, he saw the butt of a pistol being held by one of the Chinese. Thompson's guard turned, saw the gun in Mark's side, then drew his own. He pointed it at the Chinese and said, "I'm paid to guard this man." He pushed Thompson forward a foot. "You let the two of us through, you'll have no problems."

"*Búyào pèng wǒ!*" said Thompson. *Don't touch me!*

The two Chinese in front appeared ready to back down and let Thompson go, but then one put a hand to his earpiece and nodded. A second later, a single sharp shot rang out. Mark ducked just as Thompson's guard slumped forward and fell to his knees.

One of the Chinese grabbed Thompson and started shouting commands as he pulled the CIA station chief over to the gray BMW.

Mark pivoted and tried to punch the Chinese behind him but his fist slipped off the man's chin. Another shot was fired and one of the Turkmen soldiers fell. Mark felt a blow to the head. He didn't pass out, but was dazed enough that he could do nothing to prevent being dragged over to the BMW.

33

D ECKER COULD HEAR HIS CAPTORS FRANTICALLY SEARCHING
for him, but the ravine was a large area to cover, and Decker
had been trained to be patient and use natural cover to his advantage.

When he'd slowly picked his way far enough through the
junipers that he could see the twisting mountain road at the
end of the driveway, he took out the pruning shears and tried to
loosen the nut and bolt that held the blades together. His fingers
trembled and were so weak that he gave up and used his teeth,
chipping one of his rear molars in the process. When he finally
got the blades separated, a stiff wire spring fell to the ground.
He straightened the spring and used it to pick the lock on his
handcuffs. He spread juniper needles over the discarded cuffs
and stuck the two loose blades in his pocket.

By methodically threading his way through the trees, lying
flat on the ground and covering himself with dead branches
whenever one of the guards came near, he eventually half-
crawled, half-limped to within a hundred yards of the mountain
road. He took his time, remaining perfectly still for minutes on
end and willing himself not to pass out. The longer they searched,
he knew, the wider the search perimeter would need to become.
Time was his friend if he could force his body to keep going.

Eventually, one of his captors sped off in a car.

Decker edged forward on his belly until he was within fifty
feet of the road. The driveway intersected the road maybe a quarter mile below him. He tried to shake the dirt out of his hair

and wipe his face clean, but all the cuts and bruises made it a painful process. There was no way he was going to look anything approaching normal anyway, so he gave up and started crawling up and away from the driveway, paralleling the road as he did so. He was able to advance maybe a quarter mile more, until the terrain became too steep and the road ducked into a small canyon. To continue forward would mean he'd have to come closer to the road, potentially exposing his position.

He lay there, perfectly still, for an hour—listening to the traffic pass. Early on, one car sped up the hill as if in pursuit of something, but after that, all appeared to be normal.

It was his extreme thirst that finally led him to inch closer to the road.

When he caught a glimpse of a white van slowly winding its way up a section of road below him, he checked for guards. None were visible, so he crawled the rest of the way to the pavement, stood next to a rock that concealed his bare feet, and stuck out his thumb. It was a wild, but calculated, risk. He was barely able to maintain consciousness, he couldn't stay hidden in the trees forever, and on foot he would be too weak to put any real distance between himself and his captors.

He faced uphill, so that the driver of the van wouldn't be able to see him, and tried to stand in a way that didn't draw attention to his injured left leg. The van slowed down, but only so that the driver could honk his horn at Decker and curse him.

The sound of the horn cutting through the silence of a peaceful sunny day was jarring. His captors must have heard it as far back as the house.

Another car appeared. Decker stuck out his thumb again. This time the driver just slowed down and gave him a nasty look. A man in a car going down the hill took one look at Decker's face and turned away.

But then a black sedan that was slowly laboring up the hill, its tailpipe smoking a bit as it burned oil, pulled over to the side of the road a few yards ahead of Decker. Two pairs of skis had been affixed to a roof rack. Decker dipped his head down, trying to hide his face as he approached the car. The rear door opened.

"Where do you go, my friend?"

The question was in English. They must have known, just from looking at him, that he was a foreigner. He collapsed in the backseat.

"*Merci*," he said. His voice came out as a low croak. He kept his head down, eyes pointed to the floor of the car. He thought that if he could just get to the Caspian, he could steal a boat. Water was his ally. "The coast," he said.

"We can take you part of the way, we go skiing at Dizin— look at me, please."

Decker raised his head up a fraction of an inch and made eye contact with the driver.

"*A'udhu billah!*" *I seek refuge with God.*

"I was robbed. Drive. Please."

The driver frowned deeply. As though he'd just realized that he may have picked up a complete psychopath.

When the car didn't move, Decker said, "Drive! Please!"

The driver slowly pulled away. Through the rear windshield Decker saw one of his captors—a man with a short-cropped beard—running after them.

34
Ashgabat, Turkmenistan

————O————

" I AM THE POLITICAL LIAISON TO THE AMERICAN AMBASSA-
dor!" yelled William Thompson.

Mark's vision was blurry. He put a hand on the back of his head because it felt as if he were bleeding there, but everything was dry—just a bruise, he concluded, filling with blood from the inside.

The Chinese hadn't killed him in the square. Which meant that now, despite the attempt on his life in Baku, they must want to talk to him. They'd probably want to kill him afterward, but for the moment they wanted him alive. That bit of knowledge was a tactical advantage.

"I am a diplomat, do you hear me?" said Thompson. "And I know damn well you all work for the Guoanbu. I know this! My government will soon know this. Are you trying to start a goddamn war?"

"Quiet!"

Mark and Thompson had been stuffed into the backseat of the gray BMW, squeezed together by a Chinese who sat on their right, clutching a gun. The Chinese in the front passenger seat was also pointing a gun at Mark and Thompson. The driver made a sharp turn, and the car's tires squealed. Mark felt for his wallet. It was gone. So were his cell phone and passport.

Thompson turned to Mark. "Why is this happening, Sava!"

The car made another sharp turn. They had left the showy white-marble part of the city and entered a neighborhood lined with old mustard-colored Soviet apartment buildings festooned with a riot of satellite dishes and air conditioners and rotting wood shutters.

"Quiet!" said the Guoanbu agent in the passenger seat of the car.

"I don't know." Mark wished everyone would stop yelling.

After speeding through the glum Soviet part of town, they came to a warren of dirt lanes framed by small houses with ramshackle fences protecting little gardens. A couple of minutes later, they skidded to a stop next to an old Russian Lada with bald tires. Everyone climbed out of the BMW and into the Lada.

They took off again, this time more slowly, in the direction of the vast Kara-Kum Desert that began just beyond city the limits. It occurred to Mark that the dunes of the Kara-Kum would be a convenient place to dispose of bodies.

But then they circled back toward downtown Ashgabat. Soon Mark saw the white marble and blue-tinted glass of the President Hotel looming in the distance.

It was Thompson who finally said, "They're taking us to the Chinese embassy. You will all regret this."

The Chinese sitting next to Thompson in the backseat smashed the butt of his gun into Thompson's temple, knocking the station chief's glasses off his face and opening an inch-long gash that started to bleed.

"Quiet."

They passed the enormous white-marble embassy of the United Arab Emirates. In the distance, a soldier in an olive-green uniform stood in front of a tall fence. A large red-and-yellow Chinese flag hung from a tall flagpole behind him.

The Chinese in the driver's seat pulled out an identification badge, as though getting ready to show it to the embassy guard.

Mark figured it was a near certainty that if they drove through those gates, he and Thompson weren't ever getting out. You don't abduct and rough up a US station chief and then let him live to tell Washington who did it. After the interrogation, that would be it. He glanced at the Chinese with the exposed gun in the front passenger seat.

The Chinese stared back at Mark and slowly shook his head, as if to say *don't even think about it.*

The entrance gate to the Chinese embassy was less than a hundred feet away.

Mark visualized manually unlocking the car door he was pushed up against and rolling out onto the road. They wanted him alive to interrogate him? Well, he'd run and dare them to shoot him. Alone, without Thompson dragging him down, it'd be a footrace, and he'd have a head start.

The car slowed to make the turn into the embassy. Mark was about to go for the lock when out of the corner of his eye he saw a police car on the opposite side of the road careen up onto the grassy median. The police car bounced over the curb, swerved sharply, and then lurched into their lane, going against traffic.

The Chinese driving the Lada cried out and yanked the steering wheel to the right, but the momentum of the two cars speeding toward each other was too much to overcome.

Mark put his arms out and braced himself against the rear of the front seat.

35

---○---

DECKER EYED THE COUPLE WHO'D PICKED HIM UP. BOTH early twenties, he figured. The driver wore sunglasses and a tight red ski sweater. He'd combed his longish jet-black hair straight back, exposing a high forehead. The young woman wore makeup and had plucked her eyebrows. Her green headscarf had slipped down to her shoulders, revealing long brown hair that framed a pretty face.

It pained Decker when she looked at him with such horror.

"I'm sorry," he said. He glanced out the rear windshield. They'd left the guard who'd been running after them behind. But that guard would have sounded the alarm.

"Where do you come from?" The driver spoke in heavily accented English. A tape cassette of a woman singing a plaintive song in Farsi played on the stereo.

"Canada."

"I never go to Canada."

"I was robbed." It was hard for Decker to speak. All his words came out so raspy that he didn't even recognize his own voice. "I was hitchhiking and they beat me and robbed me."

"Maybe because you show the thumb. Here, that is like, how do you say? F-U-C-K you. Some of the people in the mountains are not so smart, maybe they think you insult them. For hitchhiking you must wave the hand. I hitchhiked once in California. You need a doctor."

"No." Decker shook his head. "No doctor. I'm OK."

After an uncomfortable silence, the driver said, "Maybe the police can find these people who beat you. We will take you to the police."

Decker looked out the rear window. They passed a roadside kebab restaurant. A few modest houses lined the steep banks on either side of the road. He wished the guy would drive faster, but when he looked he saw the gas pedal was already pushed to the floor. At the next cluster of houses he'd have them stop, he thought. Maybe he could steal a car. He thought of trying to steal the car he was in, but didn't feel up to overpowering its current occupants.

"No. No police. Do you have anything to drink?"

The driver lifted up a ski jacket from the space on the front seat between him and the woman, revealing a six-pack of Coke. The woman handed Decker one, but when he tried to open it, his swollen fingers couldn't do it. The woman's eyes widened when she saw Decker's mutilated hands. Decker looked back right at her, thinking, *let it go.*

He handed her the Coke. "Could you open this for me?"

His voice trembled. She popped the can open and handed it back to him. He tried to take a big gulp, but the liquid was cold. His throat convulsed and he spit it up into his hands.

He felt like an alien.

"I'll go soon." He looked out the rear window again. A street sign said *Fasten your seat belt* in English. Between the Coke and the sign in English, Decker wondered whether he was going crazy.

"Doctor," said the girlfriend.

"No." Decker took another sip of the Coke, and this time the liquid went down, so he took another sip, and then another until he'd finished the can.

The girlfriend opened another and handed it to him. Decker finished that one too. The car came to a long ridge, and Decker turned to look behind him. He could see the better part of a mile or so of the road they'd just climbed. Two lanes wide, it wound down through the steep brown hills. An electric power line, with gray metal towers spaced every few hundred feet, paralleled the road.

A green Peugeot was about a half mile behind them and gaining fast, accelerating through the curves.

At the end of the ridge, at a spot where there was a ravine not unlike the one from which he'd escaped, Decker said, "Stop."

"A town," said the driver. "Three kilometers. We'll take you. We'll stop there."

"Here," said Decker. He should have gotten out at the cluster of houses he'd seen back down the road. He wasn't thinking clearly.

"Three kilometers. The town will be better."

By then the green Peugeot would have caught up. Decker gripped the driver's shoulder with his wounded hand and gave a violent squeeze. "Here, goddammit! Here!"

The car slowed to a stop and backfired.

"I'm sorry," said Decker.

"American?" said the woman.

"I need the rest of the soda!"

"Get out," said the driver.

The girlfriend quickly handed Decker four more cans of Coke, along with a large bag of sugared almonds. Decker mumbled his thanks and opened the door. As he was stumbling out of the car, she pulled out a half-full bottle of Smirnoff vodka from underneath the passenger seat.

"*Na!*" said the driver to his girlfriend. The look on his face said *no way in hell are we giving him that.*

"For face," said the girlfriend, looking at Decker. "For clean." She touched her face, as if swabbing it with a cotton ball, and pushed the bottle of vodka into his hands.

36
Ashgabat, Turkmenistan

———————o———————

WHEN MARK REGAINED CONSCIOUSNESS, HE WAS IN THE front seat of the Lada, his face mashed up against the dashboard and surrounded by shattered glass. A police car, its hood reduced to an accordion-like crumple, lay a couple of feet in front of him.

A strange silence persisted, as though time had stopped. For a moment Mark wondered if he'd been rendered deaf.

Broken glass tinkled as it fell to the asphalt.

Someone groaned. Mark lifted his head. The Lada hadn't been equipped with airbags and the seat belts had been removed, so the two Chinese who'd been in the front seat had been thrown outside—one lay facedown on the pavement, the other sprawled awkwardly on the hood of the police car. Both were motionless and bleeding, their bodies twisted into unnatural positions. Thompson was unconscious in the back of the Lada, slumped in a kneeling position on the floor. The groaning had come from the Chinese who was still in the backseat next to Thompson.

The driver's side door of the police car opened. Daria unbuckled her seat belt, pushed away the deflated airbag, and stumbled out.

The Chinese next to Thompson groaned again, so Mark aimed a foot at the man's head and kicked him as hard as he could until Daria climbed onto the hood of the car. "Gotta get out of here, Mark."

She pulled him out through the front windshield. His face and hands scraped against the broken glass. He rolled off what was left of the hood of the car and hit the pavement on his knees.

"Can you stand?" asked Daria.

Mark forced himself to do so. The world was spinning. He felt nauseous and had an unsettling feeling that his head wasn't properly attached to his neck.

"I'm good."

Quick footsteps sounded behind him. He turned to see a single Chinese embassy soldier sprinting toward them with a worried look on his face and an automatic rifle slung across his back.

Mark stumbled to the Lada, pried open one of the back doors, and grabbed a pistol from the Chinese he'd been kicking. Gripping it with both hands, he swiveled and fired a warning shot.

The embassy soldier stopped short. He'd clearly been expecting to help with an accident, not become a part of a firefight.

Mark fired another shot above the guy's head.

Daria screamed out something in Mandarin Chinese. The soldier let his rifle slip off his back and sprinted back to the embassy gate. He'd return within a minute, Mark knew. With reinforcements.

Daria retrieved the soldier's rifle. "We're outta here!"

"Thompson." Mark's head was pounding. Blood from little cuts on his head dripped into his eyes.

Sirens wailed in the distance. "No time."

"Help me get him out."

Daria face registered exasperation. "You get him out, I'll get us a car."

Mark pocketed the gun of the Chinese who remained unconscious in the Lada and dragged Thompson out of the backseat.

Thompson was a thin but tall man, and Mark struggled with the dead weight.

Fifty feet behind him, Daria commandeered a Volga sedan at gunpoint from a man who had stopped to gawk at the accident. She pulled up next to the ruined Lada and skidded to a stop.

Mark yanked open the rear door, clasped his hands around Thompson's chest, and heaved him into the backseat of the Volga.

37
Washington, DC

———————○———————

"**A**IM POINT ONE, ARAK."

A satellite image appeared on an LCD monitor. The monitor was embedded in a sound-dampening fabric wall at the far end of the conference table in the White House situation room. A PowerPoint slide with a series of bullet points popped up on an adjacent monitor: *40 megawatt heavy water reactor, air defense protection, onsite government housing, collateral damage risk: low.*

"Accepted," said the president's national security advisor. The secretary of defense, the director of national intelligence, the commander of CENTCOM, and the secretary of state—all members of the principal's committee—concurred.

"Confirmed," said the president. He took a big sip of his black coffee. It was six in the morning. He'd made his decision.

"Aim point two, Natanz."

The satellite image showed a lonely collection of buildings right where the desert met the Zagros Mountains.

The bullet points on the PowerPoint slide said: *Uranium enrichment site, 9000 centrifuges confirmed, heavily fortified, collateral damage risk: low.*

"This slide bears some additional explanation," said the secretary of defense. "Note that the armaments slated for the first attack include three twenty-two-thousand-pound MOAB bombs to clear the surface, followed by four of our thirty-thousand-pound bunker busters. When those go off in quick succession, it may cause enough of a seismic event that the Russians and Chinese will assume we've hit the Iranians with a tactical nuke. We'll have to have our diplomats ready to shoot that theory down pronto before it gets out of hand."

"Understood," said the secretary of state.

"Also, there could be a decent amount of both low and highly enriched uranium at the bomb site, which will complicate onsite confirmation of complete destruction. The cleanup team that goes in will have to be prepared for the radiation factor."

The CENTCOM commander said, "They are. But when it comes to Natanz, everyone needs to understand that heavily fortified means that the two main centrifuge halls we know of are both protected by two-point-five-meter-thick walls made of reinforced concrete, are buried at least ten meters in the ground, and further protected by a thick surface layer of concrete. Even with the new bunker busters, those underground halls are a tough aim point. The only way the air force feels comfortable guaranteeing their demolition is with an actual tactical nuke."

"We've talked about this," said the national security advisor.

"We'll hit it with the bunker busters until we get the job done," said the president. "If the SEAL team we send down to confirm destruction needs to finish the job, then that's what they'll do. We'll need boots on the ground to take out Fordo anyway."

"Target accepted with conventional armaments," said the national security advisor.

The rest concurred and the president confirmed the decision, as he did the decision to hit Fordo—a heavily fortified uranium-enrichment site that the Iranians had built under a mountain—with a combination of conventional armaments and a Special Forces cleanup team.

"Aim point four, Tehran Nuclear Research Reactor."

"Obviously this is a tough one," said the secretary of defense.

The satellite image showed a red dot in the middle of an urban area in northern Tehran.

"Define high collateral damage," said the president, after reading the accompanying slide.

"Two to three hundred civilians plus the technicians on site. Plus they use the reactor for medical purposes. Somewhere in the neighborhood of ten thousand patients a week are dependent on it."

"Are the heavy bombs necessary?"

"If we play it safe and dial down the armaments, we'd probably be able to limit immediate collateral damage to the technicians on site. But if we want to be sure we've taken it out completely, including the tunnels we believe are buried beneath the visible buildings, then we should go with the targeteers' recommendation."

"North Tehran is the stronghold of the reformists," said the secretary of state. "If we kill large numbers of civilians there, it will only drive them to the hard-liners. Intelligence is spotty about the tunnels and what they might contain. I'll accept the aim point, but with reduced armaments."

"My view is that the aim point should be accepted with recommended armaments," said the national security advisor. "The reformists will rally around the flag the second the first bomb falls, collateral damage or not."

"I agree," said the president. "Level the place."

The rest of the committee concurred.

38
Ashgabat, Turkmenistan

———————○———————

"IS HE ALIVE?" ASKED DARIA.

Mark sat beside Thompson in the rear seat of the commandeered Volga. He put his finger on Thompson's neck, feeling for the carotid artery.

"Yeah." He gave Thompson a light tap on the stomach. "William, you with us!"

There was no response.

"What do we do with him?"

Mark's head was pounding. "The US embassy. We'll leave him there. How did you find me?"

Daria explained how she'd gotten the message he'd left on her phone and set up a surveillance post with a view of the arch. After the Chinese had closed in and shot the Turkmen soldier, police from all over the city had descended on the scene within minutes. One of them had left his car running, so she'd stolen it—with all that was happening in the square, no one noticed her driving off—and had headed to the Chinese embassy. "I recognized a few of the guys who grabbed you. They're definitely Chinese Guoanbu. I knew they operated out of the embassy. So I took my best guess and drove right there."

"And ran straight into us."

"The Turkmen spent a ton on new Mercedes police cars last year. I figured the Mercedes had airbags and I was hoping you were in the backseat of that Lada."

"Lucky guess."

"My options were limited."

Mark couldn't argue with that.

"I couldn't let them take you past the embassy gates," she added. "If that happened—"

"You did the right thing." He'd been planning on running, but he might not have made it. "Thanks." He turned to face her, and they locked eyes for a moment. "Really, I appreciate what you did."

The US embassy in Ashgabat, a boxy, low-slung building clad in bluish-gray tiles, reminded Mark of a shower stall. The only remarkable thing about it was the massive satellite dish mounted in the rear of the property and the bristling nest of antennae protruding from its roof.

A guy in a black T-shirt with bulging arms and a radio headset kept watch from behind the tall, wrought-iron perimeter fence. A couple of Turkmen soldiers in camouflage uniforms walked back and forth along the outside of the fence.

Daria stopped about fifty feet from the entrance. Mark opened the rear door and dragged Thompson out onto the sidewalk. One of the Turkmen soldiers yelled at him to stop.

Mark hopped back in the car as Daria punched her foot down on the accelerator.

As they sped off toward the northern outskirts of the city, Daria said, "They're going to come looking for us. The Americans. The Chinese. The Turkmen. Everyone."

Mark didn't respond for a while. But as they were passing over the bridge that spanned the Kara-Kum Canal, the artificial waterway that ran almost the entire length of the country, he said, "They'll come looking for me, you mean. You're not on the CIA's radar, and no one saw you at the arch. If you act now, you can probably make it out of the country safely."

"We need to call Holtz."

"Did you hear what I said?"

"And we should call him now, before the Agency puts someone on him. He's our only lead on Decker."

39

---o---

D ECKER HOBBLED DOWN THE GENTLE SLOPE ON THE RIGHT side of the road, but as soon as the couple who'd helped him had driven out of sight, he retraced his steps, climbing backward so the prints made by his bare feet would still appear to be going downhill. He couldn't bend his left leg, but by keeping it locked at the knee, he was able to use it like a crutch.

Fighting through the pain, he half jogged, half limped up the road a bit then began to climb the steep slope above it. About halfway up, he collapsed behind a large rock as his pursuers raced by in the green Peugeot. They would catch up with the couple soon, he knew. And when they did, the couple would bring everyone back to this place. But with any luck, his pursuers would think that he'd gone down the hill in the direction of the houses below. That's what a rational person would do.

He still had a chance. The mountains here were huge. Desolate and bare, but huge. All he needed was someplace safe to hole up in for a day, so that his pursuers would be forced to further widen their search and spread themselves thin. The terrain would be as unforgiving for them as it was for him.

Decker took out one of the pruning shears' blades and used it to stab open one of the Coke cans. He downed it all in a few seconds, carefully put the empty in one of his jacket pockets, ate two handfuls of sugared almonds, and began to climb again. The pain in his leg from the bullet wound was excruciating, but the pain in his bare feet, swollen from the bastinado and bleeding from the sharp rocks on the mountainside that had pierced his soles, was worse. After five minutes, he collapsed.

He ate more sugared almonds, drank another can of Coke, and forced himself to continue.

At the top of the ravine, a long patch of melting snow lay in a hollow hidden from the road but exposed to the surrounding hills. Decker placed his hands on top of the snow and let them numb up while the sun warmed his face. For there to be snow in April, he reasoned, he had to be at a relatively high altitude.

Which way was the coast? He looked up at the sky, blinking from the brightness. The sun was halfway between high noon and the horizon. Was it morning or afternoon? Which direction was he facing?

He was trained to survive in the wilderness for weeks on end, to orient himself by the sun and stars, to use natural cover as camouflage. But his mind was freezing up. He looked at the whiteness of the snow and began to get dizzy. Moss grew on the north sides of trees, but nothing at all grew up here. Deep in his gut he felt a sharp stab of pain, his stomach revolting against the sudden influx of food and drink.

He should find a hole to hide in and camouflage himself.

Far below, where he knew the road must be, a car skidded to a stop.

The bottle of Smirnoff slipped out of his jacket as he struggled to stand. He slumped back down into the snow, opened the vodka, and poured it over where he knew the bullet wounds on his leg must be. The vodka soaked into the grease-stained work pants and the wound beneath burned. Decker clenched his teeth. His eyes wanted to tear up, but he was still too dehydrated to form tears.

The air was cool and fresh, and he breathed in as deeply as he could, savoring the clean taste of it.

He poured vodka into his swollen hands, soaking his fingers, then poured all that was left into his cupped palms and brought the alcohol to his face, trying to disinfect the cuts as best he could.

Buying time, that's all you're doing. Fighting off infection for as long as you can.

His face felt as though it had been doused with acid. He struggled to stand but wobbled on his feet. The blue sky and white snow swirled around him like a kaleidoscope.

Still hidden from the road below, he began to walk slowly uphill again, resting after each step but making steady progress toward a pass between two low hills. When he was halfway to the top, the green metal roof of a house emerged, and then windows with decorative Persian arches. A mountain refuge. He hoped that no one was home, and that he could break in and hide there.

The sun was hot on his neck. He finished the sugared almonds and drank another can of Coke. But when he went to put the empty can back in his coat pocket, he realized that the other empties were gone. They must have fallen out, he realized, left like a bread-crumb trail for his pursuers to follow. And he'd left the vodka bottle on the patch of snow.

He was losing his mind. His feet no longer hurt because he couldn't even feel them.

Decker looked behind him. And wondered whether the black figure he saw below was a mirage. He looked up to the sky, half expecting to see a dragon from Middle Earth.

When he glanced behind him again, the black figure was still there, climbing fast up the hill.

Decker eyed the house. It was no more than a few hundred feet away, but up a long steep slope. If he could get there and get inside, he might have a chance. There might be a gun, or a car.

He climbed, going faster now, no longer resting between steps, driven by a hidden store of adrenaline. He kept his eyes focused on the ground and began to count his steps...*one, two*...

A voice called out for him to stop, but he ignored it. When he glanced behind him, it looked as though the black figure hadn't gained much ground.

A few steps later he fell, but he instantly lifted himself up from the dirt and continued his march. *Hundred ten, hundred eleven...*He concentrated on the ground immediately in front of him, taking care with each quick step and only occasionally glancing up at the house to gauge his progress.

His eyes registered a flattening of the ground, followed by the black macadam of a road that had been cut into the side of the mountain, a road that had been hidden from below.

Decker looked up.

Two men, both carrying AK-47s, sprang up from a drainage ditch and rushed at him from opposite sides.

One guy below to flush him out, the other two to capture, Decker realized.

He spun around, took a step back toward the hill, stuck his hand in his coat pocket, and fingered one of the blades from the pruning shears.

The first guard hit him in the gut with a football tackle. As they tumbled to the ground as one, Decker whipped out the blade and stabbed the man's carotid artery.

The second guard lit into Decker with the butt of his gun, swinging it like an ax. Decker absorbed a few blows to his head and thighs and a glancing blow to a knee. He pulled out the second blade from the pruning shears, stabbed the guy's Achilles tendon, and was about to try for the femoral artery when a volley of twenty or so bullets flew over him, inches from his head. A hit to his ankle connected, breaking bone. Two men grabbed his arms, pinning them to the asphalt. Another kicked him repeatedly in the balls and guts.

A few seconds later, a sweaty nervous man with ugly cauliflower ears that poked out from beneath his black turban stood over Decker. "You'll pay for this," he said.

40
Ashgabat, Turkmenistan

M ARK AND DARIA ABANDONED THE STOLEN VOLGA IN A vast dirt parking lot crammed almost as far as the eye could see with old trucks and cars and hordes of Turkmen.

The Tolkuchka Bazaar was only a few miles from the sterile white buildings of downtown Ashgabat, but it might as well have been a different country; it was as if all the messiness of human life had been swept up from the streets of the capital and deposited in a stinking heap on the edge of the Kara-Kum Desert.

There were carpets, giant crates of fruit, boxes of hard candy, clothes, spices, stacks of Barf laundry detergent, electronics from China, dromedary camels...It smelled of lamb roasting on ancient iron grills and human sweat and mud. Squat old women with gold teeth and bright, tightly tied headscarves sat on little crates and called out for people to inspect their wares.

Daria bought an embroidered traditional Turkmen robe and several imitation-silk headscarves. Mark bought shoes, shirts, and pants, all locally made, hair dye, and a new wallet, which he filled with Daria's counterfeit manats. Then he used Daria's phone to call Holtz.

"Sava, I'm sorry. Thompson pulled a fucking bait and switch—"

"Main entrance to the Tolkuchka Bazaar. Be here at noon."

"It's almost noon now."

"I'm aware of that."

"Aren't you supposed to be at the air—"

"Take surveillance-detection measures, but be quick about it. You rat me out to the Agency or come with a tail on your ass, I'll shoot you myself."

Mark hung up without waiting for Holtz's response, walked back to the parking lot, and haggled with a merchant over the price of a used four-wheel-drive Niva—the Russian version of a jeep. He paid the equivalent of fifteen hundred dollars in cash and drove it to the edge of the parking lot, where Daria cut his hair and helped him dye what remained black. By the time they'd finished, Holtz was there.

Mark saw him scanning the crowd near the entrance to the bazaar, his head protruding a good foot above the crush of bodies flowing past him as if he were a rock in the middle of a fast-moving river.

He called Holtz and told him to meet him inside the bazaar, in the far southern corner. And then, when Holtz was almost there, he called back to tell him to instead meet him in the far northern corner. And then outside the bazaar, in the parking lot by the camels.

"What is this crap?" Holtz said, when Mark finally approached from behind. "Man, what happened to your face?"

"Congratulations, you're alone."

"I told you I'd do an SD run," said Holtz, as if offended that Mark hadn't trusted him to shake a tail.

"Walk with me." When Holtz began to follow him, Mark said, "Thompson and I were attacked on the way to the airport. At least one Turkmen soldier was shot, probably fatally. A couple Guoanbu agents are probably also dead. Thompson may or may not survive. Tell me about Decker."

"A Turkmen soldier was shot?"

"That's what I said."

"The city's going to be in lockdown mode. I mean, this is a fucking police state. The Turkmen don't screw around with this kind of thing." Holtz scanned the crowds. "Did *you* shoot the soldier?"

"No."

Holtz looked both worried and indignant. "And are you sure you weren't followed here, dude?"

They'd arrived at the parking lot. Instead of answering Holtz, Mark pointed to an open patch of dirt between a cluster of haphazardly parked cars. "Sit down. You're easy to spot.

Eventually Holtz did, although he looked uncomfortable doing so.

"Talk to us about Decker," said Mark.

"Us?"

Daria appeared and took a seat next to Mark. She'd been following them from a distance, ready to provide backup for Mark if he got into trouble.

Holtz looked at her and rolled his eyes. "Oh, great."

"So this is the deal," said Holtz. "A few weeks ago, inflation starts going through the roof here—"

"Daria already told me about all that," said Mark.

"Yeah, well, what she doesn't know is that Decker figured out why. Turns out it was the ChiComs. They were printing counterfeit money. Tons of it, just dumping it on the market."

"*I* told you I thought it was the Chinese before I left," said Daria. "You wouldn't listen. I told Decker that too. *That's* how he figured it out."

"You told me rumors. Decker brought me evidence."

"What evidence?" asked Mark.

"Decker knew this bartender. Hell, he knew a lot of bartenders, which was kind of an issue with me, but one did black market currency exchange on the side."

"Got a name?"

"Decker wouldn't tell me, said he'd promised not to. Anyway, this bartender tells him the ChiComs are buying up US dollars all over the city."

"With counterfeit manats," said Mark.

"Yep."

"What bar was this at?"

"Decker wouldn't tell me that either, said he'd be compromising his source. Which was a problem. I couldn't rat out the ChiComs to the Turkmen just because Decker heard something at a bar; I needed real evidence if the charge was going to stick. So I thought, why not find a way to trace all these dollars that were being bought up? If I could show the Turkmen that they were going straight to the ChiComs, well, then the Turkmen would *have* to boot the bastards. You familiar with RFID technology?"

"No," said Mark.

Holtz appeared satisfied, but not surprised, by Mark's ignorance.

"It stands for radio frequency identification," said Daria. "It's a—"

"—way to track things," said Holtz. "Big businesses have starting using it instead of bar codes. They even have passive RFIDs that are like the-head-of-a-pin small and don't need batteries in the transmitter. With the right transmitter and right receiver, you can track a signal from like a kilometer away. What I did was supply Decker with a one-hundred-dollar bill that had one of these tiny RFIDs inserted into a slice in it. The idea being that Decker's bartender friend would sell this bill to the ChiComs and then Decker would track where they went. And that's actually what happened."

"So where'd he track it to?" asked Mark.

"Last I know he was driving east on the M-thirty-seven toward Dushakh. His bartender buddy was with him."

"That's no-man's-land out there. Who else besides the bartender was helping Decker at this point?"

"I gave him some tips," said Holtz.

"He's trained as a SEAL, not as a spy. They're different crafts."

"Decker wanted the job, and he was the one who recruited the bartender."

"Did State know what he was doing?"

"Oh yeah, and by now the Defense Department was in on the action too. Once I told them what the ChiComs were up to, everybody's interest perked up real good. They were pushing me to find out anything I could, especially since the CIA was just holed up in the embassy, playing it safe."

"Deck's a six-foot-four SEAL with blond hair and no formal intelligence training. And he doesn't speak a word of Turkmen or any other foreign language for that matter."

"Like I said, his bartender friend was helping him. They were working as a team."

"You were bullshitting State and DoD, weren't you?" said Daria.

"What are you talking about?"

"You inflated John's résumé before being hired by State. So you could charge more for him."

"Who the hell is John?"

"John Decker. The guy we're talking about."

"You don't know jack shit, Daria."

"I saw the write-up you provided to State selling them on me. You said—"

"That was a classified document."

"You said I had extensive paramilitary experience and had operated in war zones. That I had experience with explosives and had been trained as a sniper."

"You got weapons training with the CIA, along with some paramilitary training. We all did."

"You lied, Bruce. And you did it because it allowed you to charge State more per day for me. And you did the same thing with Decker. That's why State and DoD were comfortable with him working in the field. What'd you tell them? That he was trained by one of the CIA's best?" Daria turned to Mark. "That would be you."

"I never trained him for an operation like this," noted Mark, though, now that he thought about it, when Decker had stayed with him in Baku, they'd spent a lot of time discussing things like surveillance detection techniques, tracking techniques, dead drops, ways to read people's body language...Decker had been eager to learn everything he could of spycraft. Maybe too eager, Mark thought now.

Daria turned back to Holtz. "How many languages did you say he spoke?"

Holtz turned to Mark. "You know why I had to fire her? Because she was fucking for information. Thought she'd do a little moonlighting, play superspy instead of just doing her damn work as a translator. So she starts balling—"

"You are so full of it," said Daria.

"—this fat Turkmen deputy energy minister, and the guy's wife finds out and raises a stink."

"That's a total lie."

"Check with State," said Holtz to Mark. "They know what happened."

"You sold John out," said Daria. "You presented him as something he wasn't to State, State passed that bad information on to DoD, and because of it—"

"Enough," said Mark. He turned to Holtz. "When's the last time you heard from Deck?"

A group of five women, each stooped over and carrying a rolled-up carpet on her back, passed by in front of the Niva. Holtz and Daria and Mark stayed quiet until they were gone.

"After Decker left Ashgabat, we agreed that he wouldn't try to communicate with me unless he knew he could do so securely. The idea, though, was that he'd only be gone for a day or two tops, just enough time to document where the money went to."

"What kind of equipment was he carrying?"

"The RFID tracker, a digital recorder with a directional microphone and wire probes, and a digital camera with a high-powered telephoto. He had top-of-the-line surveillance equipment. I paid out the ass for it."

"Give me your phone," said Mark to Daria. When she'd handed it over, Mark pulled up the photos Alty8 had sent them and tossed the phone to Holtz. "These mean anything to you?"

Holtz didn't recognize the mansion and didn't appear to recognize Decker's arm. But when he came to the photo of the two men exchanging a briefcase, he said, "Holy shit. That's Li Zemin, the head of the Guoanbu here in Ashgabat. Did Decker take this picture?"

"Maybe."

"How much do you want to bet that briefcase is full of hundred-dollar bills? And that one of those bills has an RFID tracker on it?"

"What about the guy with the black turban?"

"Him I've never seen before."

They were quiet for a moment. Mark felt a warm desert breeze on his cheek. He stood up.

Daria stood up too and brushed the fine dirt off the rear of her Turkmen dress. "By the way, Bruce, you can take your non-compete contract and stuff it up your dirty ass."

"When you get back to the States, and you will, someday you will, honey, I'll have my lawyers draw up a suit that'll leave you in the gutter."

"I'm not going back to the States, and if I ever did, I wouldn't have a penny to my name." She opened the driver's side door to the Niva. "There'd be nothing for you to take."

PART III

41

Turkmenistan, Near the Afghan Border

————○————

THE MUD-BRICK HOUSE ROSE UP LIKE A LITTLE KNOLL ON THE surface of the flat grassy plain.

Behind the house, an old pickup truck had been driven into a drainage ditch next to an outhouse and a solitary apple tree. A cow stood in the wooden bed of the pickup, unable to lie down because of the way she'd been tied to the cab. Goats had wandered through a hole in the stick-fence enclosure and were grazing on either side of the road.

Li Zemin, chief of mission for the Guoanbu in Ashgabat, pulled up in a jeep with his driver.

He was a tall man with sunken cheeks and an angular jawline. His lips were pressed together in a tight, controlled line that was neither a smile nor a frown, and his alert-looking eyes suggested intelligence. Although he held no military rank, his uncle—the man who'd raised him from the age of two—was a high-ranking army general and member of China's powerful Central Military Commission. Partially because of this connection to power, but also because rumors of Zemin's ruthless management of the Turkmen Guoanbu had reached the army, the special forces Chinese soldiers who stood in front of the house snapped to attention as Zemin passed by.

Zemin tipped his head in acknowledgment. Then he ordered one of the soldiers to get the cow down from the pickup truck and set it free to graze in the surrounding grassland.

His inspection of the site was perfunctory. The men who had been killed in the raid were Chinese Uighur separatists who had been harbored by the Taliban, then driven by the Afghan government across the border into Turkmenistan.

As Zemin was paging through a Qur'an that had belonged to one of the separatists, checking it for handwritten codes that the military might have missed, a call came through on his satellite phone. When he saw where it was from, he excused himself and walked alone back to his stripped-down Chinese-made Hafei minitruck.

He picked up the phone, spoke his name, and then listened to the circumstances of John Decker's escape and recapture.

"I must also inform you that the interrogation is not going well," said the caller. "My men are not properly trained for such work."

"Perhaps it is possible to get men that are?" Zemin was careful not to let sarcasm seep into his tone.

"Certainly. But not men that I trust. Understand, I did not anticipate that you would be followed. Had I known this to be a possibility, I would have made different arrangements."

I did not anticipate you would be followed.

Over the years, Zemin had learned to consider his emotions as he might a wild dog on the street, as something outside of himself that one should keep an eye on but not be controlled by.

But the American John Decker *had* followed him. That Zemin couldn't deny.

And that failure had been compounded by the Guoanbu's inability to contain Sava. Yet.

"I will have two men for you within twenty-four hours," said Zemin.

"Set a flight plan for Tehran, divert to Karaj. I'll have them met at the airport so they won't need to go through customs."

42

D ECKER WAS BROUGHT BACK TO THE HOUSE FROM WHICH he'd escaped, stripped, and thrown to the basement floor. His hands were once again handcuffed and his legs bound with rope. Two armed guards stood over him at all times. After a few hours, a two-man crew arrived carrying an enormous drill with an eighteen-inch bit attached to it. Decker worried for a moment that it was to be used on him, but the men just pulled up the trapdoor and descended a ladder into the pit. He heard the high-pitched whine of what sounded like the drill piercing metal.

The man in the black turban came down to the basement just after the men with the drill had emerged from the pit.

"I have made new arrangements for you."

Decker ignored him, as he always did. He kept his eyes focused on the arabesque swirls in the carpet, trying to shut down his ability to hear.

"You will have new friends soon. Look at me!"

Decker pretended that he was still outside, climbing a mountain.

Someone kicked him in the stomach.

Orders were given, prompting one of the men to throw Decker face-first down the steps into the pit. He saw that the hole he'd dug out had been filled in. And that the door to the safe was open. A guard followed him down and tried to grab him under the armpits, but Decker was feeling stronger from the food and drink, and as he stood he twisted and head-butted the guard in the nose.

The guard was taken by surprise and fell back. Decker was on him instantly, using his head like a sledgehammer to pound the man's face.

It was futile, though. The guard had no gun to steal, and two more guards were in the pit within seconds. Though they beat the hell out of him, Decker didn't regret it. If he was capable of fighting back, he'd fight.

Keep pushing.

The guards threw him into the safe and stuffed his legs up into his chest.

Decker screamed. The pain in his wounded leg was unbearable. He was shaking uncontrollably. The interior walls of the safe pressed against his shoulders. Even with his knees touching his chest, he barely fit in the space.

As the door clanged shut and blackness descended, Decker put his mouth next to one of the air holes that had been drilled through the thick metal. He closed his eyes and began to count again. He was climbing, slowly, steadily, one foot after the other. The sun was shining, the sky was blue, the air was clean.

43
Ashgabat, Turkmenistan

———————o———————

D ARIA MANEUVERED THE NIVA THROUGH THE CROWDS OUT-
side the Tolkuchka Bazaar. Manhandling the stick shift and
honking the horn at everyone who got in front of her helped dis-
sipate some of her anger.

When they reached the road back to Ashgabat, she said,
"Holtz was lying about firing me, you know. I don't do that kind
of thing anymore."

"What bars did Deck hang out at here in Ashgabat?"

"You don't believe me about Holtz, do you?" she asked.

"I believe you."

"No, you don't. But you should. I know you don't think much
of me—"

"That's not true."

"People change, Mark. I wouldn't stoop that low. Not to
make money for a piece of shit like Holtz, anyway. You know, he
probably told the State Department people the same lie he just
told you, just to spite me because I quit."

"Holtz is a bottom-feeder. There's nothing you can do about
it. That's just the way he is."

Daria thought Mark sounded bored by Holtz's lies. Bored.
Which told her exactly where things stood between them. She
glanced at him. His eyes looked even more heavy lidded and
deep set than usual. He hadn't shaved in days. It was hard for her
to believe that this was the same professorial guy who'd spent
over a month nursing her back to health.

167

She pulled open the dash compartment. "Jesus, I need a cigarette." She rifled through some papers but came up short.

"When did you start smoking?"

"A week ago, as part of my cover."

"Forget Holtz. He's just trying to get inside your head. Don't let him."

She wanted to blurt out that it wasn't Holtz that was getting inside her head, it was him. It was being close to him, without really being close. Talking to him, without really talking.

She considered what little she knew about him, starting with the fact that Mark Sava wasn't even his real name.

He'd always been guarded, especially about his past. But once he *had* let slip—this a month into their relationship—that he'd grown up in a run-down neighborhood in Elizabeth, New Jersey, and had gone to public schools there. When she'd gone back to the States, she'd done some snooping and hadn't been able to find any record of him in Elizabeth. At least not until she'd paged through several old public school yearbooks and discovered that he'd grown up not as Mark Sava, but rather Marko Saveljic. That had thrown her for a loop. CIA operations officers used aliases all the time, but Mark had been a station chief when he'd left the CIA; he'd been declared to the Azeris and shouldn't have needed to use an alias. At the very least, once they'd become intimate, Daria thought he should have mentioned what his real name was. She'd also learned—from an obituary on file with a local newspaper—that Mark's mother had died when he was in his teens.

She tried to imagine him as a young kid, before his mom had died, before life had roughed him up. She tried to picture him as a normal, innocent child playing with his older sister and two younger brothers, climbing on jungle gyms and running through sprinklers.

Back when they'd been living together in his apartment, she might have been able to imagine it. But now? No way. All she saw was a serious kid, back to the wall, sizing up every other kid in the sandbox as he looked for weaknesses to exploit, angles to work. His mind packed with dark secrets. She had no doubt his mom's death had been a hard blow, but she guessed it was a blow that, if anything, had just pushed him in a direction he'd already been going.

"So are you going to answer my question?" asked Mark, interrupting her thoughts.

"You had one?"

He was a strange man, Daria thought, born with a rare ability to separate his life into distinct and often contradictory compartments, some of which he'd shared with her, most of which he hadn't and, she was sure, never would.

"Bars. Decker. Where did he hang out? Focus, Daria."

Daria downshifted as she entered a traffic circle. The transmission whined. "I know Holtz wouldn't let him drink at the President, so we can cross that off the list. He took me out to the Grand Turkmen once. We could start there."

Daria remembered an awkward night. Polite dinner conversation, mostly about how crazy Turkmenistan was—Beards outlawed! Compulsory hockey! Bubonic plague! Decker had been nervous during dinner. They'd both had too much wine. Afterward, he'd pulled her onto a nearly empty dance floor. A cringe-inducing gyration to "Tainted Love" with a disco ball right out of *Saturday Night Fever* spinning above them had followed. They'd played blackjack for an hour at the casino. He'd won—she remembered him high-fiving her and that it hurt—and she'd lost, badly.

"They have a bar at the Grand Turkmen?" asked Mark.

"It's part of the restaurant."

Then there was that good-night kiss that she'd been a little too boozy to deflect and that had made her feel as if she were being mauled by a bear.

Objectively, she knew that Deck was a seriously handsome guy, with a body that really was a marvel to behold. She loved looking at him. And she liked him on a personal level—a lot. She'd never seen him in a bad mood, and that counted for something. But she was barely five feet tall and he was six foot four. And he was still in his twenties, with the cares and concerns of a guy in his twenties. What he needed was a young buxom Russian weightlifter who liked to pound shots and trade punches. And that just wasn't her.

They tried the Grand Turkmen Hotel, then the Nissa Hotel, and then a few of the seedier joints like the Vavilov and the Mopra Club—tired places with stained carpets, stale air, and watered-down drinks. Mark always started by ordering something at the bar and grossly overtipping. Then Daria would show the bartender a photo she'd taken of Decker on their night out together.

No one recognized him, or would admit to it. As soon as they were sure a place was a bust, they'd leave in a hurry, without finishing their drinks.

They tried seedier places still, until Daria had the sense that she'd fallen into a toilet and was slowly circling the bowl. But that's when they started to get some real hits.

At the Flamingo Disco, an expat-German waitress with pierced eyebrows and a cattle-style nose ring remembered Deck, though she said he'd only been in a couple of times and had hung out more at the bar than on the dance floor.

At the City Pub—where the guy watching the door informed Daria that if she was there as a whore, she'd need to give the house a percentage of her take—they seemed to know Decker well. He evidently was a big tipper who'd been known to buy rounds for everyone at the bar, on multiple occasions. But no one had heard anything about his taking off with one of the bartenders. An offer of one hundred, then two hundred dollars for more information didn't jog anyone's memory.

"Try the British Pub," the bartender told them on the way out. "I know he used to hang out there too."

44

Ashgabat, Turkmenistan

———o———

N O SIGN HUNG OUTSIDE THE BASEMENT-LEVEL BRITISH PUB, just a coat of arms on a nondescript door. Inside, faded pictures of a young John Lennon and Paul McCartney lined the entrance foyer. Dark curtains hung over fake windows. When Mark's eyes had adjusted to the gloom, he saw a sitting area near the entrance where two women—prostitutes, he guessed—were chatting on one of several couches. A bar with mirrored shelves displayed a meager selection of foreign booze under purple lights. Brick-patterned wallpaper had been pasted on the floor-to-ceiling columns near the bar. A dartboard hung on a nearby pine-paneled wall that was riddled with dart holes. Farther in was a band area, then a billiard table, its stained baize more shit brown than green.

It was one thirty in the afternoon. Aside from the prostitutes and the staff, the pub was empty.

Mark ordered a beer, overtipping as usual.

Daria stuck with bottled water and showed the bartender—a big Russian with a facial tick—her photo of Decker.

"He drinks Tuborg?"

Mark glanced at the beer menu to the side of the bar. Tuborg was the cheapest. And it came in half-liter bottles. It also happened to be what he was drinking. "Yeah."

"The Decker!" The bartender's face twitched as he smiled.

"That's him," said Mark.

"He is here all the time, he loves the karaoke."

"I wasn't aware."

"Very good singer. Very good, just like the Meat Loaf."

Mark raised his eyebrows and exchanged a look with Daria. "Have you seen him recently?"

"Not since many days, I think."

The bartender added that Decker had often bought rounds of drinks for everyone at the bar. And that he was a good tipper and extremely popular with the female waitresses. And that he also sometimes hung out at the Flamingo disco next door.

"Sounds like he was the life of the party," said Mark, wondering how much of the Decker party-guy routine was a just calculated act—a way for Decker to quickly learn far more about what was going on in Ashgabat than he could hanging around with fusty State Department diplomats—and how much of it was just that Decker liked a good time. Fifty-fifty, Mark guessed.

"Yes, of course, all the time."

The bartender started washing glasses in his utility sink.

"By any chance was he friends with one of the bartenders here?" Mark wrote *Alty8@online.tm* on a bar napkin. "Or someone who used this e-mail address."

The bartender frowned and stopped washing. "Alty was another bartender here."

"Was?"

"He quit around the same time I last saw the Decker."

"Quit?"

"He didn't show up for work."

"Do you have any idea where he is now?" said Mark.

"No."

"Know anyone that might?"

The Walk of Health, as it was called, was a wide concrete path that wound for over twenty miles through the desolate hills just south of Ashgabat. It had been built at great expense to promote exercise, but except for the one day each year when all government employees were required to hike the thing from beginning to end, no one actually used it. Which is why Mark had wanted to meet there, so that he could be sure that Alty's brother—a man named Atamyrat Nuriyev—had come alone.

They converged on the path about a mile south of the Eternally Great Park, where the path started. Mark approached from the north—after hiking cross-country to reach the path; Nuriyev from the southern park entrance.

Before speaking, Mark studied Nuriyev.

The drooping shoulders and hangdog look suggested that Nuriyev had no news or bad news regarding his missing younger brother; the cheap domestic suit told him that Nuriyev's government job—assistant to the minister of culture—hadn't translated into any real power for him; the plastic digital wristwatch he wore, which he'd probably bought for a dollar at the Tolkuchka Bazaar, confirmed this; the broad flat face and almond-shaped eyes told him that Nuriyev was a native Turkmen and not a Russian transplant, which in turn suggested that Nuriyev had grown up dirt-poor during the long Soviet occupation.

Still, Nuriyev was of average height, so he likely hadn't grown up so poor that his growth had been stunted as a child. His relatively clear complexion suggested that he didn't smoke and hadn't adopted the Russian predilection for extreme drinking. And the fact that he hadn't bought a fake Rolex wristwatch for two dollars, also on sale at the Tolkuchka Bazaar and popular with many Turkmen, suggested a personal modesty.

It was the watch that made Mark decide he would try being honest with Nuriyev. "Thank you for coming so quickly." Mark spoke the greeting in Turkmen, with what he knew was a heavy Azeri accent.

Nuriyev had removed his government-gray suit jacket, revealing sweat stains underneath his armpits. His pressed suit pants were an inch too long and the cuffs grazed the ground. Mark was sweating too. He'd climbed three miles to get to their meeting spot, much of it up steep slopes. By now it was three in the afternoon, and the sun was intense. Nuriyev had come straight from work.

Far below them, Ashgabat, hazy and bright, rose out of the desert. A couple of helicopters circled over the city center; evidence, Mark thought, of a security crackdown following the shooting of the Turkmen soldier.

Nuriyev acknowledged Mark with a nod, but didn't speak. Mark wasn't surprised. Even in normal situations, most Turkmen were usually so reserved that they made their former Russian overlords look positively friendly—no easy task.

Mark kept both his hands in front of him and in sight so as not to give Nuriyev cause to worry.

After he'd rested a moment, Mark launched into an explanation about Decker, how the cryptic e-mail he'd received had contained the name Alty in it, and how he'd wound up at the British Pub. At the bazaar he'd needed to speak slowly for the merchants to understand him, so he took care to speak slowly now. Eventually, he took out Daria's phone and clicked open the first of the three photos that had been sent by Alty8. Nuriyev studied it for a moment, but it was as though he were staring through the photo, not really seeing it. Mark clicked on the next one, then the next. "Do these mean anything to you?"

Instead of answering, Nuriyev said, "Alty is my youngest brother."

"So I've been told."

"He's only eighteen years old. My family has not heard from him in four days."

"I see."

"I don't think you do."

"Then explain it to me."

For the first time, Nuriyev looked Mark right in the eye. "Your colleague shouldn't have used my brother."

"What are you talking about?"

"I know these things. Your colleague, he's a CIA spy."

"No he isn't."

"I'm not stupid."

Mark turned back toward Ashgabat and spent the next half hour explaining everything he knew about why Decker had been in Turkmenistan—the counterfeit money, the rivalry between the United States and China and Russia, CAIN's role, how Decker and Alty had wound up working together...he didn't hold back a thing.

At one point Nuriyev put his hand up, as if to say *stop, you are telling me that which I should not be allowed to hear.* But Mark kept talking. He figured he had nothing to lose. The secrets he was divulging weren't ones he'd been charged with keeping.

He finished by telling Nuriyev that he, Mark, used to work for the CIA but no longer did. And that anyway, the CIA wasn't the all-powerful force that Nuriyev seemed to think it was.

"Even if your colleague wasn't working for the CIA, he used my brother in an investigation that was paid for by the US government. My brother is eighteen years old. He should not have been involved. Your government used him. This John Decker used him."

Nuriyev spoke emphatically, but with his sweaty shirt and rumpled hair, he looked unsure of himself. A hot breeze started blowing and his shirt billowed up.

Mark was thirsty. Which made him think of another time when he'd been thirsty.

A few days after Decker had showed up in Baku, looking for a place to stay, Mark had needed to drive out to the mountains west of the city, to interview a 102-year-old Azeri man who'd worked with Soviet intelligence in the 1920s. It was research for his book.

Mark had been reluctant when Decker asked to come along, but Decker had proved to be a decent traveling companion—he'd just bought a copy of *Interview with the Vampire* from a second-hand bookstore in Baku, and had read for most of the car ride out. Which had been fine with Mark—small talk annoyed him.

The only problem was that the final seven-mile stretch of road to the village where the old man lived had washed out the week before. Finishing the journey on foot wouldn't have been a big deal, except that Mark took a wrong turn early on—a mistake he only figured out after he and Decker had been climbing for three hours. They'd been forced to slog back down the way they came. And then start up the right trail.

The thing was, Mark had been sweating like crazy, and he hadn't packed any water for the trip. After several hours of hard hiking, Decker had offered him his half-full water bottle. Mark had refused it at first, but Decker had insisted that he didn't need it because he had a second one in his pack.

Mark had been grateful for that water. But then he realized he'd never seen Decker pull out a second bottle. So when they finally got to the village, and Decker went to take a leak, Mark had opened Deck's backpack. There was no other water bottle. Decker had given away his only one.

Mark had never mentioned the incident, but he thought about it now. A guy who would give his only water bottle away to a jackass who had just led him hours up a wrong trail wasn't the kind of guy who would intentionally screw over an eighteen-year-old kid.

Mark turned to Nuriyev.

"Did Decker know how young Alty was? Would Alty have told him?" Mark let that sit for a moment. "Listen, my colleague and your brother are missing. My government won't lift a finger to help get them back and neither will yours. I'm trying to help on my own."

After seeming to consider Mark's remarks for a while, Nuriyev finally said, "When Alty started working at the British Pub, he became obsessed with all things foreign. And the more he learned, the more unhappy he became in his own country."

"I'm sorry."

"Those photos you showed me. I believe they were taken with Alty's iPhone. I told Alty the phone was a stupid waste of money, but he insisted on buying it."

"Was it a new iPhone?" Mark remembered that Daria had said the quality of the photos was poor.

"No. Used. He didn't have money for a new one."

They stood in silence for a long time. Eventually Mark said, "You said you haven't heard from your brother in four days."

Nuriyev didn't respond.

"But the bartender at the British Pub said Alty has been gone for a week."

"He wanted me to try to save his job. To make an excuse for him. So he called me. That was the last time I heard from him."

"Where was he when he called?"

"Iran."

"Where in Iran?"

"I don't know."

"Was my colleague with him?"

Nuriyev sighed. "Come, we must drive to south, toward the mountains."

45
Washington, DC

―――――――○―――――――

THE MEETING HAD BEEN DRAGGING ON FOR HOURS. HUNDREDS of aim points had been considered. Most were easy to approve—radar installations, Revolutionary Guard bases, anti-aircraft batteries…it only took fifteen seconds a slide on average, but every so often they hit a hard one.

"Aim point one thousand sixty-seven," said the secretary of defense. An address in Esfahan, Iran, came up on the white-board. "Home of Dr. Farid Kermani. Director of the Esfahan Nuclear Technology Center."

"He lives in a housing complex," said the national security advisor, "so there is a certainty of civilian casualties, perhaps significant. The complex is located within a quarter mile of the Khaju Bridge, which is around four hundred years old and a big tourist site. If we screw up and hit that bridge, we'll suffer serious backlash beyond what we're already in for."

"How many individuals are on the aim point list?" asked the president.

"Eight, beginning with Dr. Kermani. They represent our best estimate of what constitutes the top nuclear minds in the country. If we can eliminate these people from the equation, the Iranians could be set back several years on top of the time it will take them to rebuild the infrastructure damage we'll inflict."

"This is one of the many reasons why we're not consulting with the Europeans," added the national security advisor. "We choose the aim points, we take all the blame and all the backlash.

We'll get hammered for it, and it might mean we'll be ceding the initiative on some foreign policy goals for the next few years, but we'll just have to live with that. It's better than the alternative. Aim point accepted."

Everyone else concurred.

"Aim point confirmed," said the president.

46

Turkmenistan, Near the Border with Iran

———————o———————

MARK AND NURIYEV DROVE SOUTH IN NURIYEV'S OLD white Volga toward the foothills of the Kopet Dag Mountains, which paralleled the border with Iran. It was desolate country, dotted with only occasional clusters of small houses, and the scorched hills made Mark long for the relative luxury of his apartment in Baku.

After a half hour they turned down a dirt road where chickens roamed free. The little whitewashed houses all had rusting corrugated-metal roofs with satellite dishes nailed haphazardly to their sides. Laundry lines had been strung between stunted palm trees.

Nuriyev pulled up to the last house on the street. A shiny blue BMW 3 Series was parked out front, and two little girls were chasing a big cream-colored *Alabai* dog and laughing. Nearby a camel poked its head out from a backyard that had been fenced in with old doors.

Nuriyev announced that they'd arrived at his uncle's house. And that his uncle was a smuggler.

"Of?"

"Mostly alcohol and Western cigarettes. That they bring to Iran."

Mark wondered what 'mostly' meant.

"They have—"

"Who is they?"

"My uncle and his family. They have an arrangement with the border guards." Nuriyev muscled the steering wheel as he parked. "If Alty crossed into Iran, he may have turned to them for help."

As they approached the house, a stooped old man appeared in the front door, beneath a cluster of dried chili peppers that had been nailed to the top of the doorframe for good luck. Although it was hot out, he wore a long-sleeved Turkmen robe under a soiled North Face vest. His face was creased with deep wrinkles, his mouth set in an unfriendly frown.

Nuriyev put his right hand over his heart and dipped his head a bit.

The old man didn't reciprocate. After standing in the doorway for a while, as if to block their entrance, he simply said, "Well, you must come in for tea." He turned, with little enthusiasm, into the house.

In the main room, floor pillows, shiny with hair grease, ringed a large red Turkmen carpet. Mark detected the smell of both cigarette and opium smoke. In a corner, an intricately carved opium pipe sat next to a paraffin lamp. The sole piece of furniture was a low table, reinforced with several pieces of scrap wood, on top of which sat a decent-sized LCD Sony television. A boy of about ten sat in front of it, watching two American professional wrestlers beat each other over the head with chairs.

Nuriyev's uncle gestured to the floor. "Sit." He called loudly for tea, and his wife appeared, wearing a bright yellow-and-blue headscarf. Behind her stood the two girls who'd been chasing the dog on the street.

Mark wondered whether Decker had visited this house. He scanned the room for signs of Deck as Nuriyev and his uncle discussed the price of cottonseed oil and the recent inflation crisis.

"He likes us to smoke," said Nuriyev in halting English, interrupting Mark's thoughts.

"I quit cigarettes," responded Mark, also switching to English.

"He means the opium."

Even if staying sharp hadn't been a factor, which it was, Mark didn't trust himself with opiates. It had been over twenty years ago, but for a short time he had been a heroin addict—the result of being abducted and interrogated for months on end by the KGB. The idea had been to get him hooked and then withhold the drug to entice him to talk. The tactic would have worked if he'd had anything of value to tell his captors. Since then he'd stayed away from the stuff.

"Tell him I'm sick and that tea will be more than enough."

Sounding embarrassed, Nuriyev said, "I already tell him I am sick."

"Then I guess I caught what you had."

Nuriyev's uncle looked unhappy about the refusal. Mark figured the old man needed his fix but didn't want to violate some unwritten rule of hospitality by smoking alone. The tea soon came, brought out in a metal thermos. Mark accepted a cup and a cube of sugar.

Switching back to Turkmen, Nuriyev said, "I must tell you this is not entirely a social visit, Uncle. Do you remember my brother Alty?"

Nuriyev's uncle placed three cubes of sugar into his tea and listened with a bored look on his face as Nuriyev launched into a mostly fictional account of why he thought his brother may have crossed into Iran.

"Have you seen him recently?" asked Nuriyev.

His uncle began to cough, and then he took a Camel cigarette—a rare luxury in Turkmenistan—from a pack that lay on the floor by his feet. "Your father is a stubborn man." He rolled the cigarette between his tobacco-stained thumb and index finger. "Surely you know that he would not allow Alty to visit us."

"I am here."

"And does your father know?"

"I am not my father."

Nuriyev's uncle lit his cigarette with a wooden match, which he then blew out and carefully placed on top of an overflowing ashtray. "I have not seen your brother. If I do, I will send word."

"What about Murat?"

"My son has not seen Alty either."

"They used to be friends."

"Your father ended that."

The power went off, causing Nuriyev's uncle to yell something about a generator to his wife. Then he turned to Mark. "Every day at this time the electricity goes off. But does it ever go off in Ashgabat? No, there they have all the electricity they want. Nobody cares about the villages." A minute later a loud engine started rumbling, the television came back on, and the house began to smell of diesel exhaust.

"Alty told me that Murat came to see him at the British Pub one year ago," said Nuriyev. "They have been in contact since then, I'm sure of it."

The old man took a sip of his tea.

Nuriyev said, "I need you to ask Murat about Alty."

"You don't tell me what I need to do."

Nuriyev lowered his head. After a time he said, "I am not telling you, I am asking you, Uncle. I am asking you to help me."

Mark waited a moment for Nuriyev's uncle to respond. But the old Turkmen just sat there smoking like some debauched Buddha, so Mark stood up.

"Enough of this crap," he said in English. With one kick, he sent the old man's tea thermos and pack of Camel cigarettes sailing across the room. The thermos hit the far wall and splattered tea everywhere, and the cigarettes flew out of their box. Switching to Turkmen, he said, "I'm here as an observer from the United Nations, as part of a group that is monitoring opium trafficking. Alty is important to us, for reasons I don't intend to discuss with you. If you want to stay in business, you'll help us find him. If you don't, I'll have your pathetic smuggling operation shut down tomorrow."

The room went silent.

Nuriyev looked utterly appalled at what Mark had done. To his uncle he said, "I did not come here with the intention of interfering with your business."

"I only trade alcohol now," muttered Nuriyev's uncle. Mark observed the old man's fingers shaking slightly as he took a long drag off his cigarette.

Wagging his finger, Mark said, "I can tell you this—nobody gives a donkey's ass about your business right now. But they will soon if you don't answer the questions."

The old man turned to Nuriyev. "You bring this filth into my home?"

"Get Murat," said Mark.

At that moment the front door opened. A stunted, emaciated young man of about twenty, with the same olive skin and almond-shaped eyes as Nuriyev, appeared. He wore a button-down short-sleeve polyester dress shirt and an old World Wide Wrestling Federation baseball cap that accentuated his big ears. Mark noticed his thumb and index finger were tobacco stained, like the old man's.

"Leave, boy!"

Murat dismissed the old man's order with a disgusted wave of his hand. "Come," he said to Nuriyev and Mark. "I heard what you need."

"Did you help Alty cross to Iran?" asked Nuriyev.

"Yes, yes."

"I knew it," said Nuriyev. "Alty denied it when I asked him, but I knew if he made it to Iran, you must have helped him."

"My father's brain doesn't work right anymore. All he does is smoke all day. I have run the business myself for the past two years."

"Murat!"

Murat gestured to his father. "He knows it's true. And he knows I helped Alty and an American cross the border—last I heard they are in Mashhad."

Mark had never been to Mashhad, but he knew it was close to the border with Turkmenistan and one of Iran's most important cities. Millions of devout pilgrims flocked to it each year to visit a holy shrine in the center of the city. Which meant Decker would have been ridiculously conspicuous there. The image was almost comical.

"When was this?" asked Mark.

"Four days ago. They crossed in a supply truck, on one of our regular runs."

Mark counted the days back in his head. The photo of the man in the black turban exchanging a briefcase with Li Zemin—the one sent from Alty's iPhone—must have been taken in Mashhad.

"My colleague is a big man," said Mark.

"A giant!" said Murat with enthusiasm. "My brother thought he was a wrestler. Like maybe the brother of Edge."

"How would such a man go unnoticed?"

Murat shrugged. "He was not unnoticed. I paid the border guards a percentage of the money your friend gave me, so there was no problem."

"Were they supposed to come back?"

"The next day."

"What happened?"

"Alty called from Mashhad. He said there was a delay and he'd call again when he needs me. Then I don't hear from him."

"Where in Mashhad was he staying?" asked Mark.

"He didn't say."

"Where was he going after Mashhad?"

"I don't know."

Mark took out Daria's phone and brought up the photo of a man in the black turban exchanging a briefcase with Li Zemin. "This photo was taken by either my colleague or by Alty. From what you just told me, and by the time stamp on this photo, it must have been while they were in Mashhad. Do you recognize the man in the black turban?"

Murat studied it. "No."

"How much to smuggle me and an associate into Iran?"

"When?"

"Now."

"No, there was a shooting in Ashgabat today. There will be more security on the borders. And the time, it's late, too late to arrange."

Mark checked the sun. He estimated it was around four thirty. But the border was close, he knew. No more than an hour away. "I can't wait."

Murat shrugged. "Then three thousand dollars. One way. This is double what it usually costs. Today there will be more people to pay, and if you want to leave today I must offer more money. Even so, it will take some time to arrange."

"How much time?"

"I don't know, maybe an hour, maybe two. I will tell you where to meet your driver and I will bring him there as soon as I can."

"I'll also need you to exchange four thousand dollars of manats into Iranian rials for me."

Murat smiled. His teeth were deteriorating where they met his gums. "OK." He named a price that included a five-hundred-dollar service charge for himself. Mark let it go. There was a time to bargain and a time to pony up.

47
Washington, DC

THE PRESIDENT LEANED FORWARD AND RESTED BOTH FORE-arms on his desk in the Oval Office, exhausted after sitting through the four-hour targeting meeting in the situation room on only two hours of sleep. And it was only nine in the morning. He still had the whole day ahead of him.

In front of him sat Melissa Bates, formerly the head of the CIA's Office of Near East Analysis, now a member of the CIA's Persia House.

"What have you got for me?"

"You asked for a quantitative analysis regarding the likelihood that intelligence reports regarding Khorasani are correct."

The president opened his palms. Get on with it already.

After reviewing the essentials of what the CIA knew about Iran's dictator, Supreme Leader Ayatollah Khorasani, Bates got to the point: "The question becomes, what is the likelihood that someone like Khorasani would seek revenge, given what we believe happened to his daughter? In an attempt to answer that question, our statisticians compiled data from other Iranian fathers who have experienced similar situations. Data from Iran itself wasn't available, but there are millions of Iranians spread out across the world, in Bahrain, Turkey, Azerbaijan, Kuwait, Saudi Arabia, the United States..."

After twenty minutes of listening to Bates walk him through all the figures, the president rubbed his temples. "What's the bottom line here?"

Bates pulled out a series of charts, which she explained were regression analyses that took into account the age, religiosity, and social status of the fathers as a predictive measure of whether they would seek revenge.

"The bottom line is this—the older a man is, and the higher his social status, the less likely he is to seek revenge. For someone like Khorasani, you're talking about less than a one percent chance that he's going to resort to violence. But even that figure doesn't tell the real story, because it doesn't distinguish an eye-for-an-eye kind of revenge from what Khorasani, as the leader of a nation, is theoretically capable of. Most of the revenge killings we studied were rational, from the point of the killer. They redressed a wrong in a way that fit with the perpetrator's worldview—an eye for an eye. In only two instances was revenge exacted in a way that could be considered irrational—in Turkey when a father went on a monthlong arson spree, killing twenty, and in Bahrain where a father drowned the five young children of his daughter's rapist. In the case of Khorasani, all the evidence my office has compiled indicates that, despite his willingness to support groups that kill innocents, the intelligence reports we're receiving would represent a break from his rational model. There's not enough data to perform a decent analysis on the probability of his breaking with his rational model, but when we just plug in what numbers we have, you're talking close to nil."

"Except that the Mossad says it's going to happen."

"Except that the Mossad says it's going to happen," Bates confirmed. "And I trust their intelligence operation. And the Mossad report has been confirmed by our own sources in the MEK. "

The president rubbed his temples. "Are you saying you lack confidence in the assessment you just gave me?"

"I am, Mr. President. You know the rule—garbage in, garbage out. We did our absolute best to meet your mandate in a time frame that would prove useful to you. But we were assembling data, sometimes incomplete, from a variety of countries, all of whom treat crime statistics differently. Not to mention the fact that comparing the actions of your regular man on the street with a ruler like Khorasani is sketchy at best. I wouldn't trust this analysis."

After Melissa Bates left, the president leaned back in his chair, removed his watch, placed it on his desk, and ran his hand through his thin hair. White stubble covered his chin.

"I want every intelligence agency working overtime, vacuuming up every scrap of information they can about what the Iranians are up to," he said to his chief of staff. "Open wallets, crack heads. Anything you get comes straight to me ASAP."

"Wallets are already open. Heads are already being cracked."

"I'd feel a lot better if we had *some* kind of confirmation, from a source outside the Mossad and MEK, that we're not being jerked around and acting on bad intel."

48
Turkmenistan, Near the Border with Iran

————————o————————

MARK MET MURAT AT A ROADSIDE TRUCK STOP ON THE OUT-
skirts of Ashgabat. The dirt parking lot was littered with
little straws and burned metal wires, evidence of truckers dosing
themselves with opium before venturing across the bleak Kara-
Kum Desert.

"Chadors for the religious ladies!" Murat, slouching, pointed
to the dusty rolls of black fabric that filled most of the Russian
18-wheeler. The truck trailer's canvas sides had been ratcheted
down, but sand and road filth had swirled in through the gaps.
"The chadors protect the vodka we hide inside them!" Murat
seemed to think that was funny. "Call when you make it through."
He took a cheap cell phone out of his front pocket. "This will work
in Iran and even at the border you will have good antenna. When
you cross, give the soldiers this." He handed over an Iranian passport that had been stamped with an expired visa. "Tell them you
went to Ashgabat to gamble and are now paying the truck driver
a fee to take you back to Iran. The soldiers on both sides of the
border will accept the visa. Everything has been arranged."

"And if they don't?"

"They will not be paid. Which is why the documentation is
always accepted. Where is the woman?"

"She'll be going alone." Daria, it turned out, had a perfectly
valid Iranian passport—one that she'd neglected to surrender
after leaving the Agency. So she was just going to drive across the
border.

Murat eyed him. "No refund. Our agreement was for two."

"I didn't ask for a refund."

Mark climbed into the cab of the truck. A Russian driver wearing a soiled dress shirt and a red bandana on his head acknowledged him with a surly nod.

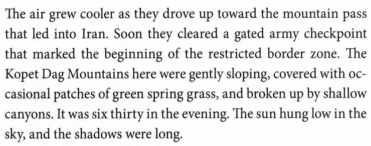

The air grew cooler as they drove up toward the mountain pass that led into Iran. Soon they cleared a gated army checkpoint that marked the beginning of the restricted border zone. The Kopet Dag Mountains here were gently sloping, covered with occasional patches of green spring grass, and broken up by shallow canyons. It was six thirty in the evening. The sun hung low in the sky, and the shadows were long.

Eventually the road leveled out and the truck's air brakes hissed as it ground to a stop. They'd reached the border. Mark counted six trucks and two cars ahead of them.

The truck at the front of the line was being inspected by Turkmen soldiers dressed in camouflage uniforms and floppy safari hats. Beyond it, Mark could see a squat white-marble building and a ten-foot-tall wrought-iron border fence.

A minute later, Daria pulled up behind them in the Niva. She wore a black headscarf and was smoking. Two more trucks pulled up behind her. Turkmen soldiers with automatic rifles paced back and forth at the very end of the line.

When the lead truck was cleared to pass, the whole line moved forward. Mark wasn't surprised when he saw the soldier who'd been guarding the Chinese embassy earlier in the day. He wore civilian clothes and stood next to an older Chinese; both men stood off to the side, eyeing the incoming vehicles as the Turkmen soldiers searched them.

Mark turned to the driver. Speaking Russian, he said, "Murat told you of the special problems we're likely to encounter?"

"Calm yourself." The driver spoke like a man who was used to dealing with panicked novices. But after a minute of silence, he asked, "What special problems?"

Mark explained that he'd been involved in the shooting in downtown Ashgabat earlier in the day and that it was entirely possible that people at the border would be looking for him, people who almost certainly wouldn't be bound by any smuggling agreement arrived at between Murat and the border soldiers.

The driver protested that Murat had said nothing of this, nothing at all! And that Mark should have said something earlier! Now that they were in line, they couldn't turn around without triggering a search.

Mark claimed that he *had* told Murat about the situation, which was a lie, and that he wished he'd said something sooner, which was another lie—in fact, he'd purposely waited to tell the Russian what was really going on until it was too late to turn around.

A minute later, the line moved forward again. The Turkmen soldiers descended on a new truck. They checked under the hood, inside and under the cab, and through everything being transported in the trailer.

The driver eyed the Chinese observers then banged his hands on the steering wheel. "Murat told me nothing of this."

"Listen, buddy. This is what we're going to have to do..."

Mark explained his plan. The driver twisted in his seat to face Mark and clenched his teeth. "Don't touch me. And keep your clothes on, *pedik*."

Mark gestured to the Chinese. "Do you have any better ideas?"

The driver didn't.

The driver threw his truck into neutral and let it slowly roll back down the hill. When Mark heard the crunch of the truck's rear bumper ramming into Daria's front bumper, he slipped out of the cab wearing the Russian driver's old shirt, pants, plastic sandals, and red-bandana head covering.

Daria climbed out of her car.

"We've switched to plan B." Mark glanced at her dented bumper.

"Yeah, I saw them."

Mark made eye contact with the trucker directly behind Daria's car and drew a finger across his throat. *Mind your own business and keep your mouth shut.* The trucker turned away just as the Russian driver joined them, wearing Mark's clothes, and began to argue with Mark about the accident. Soon one of the Turkmen soldiers from the end of the line showed up and said to take it up on the other side of the border if they needed to. The line was moving.

Fine, said Mark.

Daria climbed up into the back of the truck, where she took a seat on one of the rolls of black chadors—a religious Iranian woman would never scandalize herself by riding with an unfamiliar man in the cab.

The Russian climbed into Daria's car, while Mark took his place behind the steering wheel of the 18-wheeler. The seat was frayed, and hard springs poked into his back. He twisted the key in the ignition, shifted into first, gently raised the clutch, and stalled out. The second time he got it and pulled up to where he should have been in line. Then he studied his new passport.

Given the grisly nature of her suicide, Mark had become adept at blocking out most memories of his mother. But he thought of her now because she'd immigrated to the United States from the Soviet state of Georgia as a girl. Her father had been a Russian, and Mark had inherited some of his grandfather's Russian features—the slightly droopy eyelids, the light skin, the brown eyes. Enough so that he thought he looked at least a bit like the Russian driver, whose passport he now held in his hand.

They were also roughly the same height and age. It wouldn't hurt that the photo itself was creased and dirty.

The Russian driver's eyes were even deeper set than his own, though. With dark circles under them.

Mark wet his finger, dipped it into the coffee-can ashtray on the floor, and rubbed in some ash under each eye. Then he smeared ash on his teeth near where they met the gums.

He glanced at the passport photo again. The Russian's hair was brown and Mark had dyed his black, so he tried to push more of his hair under the bandana he now wore on his head.

Hanging from the rearview mirror was a set of well-worn worry beads. He took them down and placed them in his pocket. A half-empty pack of Java cigarettes, a Russian brand, lay on the dashboard. He pocketed those too.

Mark pulled up through the gates without stalling and stopped where he was told. The Turkmen soldiers descended, pulling up the front hood and loosening the canvas sides of the trailer. World War II–style canteens dangled from the soldiers' belts, and their pants were tucked into black army boots.

It was almost seven thirty. The sun had just dipped below the mountains, but the overhead lights hadn't been switched on yet, for which Mark was grateful—shadows would help.

He stepped out of the cab. He handed the Russian driver's passport and the inventory papers to a Turkmen official with a sergeant's chevron on his shoulder. The Chinese embassy guard and his Guoanbu minder were so focused on the search of the trailer that they hardly even glanced at Mark.

"Where do you go?"

Mark took a step to his left, so that he was in the shadow of the truck. "Mashhad."

He pulled the pack of Java cigarettes out of his front shirt pocket and silently offered one to the army officer, who shook his head no.

"And what do you carry?"

"Textiles." He spoke Russian. A hundred feet in front of him, a row of Turkmen flags hung limply by a wrought-iron gate. Past the gate stood a row of Iranian flags and a few Iranian soldiers. A sign posted in front of a beige-colored building read, in Farsi and English, *Welcome to the Islamic Republic of Iran.*

They discovered Daria in the trailer. She was dressed head to toe in a black chador and had fashioned a veil for her face.

"And who is she?"

"My brother is friends with her brother. She goes to Mashhad." Mark lit his cigarette, and the smoke swirled around his head. The clothes he was wearing stunk of vodka sweat.

"Does she pay you?"

Mark made a face, as if offended. "No. Her father has died. She goes to Mashhad to mourn."

"Does she have papers?"

"Yes, yes, of course. She is Iranian."

Mark glanced at Daria. After some commotion, a female border guard appeared. Daria was taken away to be questioned in private, without her veil. The older Chinese guard inspected the underside of the truck.

Ten minutes later, it was over. Mark's papers were signed. Daria reappeared, and the solicitous border soldiers formed a makeshift staircase out of packing crates so that it was easier for her to climb into the back of the truck's trailer. As he drove off toward the Iranian border, Mark saw the Chinese guard staring intently at the Niva, as though it might contain the people they were looking for. Instead, they'd find a Russian who would be turned away at the border because he'd left his identification papers back in Ashgabat.

The truck was searched again on the Iranian side. After having their passports stamped in the customs hall, under a large photo of Iran's supreme leader, Ayatollah Khorasani, they were told they could leave.

Mark drove toward a gate topped by a sign that read *Islamic Republic of Iran Border Terminal.* Beyond the gate, a couple of kids were kicking a soccer ball in the road, taking advantage of the bright border-terminal lights that had just come on. On the shoulder of the road, truckers stood next to their parked rigs, smoking as they waited for what could be days to cross into Turkmenistan. Even in normal times, the Turkmen were paranoid about how many trucks they let in.

An alarm began to sound.

At first Mark didn't realize it was directed at him, nor did the final Iranian border soldiers, who seemed inclined to let him pass. Then someone called out in Farsi from across the wide stretch of pavement, and one of the soldiers manning the last exit blew a whistle.

Mark laid on the horn, pushed his foot down on the accelerator, and shifted through the gears as quickly as he could. The final border checkpoint flew by him as cars veered to the side of the road.

A minute later, he was through the tiny town, thundering past little concrete-walled shops fronted by metal security gates. He began to gather speed more quickly now that he was hurtling downhill. The mountains on this side of the border loomed up as dark brown shadows, drier even than the Turkmen side, without a hint of green.

The landscape reminded Mark of the spaghetti western movies he used to watch as a kid, in which someone always wound up dying of thirst.

He floored the accelerator. From behind him, he heard a tapping at the narrow slider window in the back of the cab. Daria was perched in the space between the cab and the trailer. When they got to a relatively straight section of road, he muscled the window all the way open. Daria was just slender enough to squeeze through it.

"Welcome to Iran," she said.

"The asshole in the truck behind us must have said something. He was the only one who saw us make the switch."

An army jeep a couple of hundred feet behind them was gaining. Mark kept the accelerator floored. The whole cab rattled madly, and the steering wheel had way too much play in it.

A sets of headlights appeared in front of them.

Mark peered through the gloom. Between the approaching headlights and his current position, the road narrowed as it squeezed between the side of the mountain and the drop-off below.

"Buckle your seat belt," he said.

"There are no seat belts."

He felt for his own and grabbed air.

"Then hold on. I'm gonna—"

He gripped the wheel tighter as the truck bounced dangerously over a bump in the road.

"—try to block the road," said Daria, finishing his thought for him.

"Yeah."

"I'm with you."

When the road narrowed, Mark braked as hard as he could without skidding out. He yanked the steering wheel to the right, so that the cab of the truck smashed into the wall of the mountain and the trailer fishtailed out into the center of the road. For a moment the whole rig teetered, then the trailer slowly tipped over, pulling the cab down with it.

The front windshield shattered. Mark smelled diesel fuel. His shoulder had slammed into the asphalt. Daria had fallen on top of him.

"Go, go!" he yelled. "Out the top!"

She pushed off his shoulder and squeezed through the passenger-side window. Mark was right behind her.

The jeep that had followed them from the border was nearly upon them. A few shots rang out as they jumped to the ground, putting the truck between themselves and the bullets. The car that had been approaching came to a stop about a hundred feet down the road.

Mark sprinted over to it, reaching it in seconds.

The bearded, middle-aged man behind the wheel was frantically trying to execute a K-turn in the middle of the road, but he was constricted by the steep mountain face above him and the precipitous drop-off. No one else was in the car.

"Get out!" yelled Mark in English. He yanked the door open and pulled the man to the pavement. More gunshots rang out.

Daria reached the car and climbed into the passenger seat.

"Stand in the center of the road with your hands up," said Mark.

When the man didn't move, Daria repeated the command in Farsi.

"Tell him to stand with his hands up and not to run, or he'll get shot," said Mark.

Daria did, and the man raised his hands above his head, shaking as he did so. Mark got behind the wheel, deftly turned the car around, and slammed his foot on the accelerator.

49
Ashgabat, Turkmenistan

———————○———————

L I ZEMIN UNBUTTONED HIS PANTS AND LOOSENED HIS BELT just enough to allow himself freedom of movement. He loosened his tie and unfastened the top two buttons on his dress shirt.

The blinds were closed inside his spacious corner office at the Chinese embassy in Ashgabat, and the light was dim.

By the time he got to the twenty-fourth tai chi chuan posture—White Crane Spreads Its Wings—he was just beginning to perspire. So he was irritated when his routine was disturbed by a call from one of his field operatives.

"There was an incident."

"An incident?" repeated Zemin.

"We believe Sava has crossed into Iran."

Zemin listened carefully as he was told about the debacle at the border. Before hanging up, he noted, "This will affect your standing within the directorate."

Zemin sat down in his chair, legs spread apart, and ran a hand through his hair.

The situation had not been contained. He had to assume the worst. Which meant he would need to speak to his uncle, the fat general. In person, in Beijing.

There was no other way.

50
Quchan, Iran

⬤

ONE MOMENT THEY WERE SPEEDING ACROSS THE EMPTY
desert and the next they were careening into a roundabout
on the edge of the city of Quchan. Mark pulled off onto a side
street lined with factory buildings and crumbling walls painted
with advertisements for kitchen appliances.

The factories soon gave way to a mix of well-maintained
apartment buildings and shops. It was nine o'clock, and the
streets were crowded with people out walking and doing their
shopping. Some of the women wore chadors, but many just wore
jeans and headscarves that barely covered their hair. They passed
a pizza shop, a hardware store, clothing boutiques, and an electronics store packed with televisions and digital cameras and cell
phones. After the bizarre white-marble sterility of downtown
Ashgabat, Mark was struck by how normal it all looked.

He kept both hands on the steering wheel, still on full alert.

"Assess our current situation," he said to Daria. He'd never
been to eastern Iran before. But Daria had, many times.

Her chador had slipped from her head, and the black headscarf underneath had come loose. She tightened it with a few
quick, practiced motions, tucking her hair underneath the fabric,
then slipped the chador robe back over her head so that only her
face was exposed. Mark glanced at her as she worked, examining for the first time how she really looked in a chador. It trans-
formed her, accentuating her high cheekbones and large eyes.
Beautiful, he thought.

"Watch the road," she said.

"What's the best way to get to Mashhad?"

"It's only an hour or so away but there are always police checkpoints outside cities. Usually they're just manned by regular cops who inspect your insurance and make sure you've got proper license plates, but if word gets out in time, there'll be military looking for us."

"Can we skirt the checkpoints?"

"Depends on where and how many there are. It'd be a crapshoot."

Mark imagined the calls that were being placed right now, alerting police and army troops all over the region. It would take time for everyone to react, though. Some guys would be at home, putting their kids to sleep or drinking contraband liquor in front of the TV. Mobilizations took time.

He wondered whether they'd been photographed by security cameras at the border. Probably. Which meant that eventually the police at the checkpoints would have photos.

"What do we need to get through the checkpoints legally?"

"Valid driver's licenses, and a car with its papers in order." Daria opened the dash compartment and inspected the documents inside. "These papers are up to date, but—"

"—at a minimum we should change cars. The police will be looking for the one we're driving."

"I can hot-wire a Paykan," said Daria, referring to a popular Iranian-made car that had gone out of production a few years back.

"Really?"

"Yeah, they're like lawn mowers."

They passed a public park where Iranian families were picnicking on the grass, finishing up late dinners. Mark reflected for a moment on the huge chasm between the grotesque underworld he'd slipped back into and the placid normal world most people lived in, even in Iran. He also figured that stealing decent licenses from those normal, gullible people wouldn't be a problem. Getting the proper tools to alter them might be, though. "When do the stores close around here?"

"Probably eleven."

"Will they have what we need for the licenses?"

"Quchan isn't big, but it's big enough. There'll be a mall somewhere."

On the bed of a three-dollar-a-night hotel room, under a *qiblah* arrow that pointed praying Muslims toward Mecca, Daria arranged a pack of razor blades, rubber cement glue, a digital camera, a Lenovo laptop, a photo printer, photo paper, a couple of sheets of clear laminating paper, a scanner, hair dye, tweezers, two pairs of weak reading glasses, a travel iron, and new clothes for herself and Mark.

Next to all that, Mark placed two standard-class Iranian driver's licenses. Printed on the faces of the licenses were photos of the licensees—a married couple from Tabriz. The wife was thirty-six years old and the husband was thirty-eight. Mark had stolen their wallets while the couple tended to their crying infant. To soften the blow, he'd left two hundred dollars in Iranian rials in their coat pockets.

In preparation for their head-shot photos, they retreated to the bathroom. Daria cut Mark's hair short on the sides, so that his face looked thinner, and he lopped three inches off Daria's hair, leaving her with a bob cut.

"God, you stink," she said, as he cut her hair.

After she finished with his hair, he wiped away all the cigarette ash beneath his eyes, showered, shaved off his three-day beard, and put on new clothes. Then he cut up pieces of cardboard packaging and wedged them into the heels of his shoes, adding an inch to his height so that he stood nearly as tall as the six feet listed on his new driver's license.

Overall it wasn't much of a disguise, he thought, as he slipped on the weak reading glasses and looked in the small mirror above the toilet, standing a foot behind Daria as she worked on her own appearance. But he looked different enough that your average cop with a photo of him crossing the border earlier in the day would at least have to do a double take. He tried pushing the glasses lower, to mask the distinctive bump he had as a result of his nose being broken by KGB goons nearly two decades ago.

Daria plucked her eyebrows so that they were thinner and had more of an arch. She wiped away the makeup that had been covering the scars on her face. When she saw him looking at her, she got self-conscious and put her hands up to cover her face.

"I look like hell, I know."

Mark stood a foot behind her.

He'd actually been thinking that she was still beautiful, despite all she'd been through. She'd probably never see it that way, though.

He could see someone else's garbage—old fava beans and a bunch of used tissues—in the waste bin under the sink. The fava beans smelled sour, and a stink of sewage gas seeped up from the base of the toilet.

Daria didn't belong in this dump, he thought. No one did.

"You look fine."

51
China, Above Xinjiang

———————o———————

THE BEIJING-BOUND ARMY TRANSPORT PLANE WAS PRETTY
utilitarian inside, but Li Zemin was seated up front, where
a few comfortable captain's chairs had been bolted to the steel
floor—a first-class section of sorts, reserved for military and
intelligence bigwigs. A young lieutenant general sat beside him.

Not long into the trip, an air force steward asked Zemin and
the lieutenant general if they wanted tea and crackers.

Zemin said he'd brought his own tea. Just hot water would be
fine. He sneezed and rummaged through his shoulder bag for the
mix of oolong tea and medicinal herbs that his trusted herbalist
in Beijing had prepared for him.

"Try it with some *baijiu*," said the lieutenant general. He produced a green porcelain bottle and offered it to Zemin. "A little
bit will help clear your nose."

Zemin was about to refuse the offer—*baijiu* was a notori-
ously strong liquor that his wife had frowned upon when she'd
been alive. And Zemin had never been much of a drinker anyway. But he found himself thinking that *baijiu* might be just the
thing he needed to help him deal with his uncle. So he accepted
the bottle, and after steeping his tea in hot water for a few minutes, he poured a few ounces of the alcohol on top.

The *baijiu* had been infused with the fragrance of honey, so
despite its potency, it slipped down Zemin's throat with ease. It
did nothing to clear his nose, but he announced the success of
the treatment to the lieutenant general anyway.

"Then the bottle is yours," replied the lieutenant general, as Zemin had known he would.

"But I couldn't possibly accept."

"I insist." He explained that the brand was common in his home city of Shanghai, but hard to find in Beijing.

Zemin offered his thanks for the gift and, an hour later, when he ordered more hot water for tea, he topped off his cup with another healthy pour of the liquor.

52
Mashhad, Iran

MASHHAD AT DAWN WAS FRANTIC WITH HONKING CARS, tour buses and construction trucks, and crowds of people streaming along with great purpose. The pollution was so thick in the streets that Mark's eyes began to water as he walked. It was a city that had grown too fast, he thought, with no central planning.

In the city center, towering high above the maze of clogged streets and surrounding buildings, loomed an enormous dome tiled in solid gold and topped by a green flag. It was the shrine of Imam Reza, Daria said, one of Shiite Islam's most revered figures. Tall golden minarets rose on either side of it, and strings of lights suspended from the top of the minarets flared outward like bell-bottoms. A massive Vatican-like city-within-a-city had grown up around the shrine.

When Mark got to the high tiled walls that separated the shrine complex from the rest of Mashhad, he presented his Iranian driver's license to one of the guards standing at the men's entrance. Having already used it at two police checkpoints, when he and Daria had breezed into Mashhad early that morning, he was confident by now that it would be accepted.

The guard glanced at the license, as though to be polite, swept a hand-held metal detector across Mark's body, and asked a question in Farsi.

Mark didn't understand the question, but guessed the guard was asking him what his intentions were.

"Pilgrimage, pay my respects to Imam Reza." Mark spoke in Azeri. More Azeris lived in Iran than in Azerbaijan, and it was a common language of commerce in Iran. He figured in a place so heavily trafficked as this that the guards would understand him.

"Camera?" asked the guard, this time in Azeri. He patted Mark's body down, but stayed away from Mark's genitals, where Mark had hidden a roll of tape and a sheaf of paper fliers. Mark had figured it would be like a football game, where you were allowed to smuggle in as much booze as you could fit next to your balls.

"No."

The guard motioned for him to pass through the gates, and Mark entered the first of a series of interlocking courtyards that surrounded the shrine. In front of him, a woman in a black chador was praying, her eyes cast toward the sky, her hands held up in front of her as though holding an imaginary box. A nearby signpost pointed the way to ancient mosques, museums, religious schools, libraries, tourist centers, guest houses...

Most of the complex was technically off-limits to non-Muslims, but tests for religious purity were impossible to administer to the millions of visitors who passed through every year.

He followed the arrow pointing to the shrine itself and soon reached an inner courtyard that was ringed by a two-story arcade clad in millions of hand-painted tiles. Clusters of men in robes knelt on rugs, praying, and a gray cat walked on a roof high above the courtyard. A little girl, too young to need to cover her hair, brushed by him as she chased a little boy. As Mark traversed the courtyard, a flock of green pigeons flew up and settled on top of the gilded water station where pilgrims were washing themselves before entering the shrine to pray.

The entrance to the shrine stood under a gold-tiled vaulted Persian arch; a giant chandelier hung from its apex. To either side of the entrance were areas where pilgrims could remove their shoes before going inside. Mark approached the men's section and pulled out his sheaf of fliers.

On each flier was a photo of the man in the black turban.

Underneath the photo, it read, in Farsi, *Are you learned enough to know the name of this esteemed sayyid, next Friday's Prayer leader? The first fifty worshippers to call will be rewarded with a private sermon by this learned man, to be held at the Bala-sar Mosque. There he will enlighten all of the glory of Imam Reza, peace be upon him.* At the bottom of the flier was a telephone number and the name Center for Islamic Studies.

Mark taped three fliers to a wall where people preparing to enter the shrine were sure to see them.

Next he went to a school, where women in black chadors were seated on a carpeted floor in a central room studying the Qur'an while their children played with humidifiers, putting their hands near the steam and laughing when it touched their hands.

He taped five fliers to the green bulletin board near the entrance.

Next came a library, then a huge courtyard where he taped fliers to half the lampposts.

Outside a mosque, over a thousand people stood in bare feet or socks on prayer carpets, bowing as one. Mark walked among them as though looking for a family member, trying to avoid the men in blue suits wielding rainbow-colored feather dusters who were directing late-arriving worshippers to their proper places. He spotted fourteen black-turbaned sayyids among the crowd. None was the man he was looking for. He taped more fliers to the walls near the mosque entrance on his way out.

As he did so an old man, dressed in a torn sport coat and wool ski hat, with a face like leather, demanded to know what he was doing.

Mark flashed him a nasty look. "Contest," he said in Azeri, and taped up another flier.

He met Daria outside the main entrance to the shrine complex. She'd spent the morning posting fliers at religious universities and mosques around greater Mashhad. In her pocket was one of two cell phones they'd bought that morning, along with several prepaid SIM cards; the number for the cell phone in her pocket was the number now printed on all the fliers.

"Three calls already."

The first had been from a school administrator who was irate about the fliers that had been plastered all over his campus. The second was from someone pointing out that the prayer leader for next Friday was supposed to be Ayatollah Tabrizi, not the man pictured on the flier. The third was from a student who had mistakenly thought the man pictured was the leader of Iran's parliament.

Another call came in twenty minutes later. Daria answered as if she were the receptionist for the fictional Center for Islamic Studies, cupping the mouthpiece with her hand to muffle the street noise.

After hanging up, she said, "A woman from Ferdowsi University swears our man is a guy named Amir Bayat, owner and editor in chief of the *Enqelab*. She said she grew up in Tehran and her father worked at the paper for years. She wants to know when she's getting her pass for the sermon."

The *Enqelab*, Mark knew, was a hard-line conservative newspaper published in Tehran. When he'd been with the CIA, he'd frequently read translated versions of it. He eyed a cop directing traffic and suggested that they find an Internet café and find out everything they could about Amir Bayat.

"I've got a better idea," said Daria. "We can be in Tehran in seven hours. Once we get there, I know someone who will be able to tell us a lot more about Amir Bayat than we'd ever be able to learn online."

53
Beijing, China

———————————o———————————

L I ZEMIN DROVE UP TO A SET OF SPIKED WROUGHT-IRON GATES in his black Toyota Camry. A private security guard, wearing a uniform that mimicked those worn by the Chinese army, motioned for him to stop.

Zemin handed over his identification and looked past the gates. With its smattering of red-tiled roofs, stucco buildings, and Spanish street names, the planned community of Santa Barbara was supposed to give the wealthy Beijing residents who lived there the impression that they in fact inhabited the small California coastal town.

Zemin was not a man of strong passions—mild dislike was usually about all he could muster for even the most disagreeable elements of life—but Santa Barbara was an exception.

He loathed the place.

Forty-five years ago, during the Cultural Revolution, having been labeled a capitalist roader by forces loyal to Mao, his father had been executed. A year later, his mother had died of pneumonia in a jail, where she'd been locked up for having supported his father.

Zemin had been raised by his uncle and taught to despise his dead parents because of their alleged ties to capitalism. Santa Barbara made a mockery of that history.

Now everyone was a capitalist, and his uncle, the great general, lived like the very capitalists he'd taught Zemin to despise.

The guard waved him through.

He drove down Cabrillo Boulevard until he came to a cul-de-sac, at the end of which sat a large two-story Tudor-style house, an architectural anomaly among its Spanish-influenced neighbors. Though the grass out front was fertilizer green, the sky above was its usual sickly smog gray. He parked his car in the granite-cobbled driveway and, with a nod of his head, acknowledged the soldier standing near the garage. This one was a real Chinese army officer.

When he rang the front doorbell, he was met by a maid.

"The general is in a meeting. You'll have to wait."

Zemin wasn't surprised. The fat general always kept him waiting.

54
Tehran, Iran

―――――――――◦―――――――――

"STAY CLOSE." DARIA TOUCHED MARK'S FOREARM. "SHOVE through if you have to."

Mark turned his attention to the crush of shoppers trying to plunge into one of the main bottleneck entrances to Tehran's Grand Bazaar.

A few feet ahead of him, a man was muscling a cart, stacked six feet high with sacks of rice, through a wall of bodies. Daria fell in behind him. Mark fell in behind her.

Unlike the open-air bazaar outside of Ashgabat, this one in south Tehran was a chaotic, twisting maze composed of miles and miles of centuries-old covered alleys.

In one section were electronics, in another fine china, in another racy women's lingerie...Porters replenished the stores with goods they carried in on backpacks padded with old carpet remnants. Motorbikes occasionally wove their way through the dense crowds. In many alleys, the only light came from neon signs and strings of fluorescent bulbs hanging from low ceilings, which gave the place a cave-like feel. In others, thick shafts of bright sunlight, filled with dust motes, filtered down from open skylights that had been cut into high vaulted ceilings.

After they'd walked over a mile, Daria turned down an alley where shop after shop was packed with rolls of brightly colored fabrics stacked on shelves that reached up to the ceiling.

She approached the third shop on the left and spent a few minutes examining the fabrics that were at eye level. Eventually, a middle-aged man came over and said he would be happy to show her some of his finer rolls.

Daria said no, she was looking for a specific fabric she'd bought at the shop two years ago. It was a brocade of silver and yellow, with an image of a caged bird repeated in the pattern. It was a beautiful pattern, she said. Very rare, but the owner of the shop had been in the day she'd ordered it, and had recommended it to her. She'd used it to reupholster her couch, and now had two chairs she needed done. Did they still carry it?

The merchant inspected his inventory, but couldn't find the fabric she was looking for.

Daria asked whether he could order it.

He would have to make a call. The owner of the shop would know.

When the merchant came back, he said that Daria was indeed fortunate. The owner of the store remembered the exact fabric in question and had some at one of his stores in north Tehran. Would Daria prefer to pick it up at the other store or have it delivered?

"I'll pick it up in an hour. If the owner could have it ready, that would be wonderful."

"I will tell him."

"*Merci.*" Daria used the French word for *thank you*, as most Iranians did.

They squeezed onto a motorcycle taxi, which, fifteen minutes later, dropped them in front of a parking garage on Taleqani Avenue, just past the high brick walls that encircled the old American embassy.

On the sixth floor, Daria approached a silver Mercedes. Although it was rusting in a few places, it had recently been washed and waxed. The shiny hood stood out next to the concrete walls, which were stained with engine oil that had dripped down from the floors above. The words *Bethlehem Steel* were stamped on one of the grimy I-beams supporting the ceiling.

Daria opened the gas cap cover and pulled out a set of keys.

"He's watching us now," she said.

"From where?"

"I don't know."

She opened the trunk and listened for a moment. There were no footsteps, just the sound of the noisy city outside. "Get in."

Mark did as instructed. Daria quickly put the keys back next to the gas cap, climbed in next to him, and pulled down the lid of the trunk. To both fit, her back had to nestle up against his chest.

"He's got a thing about me seeing where he lives," Daria said, whispering in the darkness. "Which is kind of crazy because I know his name and if I wanted to figure out where he lives I could do it easily." When Mark didn't respond, she added, "When I was with the Agency, I met with him about once a month for over two years. He's one of the power brokers at the bazaar. Not the biggest, but he's got influence."

Mark forced himself to stop thinking about Daria's ass, which was pressed invitingly up against his crotch, and instead consider Tehran's Grand Bazaar. Although it had lost some of its influence lately, the bazaar was still the Wall Street of Iran; deep connections existed between many of the bazaar merchants and the government.

"If he's so paranoid, why go to his house? Why not just talk here?"

"He doesn't like to be rushed."

The front door of the car opened, then slammed shut. A muffled voice from the front seat spoke out in Farsi: "Who is he?"

"My boss," said Daria. "You have nothing to fear from him."

"In the past you have always come alone, dear."

"It's a special circumstance."

Silence, then, "Are you in danger?"

"No more so than usual."

"After so long, I was afraid I would not hear from you again."

"I'll explain everything at your home."

55

Beijing, China

"**T**HE GENERAL WILL SEE YOU NOW."

"Is my aunt here?"

"Hong Kong."

Zemin dismissed the maid and showed himself to his uncle's weekend office. The general was at his desk, signing his name to government documents.

"I meet with the transport minister at the golf clubhouse in fifteen minutes." His uncle spoke with his usual abruptness, without bothering to look up. An assistant—a young army lieutenant—stood by the side of the desk with a stack of more papers to be signed.

It was Sunday morning. The general wore a light green army shirt with dark green army slacks. His jacket, with its general's epaulets, hung on a coatrack near the door. His head was unnaturally large, even in relation to the rest of his chubby body—the result of too many Mongolian hot pots at the golf club. His cheeks sagged.

Zemin said, "I have an important matter I need to discuss with you."

"Sit."

Zemin had, in fact, been intending to sit, but now he chose to remain standing. He faced his uncle's assistant. "Leave us."

The assistant's face remained blank until the general said, "Go."

When he and his uncle were alone, Zemin said, "There are complications. With the project in Iran."

The general was seventy-four years old. His clean-shaven face showed the wrinkles that come with age. Liver spots dotted the backs of his hands.

"Stop this."

"I must tell you of these complications."

The general signed another document. "Enough! Whatever your problem is, you must solve it yourself."

"The Iranians have detained an American—"

The general smacked his palm on his desk. "One month ago you came to see me. You stood before me as you do now. You assured me, and I in turn assured the commission, that there would be no circumstances under which the commission would—"

"I provided financial support to the Iranian newspaper editor we spoke of. The sayyid Amir Bayat, the man I worked with years ago when I was in Tehran."

"Financial support that you assured me would be untraceable. You were—"

"As he promised, he was able to use that money to pay off the right generals and informants, so that false information fell into the hands of the Americans and Israelis."

"Do not tell me the nature of this information," warned the general. "There is no reason for the commission, or me, to know. We agreed on this point, Li."

"Because of complications that have arisen, you must now instruct the Guoanbu in Iran to do as I say."

"Impossible."

"Then I will tell you the specifics of the operation you authorized. So that you know the dangers involved. Two months ago, the daughter of Supreme Leader Ayatollah Khorasani was caught swimming at night, naked, on a men's beach in Kish Island.

She was arrested by local Iranian police. Of course, when they arrested her, the police had no idea who she was."

The general shook his head and narrowed his eyes. Zemin enjoyed the look of disgust on his uncle's face. Theirs was a strictly formal relationship. Certainly they had never—not even once—discussed anything remotely sexual before.

"Because she was the daughter of the supreme leader, the incident was covered up and the girl was sequestered. But rumors started…"

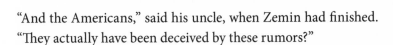

"And the Americans," said his uncle, when Zemin had finished. "They actually have been deceived by these rumors?"

"You would know better than I. How many of their aircraft carriers are within striking distance of Iran?"

Zemin took his uncle's silence as an acknowledgment that the Americans were indeed up to something. He paused, expecting some small nod of recognition from his uncle that, remarkably, the primary objective of the operation remained on track.

Instead, the general said, "This is not a Chinese operation and never was. This is your operation."

"Enough, Uncle. We are alone. We can speak the truth. You put the outline of the operation before the commission. And the commission approved it because they were afraid that, if the regime in Iran were ever to collapse, China's oil and natural gas agreements might be canceled. A new government in Iran would want to reach out to the West, and other Central Asian nations might follow suit. A US attack on Iran would ensure that that would never happen. You know that, and I know that."

"We will not acknowledge it."

"The Iranians have detained an American who knows about our involvement in the money transfer. He took a photo. It shows me delivering money to Amir Bayat. He e-mailed this photo to others."

The general looked disgusted. "This is your problem, not China's. He detected your rogue operation. Not China's."

"You approved that transfer."

"And you made commitments."

"The Americans know what we did to Turkmenistan's currency, and that I was involved, and that proceeds from that operation were transferred to Amir Bayat. These breaches are unfortunate, but not catastrophic."

"Commitments of absolute secrecy!"

"The danger is that the Americans will learn *why* we transferred money to Bayat. The only way to guarantee that that won't happen is to eliminate the two people in Iran who know both where the money came from and where the money went."

The general stared down Zemin.

"Yes, Uncle, we must kill Amir Bayat and his ayatollah brother. You must authorize the Guoanbu in Iran to do it immediately. A former CIA officer has crossed into Iran. His name is Mark Sava. He has seen the photo of me and he knows the man the Iranians have detained. He is closing in."

The general came out from behind his desk. "To come here with demands, like a pushy schoolboy. You shame yourself. The commission will not approve such a mission."

"Then you must."

"I will not. Ayatollah Bayat is a member of the Guardian Council. He could be the next supreme leader. If our involvement in his death were ever discovered—"

"It is the only way."

"I will not be interrupted and bullied by an insolent child. Now leave me be."

His uncle expected deference, Zemin knew. For the old ways to be honored, for blind obedience, for elders to be respected. But his uncle didn't respect the old ways. His uncle lived in Santa

Barbara and invested in hotel chains in Hong Kong. He only followed the old ways when it suited him.

Zemin would do the same.

"No, Uncle, that's where you're wrong. You *will* be bullied by me. You will instruct Guoanbu assets in Iran to kill Amir Bayat and his brother Muhammad Bayat. You will also instruct them to kill the Bayats' American prisoner, and the guards being used to detain him, and the American Mark Sava. And you will instruct them to do all this in direct consultation with me." He took a step toward his uncle. "If you do not do these things, I will tell the Americans myself what you and the commission and our president have planned. I will ruin you. And if it ruins me in the process, I don't care."

56
Tehran, Iran

THE OCCASIONAL STEEP SLOPE OF THE TRUNK TOLD MARK that he and Daria were ascending north into the wealthy part of Tehran, high above the dense smog and heat.

After twenty minutes, the car stopped. A gate, or perhaps a garage door, squeaked while being opened and then—after the car had pulled forward and stopped—while being closed. The trunk opened.

Standing above Mark, in a small garage, was a man of about sixty. He had a bald crown and a long, skinny, hawk-like nose. Big tufts of hair sprouted out over his ears. He offered his hand to Daria, and she took it.

"I apologize again for the inconvenience," he said in perfect, British-accented English as he helped her climb out of the trunk.

"It is no inconvenience."

"Oh but it is. A woman should not be subjected to such indignities. It is a sign of the times we live in." He nodded politely to Mark. "Had I known you would be traveling with a colleague, I would have arranged it differently."

A hallway off the garage led to a pleasant living room. It was painted a warm yellow, complementing the couch and chairs, which had been upholstered in a yellow-and-silver brocade that was notable for its caged-bird pattern—exactly as Daria had described it.

Stacked on open shelves in every corner of the living room were potted ferns and vine-like philodendrons that grew down to the floor.

"I'll make tea," said Mahmoud.

Mark checked his watch.

"Please, don't trouble yourself," said Daria.

"I insist. It is some of Darjeeling's finest; I know the man who sells it."

As Mahmoud turned toward the kitchen, Daria said, "There was a bloodletting in Baku. Eight months ago. Few survived. Part of what happened was my fault—" She glanced at Mark. "I lost my job. I was fired. That's why you haven't heard from me in so long."

Mahmoud turned back to Daria. With what sounded like genuine sadness, he said, "I grieve for you."

"Don't."

"You were hurt."

Daria touched her face. "Not badly."

"Don't trouble yourself, dear. I could hardly notice. You are still radiant, but it is not your face that worries me, it is your heart."

Mark's first reaction was to dismiss the line as nothing more than sugary nonsense, but Mahmoud said it with such genuine empathy that he couldn't.

Daria turned away. Mark had the impression she was struggling not to cry.

Mahmoud sat down. "Why are you here, Daria?"

She wiped her eye with the back of her hand. "We are searching for a friend."

"You have found him." Mahmoud opened both of his arms, gesturing to himself. "Tell me what you need."

"I speak of a friend who we believe came to Iran." She explained the nature of Decker's investigation. "Before he disappeared, he sent me three photos. We were hoping you could look at them. I can't promise that anything you do to help us will weaken the regime. I can't promise you anything, Mahmoud. It would just be a favor."

"Quiet yourself, dear. Show me the pictures."

Daria handed him a blown-up photo, cut out from one of the fliers they'd posted around Mashhad. "We believe the man in the black turban is the editor of *Enqelab*."

Mahmoud studied the photo for a moment. "It is so," he pronounced. "Amir Bayat. The dog."

"I thought you might know him," said Daria.

"Yes, the incident with my..." Mark observed that Mahmoud's hand trembled. "...my son, happened twelve years ago, around the same time this Bayat started the *Enqelab*. Bayat pressed the government's case in his paper, of course. Every day. He is a stooge of the warmongers in this country and a monkey boy for his ayatollah brother. He prints what they tell him to print." Mahmoud turned to Mark. "There is a cabal of lunatics in this country, you see, that make even Khorasani seem reasonable. Bayat is the mongrel dog of this cabal. A dog his masters use when it suits them to frighten the few reasonable people who are left in this country."

Mahmoud snapped his fingers a few times, as though to summon a dog. "Bayat's latest mission is to help destroy the conservatives who are only half-crazy, those who wish to open up limited ties to the West and lift some of the idiocy that is passed off as religion in this country. After devouring everyone decent in this country, they are now turning on their own." He smacked his knee, and then was silent, as if embarrassed by his outburst.

Mark resisted the urge to check his watch again.

Daria pulled out her phone and brought up the three photos they'd received from Decker. Mahmoud only studied the first for a moment before announcing that he didn't recognize the Asian man with whom Amir Bayat was exchanging a briefcase. But when Daria clicked on the second picture, the one that showed a mansion, he placed his fingers lightly on her hand.

He took her phone, brought it to within six inches of his long nose, handed the device back to Daria, and then closed his eyes.

A short while later, with a flourish of his long skinny hands, he said, "I know this place." With disdain, he added, "This *palace*."

Without offering further explanation, he stood and walked to a set of sliding glass doors that opened out onto a small backyard garden.

"The wild parrots came back two weeks ago." Mahmoud pointed to a bird feeder in his garden; two green parrots were indeed eating from it.

"You recognize the house?" asked Mark.

Mahmoud turned to Daria. "Have I told you the story about the caged parrot?"

"You have."

"Ah, of course, of course. I forget you know all these things." He turned to Mark. "It involves a merchant who had a caged parrot of exceptional beauty. One day the merchant told the parrot he had to go to India and asked whether there was anything the parrot wanted."

Mark wondered what this had to do with the photograph.

"The parrot said he wanted the merchant to visit wild parrots in India and tell them of how he keeps his own parrot in a cage. So the merchant went to India and did this. Immediately, one of the wild parrots fell lifeless off his branch to the ground."

Mahmoud used his hand to suggest a dead parrot.

"When the merchant returned home, he explained to his caged parrot what had happened. Moments later, his own parrot died! Grieving, the man took his parrot out of his cage and laid it beneath a tree, intending to bury it. But the moment he placed it on the ground, the parrot flew away, high into the trees. The merchant cried, "What have you done?' And the parrot said, 'I thought that by telling the Indian parrots of how you kept me caged, you would realize that what you were doing is wrong. But the free parrots knew at once that you would never change. So one of them showed me the way to my freedom.'"

Mahmoud turned back to Mark and Daria. "The photo you showed me is of a palace you will find in north Tehran. The brother of Amir Bayat lives there. He is a high-ranking ayatollah and the leader of the Guardian Council."

"I know of him," said Daria.

"I will shed no tears if harms comes to him during the hunt for your friend. But be careful, my dear. Ayatollah Bayat is a dangerous man. He is like the merchant, a man you can't reason with. He will *never* change."

Daria examined the photo. "I thought public officials were supposed to live humbly."

"The palace was one that the Shah kept for his family and guests. It is an architectural monstrosity that mocks Iran. Ayatollah Bayat gets away with living there because it is owned by the government and he occasionally uses it for official Guardian Council functions. He says he doesn't have a home, that he sleeps at his office. It is a fiction, of course. It is his home. I will make a map for you to show you where it is."

They left a few minutes later. After Mahmoud had dropped them back off in the parking garage, Mark asked, "What happened to his son?"

"He was hanged, in public."

When Daria didn't elaborate, Mark pressed her. "Because?"

"Because he was gay." After they'd walked in silence for a while, Daria added, "A year later, Mahmoud's wife killed herself. I found out about it from people at the bazaar—that's why I tried to recruit him, I thought he might still harbor a grudge."

"I take it he does."

"Yeah, you could say that."

57
Tehran, Iran

I N THE FRONT OF AYATOLLAH BAYAT'S MANSION, WIDE WHITE-marble steps led up to a spacious portico ringed by Greek columns. Deep-set balconies were lit by chandeliers on the upper levels of the house.

The mansion stood behind a tall fence and was the only structure in the vicinity surrounded by any expanse of land, consisting of nearly two acres' worth—Mark guessed—of poorly tended lawn and limbed-up plane trees. Overgrown bushes grew on the perimeter of the property, and weeds had crept up out of the cracks in the main driveway. A stagnant reflecting pool lay in front of the main entrance. Two guards stood at attention at the front gate.

Mark and Daria drove up to a point well above the mansion and parked on the street. Mark took out a pair of binoculars he'd bought downtown and studied the grounds.

"They have dogs there."

"Unlikely," said Daria. "Religious Iranians think dogs are unclean."

He handed her the binoculars. "Check out the little white flags. They're in the middle of the lawn and under the trees on the left. It's an invisible fence."

"What do they need an invisible fence for? They've got a real fence."

"To keep the dogs away from the house. *Because* religious Iranians think dogs are unclean. The way they have it set up, the

226

dogs are limited to the outside perimeter of the property, between the invisible fence and the real fence."

Daria focused the binoculars. "I heard the army started using them in some cases."

"A guy I know in Baku has a big spread." Mark was thinking of Orkhan Gambar. "He does the same thing. You get the security of the dogs without having to interact with them."

Daria looked through the binoculars a little more. "Yeah, I think you're right."

Mark noticed the white chimneys on top of the house. "Give me your phone."

Daria handed it over and Mark brought up the last of the three photos that Decker had e-mailed them, the one in which Decker's raised hand appeared against a white background. He showed it to Daria.

"That white part look anything like a chimney to you?"

Daria studied the photo. "Maybe." She looked at it some more, then down at the house itself. "Yeah, it does. What the hell was John thinking?"

"That he was trapped up on the roof and about to get caught. So he did his best under pressure to give us a trail to follow."

Mark figured that Decker had been using the roof as a surveillance post from which to spy on Ayatollah Bayat. And that he likely would have had surveillance equipment on him. Decker wouldn't have wanted that equipment to fall into the wrong hands.

"Shit," said Mark.

"Are you thinking—"

"Rally on me. That was the hand signal. And he was standing in front of one of those chimneys."

They both stared at the house for a while until Mark reluctantly said, "If I'm going to do this, we're going to need some more equipment."

58

ALTHOUGH BOTH OF HIS NEW JAILERS SPOKE FLUENT ENGLISH, Decker guessed from their facial features that they were Chinese. One wore a white T-shirt and gray slacks, the other a white T-shirt and blue slacks.

Blue apologized to Decker for his previous treatment, gave him a shirt and pants, a little food and drink, set his broken ankle, and allowed him to sleep for a few minutes.

Gray woke Decker up, stripped him naked, poured cold water all over him, hit his broken ankle with a baseball bat, and forced Decker to stand by strapping a noose made of electrical wire around his neck so that if he fell, he'd hang.

Blue said that he hated this kind of inhumane treatment and wanted to find a way to make it stop. If only Decker would help…

Beyond the good-cop-bad-cop routine, Decker knew what they were doing—they'd stripped his clothes off to strip him of his identity, in order to build a new, more dependent and compliant one. They'd had him stand with a broken ankle and a noose around his neck to make him feel that if he fell, he'd be committing suicide.

Why are you doing this to *yourself*? Let us help you.

Break apart a person's identity and then give them a false sense of being able to guide their own destiny. These guys knew exactly what they were doing.

Time bent into strange, hallucinogenic contortions. He spent long periods downstairs in the safe, his mouth pressed up to one of the holes that had been drilled through the metal, afraid that if he drifted off to sleep his mouth would fall from the hole and he'd die from lack of oxygen.

After hours or days—Decker wasn't sure—Gray hauled him up from the pit and injected him with what he said was a truth serum. Real truth serums didn't exist, Decker knew. There were drugs like sodium pentothal that could make you less inhibited, but just because you were more inclined to talk didn't mean you felt some pressing need to tell the truth while you were talking.

"There is no shame in sharing information with us," said Blue. "This drug is so strong. No one is able to resist it."

A ready-made excuse to give in. They were screwing with his mind, with his pride.

"You would personally be doing me a great favor," said Blue.

Decker said nothing. Blue left the room. Gray strung him up again with the noose around his neck. The pain that shot through Decker's ankle and wounded thigh made his legs shake. The drug compromised his ability to balance. He started wheezing and drooling.

When Blue returned he said, "I have spoken with my superiors. They have agreed that if you are generous enough to help us with this matter, we can arrange for a cash payment to you of three hundred thousand dollars plus transport to the border of your choice."

It was just a bullshit ploy to get him to talk, he knew. But there was an irrational voice inside him that wanted to believe the offer was real, that he could walk away from all this with a bit of cash and his life intact...

His legs began to buckle. He felt pressure on his neck—the weight of his own body pulling him down into the noose. White spots danced in front of his eyes. Everything started playing in slow motion.

"I beg of you," said Blue. "You can go free if you help us now."

Decker was past being able to speak.

Gray came up and kicked Decker's legs out from under him. He put his mouth right next to Decker's ear, so that he could be heard over the choking sounds.

"Soon I will start cutting. Your fingers, your eyes, your dick, your asshole. I'll keep you alive so you can watch as I cut you down to a stump. If you still don't talk, I'll pick up children from the street and kill them in front of you until you tell us what we want to know." He spoke with the quiet confidence of someone who was absolutely insane.

"Don't let him do this, friend," said Blue. "Help me to stop him. He's mad!"

Decker passed out. When he regained consciousness, he was being dragged down into the dank pit. They stuffed him in the safe and slammed the door shut.

The sound of his unsteady breathing reverberated in the small space. After a while, the air warmed up.

Decker's father was a big man, with strong arms. He felt his father's arms around him now, followed by the strange sensation of having reentered his mother's womb, of ending where he'd started.

It's over.

At least the path forward was now clear. He still had his teeth. He could kill himself by tearing open his wrist. The sodium pentothal was still coursing through him; it probably wouldn't even hurt if he did it now.

Decker twisted his head to the right and put his mouth to one of the air holes. He didn't want to do it. He loved this world, loved his family, loved himself, loved being alive. But he didn't have a choice. He had to do it soon.

Before they came back for him.

59
Tehran, Iran

———————o———————

MARK EYED THE FENCE SURROUNDING AYATOLLAH BAYAT'S estate. Made of decorative wrought iron, it was ten feet tall and topped by sharp black spikes. He figured it would have taken Decker an effortless two seconds to vault right over it.

It was one in the morning, and he was standing in an alley across the street. He was tired. He tried to do a few last-minute stretches. Crap, he thought. He was too old for this.

He tried to rile himself up by thinking about his ransacked apartment in Baku and the loss of his book.

Nothing, no anger whatsoever.

He remembered the call from Decker's father. Do this for him, do it for Decker's mother, do it for Decker.

He eyed the spikes on top of the fence again.

Or not. Suffering through god-awful, heart-wrenching tragedy was just part of the human condition. It wasn't his job to try to fix everything for everybody.

Then he thought about what Daria would think of him if he backed out.

Shit, he was really going to have to do this.

A couple of minutes later, he heard the sound of squealing tires and crunching metal. Then the horn of the stolen Paykan began to wail. That would be Daria, he knew. Evidently *she* wasn't having any last-minute doubts.

The German shepherd guard dogs that had been released at midnight started snapping their jaws and barking like crazy.

Mark counted three of them racing off. The two guards by the front gate also took off at a run.

Mark couldn't see the Paykan on the opposite side of the estate, but if Daria had done her job well, the guards would find it lodged in the fence. Spray-painted on the hood, in Farsi, would be the words *Death to the Guardian Council!* and *Independence, Freedom, Iranian Republic!*

Another guard emerged from the black woods, sprinting to the front of the mansion.

Mark eyed the fence one last time, ran at it, and found a purchase for his feet on the intricate scrollwork about halfway up. Spikes jabbed into his chest as he tried to swing his body over the top. The crotch of his pants ripped, and the five-inch knife strapped to his ankle got caught on one of the spikes.

It took him a few seconds to kick himself free.

He hit the grass and felt a sharp pain in his kidneys as he fell on his back, but in an instant was up and racing across the open lawn toward the mansion.

Within seconds he had reached a gutter downspout. The copper was green with age and anchored into the brick. He began to shimmy up as best he could.

Voices were screaming out from the site of the Paykan accident.

Although he was wiry and strong, Mark nevertheless kept slipping down until he found he could gain more traction by wedging his foot between the gutter and the wall.

About halfway up, he noticed handprints other than his own—visible because they had disturbed the copper's green patina—going up the length of the downspout.

The space between the handprints was huge.

He imagined Decker running at the wall, leaping up and grabbing the downspout ten feet off the ground, then scaling the rest within seconds.

Mark felt himself slip. If the guards had half a brain, he thought, one of them would do a perimeter sweep soon. He strained to shimmy up the rest of the way. Lifting himself over the lip of the gutter nearly proved too much. By the time he was actually sitting on the tile roof, he was exhausted, but he forced himself to keep going until he reached the ridgeline.

The first of the three chimneys was ten feet away. He checked his watch—thirty seconds behind schedule—then removed a small penlight from his pocket and inspected the exterior of the first chimney, looking for a sign from Decker. He inspected the flashing and tiles around the chimney, pulling them back, looking for a piece of paper, or anything that Decker might have left behind. He pulled himself up over the top of the chimney and stuck his head inside.

Nothing.

Below him, the guards were trying to push the Paykan off the fence. He could see them clearly, which meant they could see him too, if they chose to look up.

An inspection of the exterior of the second chimney revealed nothing, but this time, when he reached his hand into the blackened interior, he felt a collection of loose wires. The wires had been affixed to a piece of metal protruding from the interior of the chimney. When he tugged on the wires, there was resistance, as though something were tied to the end of them.

Mark pulled up a small waterproof gear bag with a shoulder strap, detached it from the wires, and stuffed it into his backpack.

Police sirens drew near.

One of the guards who had left the front gate returned to his post, putting him in a direct line of sight to the gutter downspout.

From his backpack, Mark pulled out a glass liter bottle filled with gas and screwed off the cap. He took a rag, twisted it into the narrow mouth of the bottle, held the bottle upside down for a moment to saturate the rag with gas, lit the whole contraption with a lighter, and threw it.

The Molotov cocktail arced over the edge of the roof, leaving little airborne droplets of fire in its wake. It crashed into a walled courtyard that abutted the side of the mansion opposite his exit route.

Cries rang out from inside the mansion. When the guard by the gate ran off to investigate, Mark took off across the roof, running as silently as he could on the tiles. He crawled down spider-like from the ridge and, without pausing, swung his body over the edge. His feet found the gutter downspout, and he slid down quickly, so quickly that he lost his grip halfway down.

He landed on a bush, dazed but still able to move, then pulled himself to his feet and sprinted across the lawn, making no effort now to avoid detection. Halfway across, he heard barking and glanced to his right. A lone German shepherd was coming at him at top speed, snapping its jaws. Mark tried to sprint faster, but his legs wouldn't respond—it was as if he were running through water. The fence was only a few strides away.

He turned and threw his forearm up just as the German shepherd lunged. The dog took his forearm in its jaws and bit down with an intense pressure that sent spikes of pain shooting up his arm even through his makeshift armor—five metal school rulers lashed together with surgical tape under a leather jacket. He was knocked to the ground. The dog growled and shook its head, trying to grind its teeth in deeper.

Pepper spray was illegal in Iran, but wasp spray was a decent substitute. With his free hand, Mark grabbed a small can from his jacket pocket, aimed, and shot a stream of pesticide into the dog's eyes. The dog held on to his forearm for a moment, but then let go, confused and snapping its jaws as best it could, as though unsure where this new enemy was.

"Sorry, buddy."

A guard sprinted out from the corner of the mansion.

Mark dropped the wasp spray and ran. As he was pushing himself over the points at the top of the fence, he heard gunshots. He fell to the ground on the opposite side and stumbled toward the road, where Daria was waiting for him in yet another stolen Paykan. The passenger side door opened and he fell into the car.

60
Washington, DC

THE PRESIDENT OFTEN ATE A LIGHT DINNER AT HIS DESK, BUT tonight he found the veneer of normalcy—a glass of whole milk, a chicken salad sandwich on whole wheat bread, and a bowl of baby carrots—to be strangely unsettling.

Get outside, take a walk. You'll think better.

He looked out the window to the white blossoms on the crabapple trees in the Rose Garden. The tulips were in full bloom, and there were hundreds of them, brilliant yellows and reds. Spring was his favorite time of year in Washington, he thought.

The pressure was getting to him. He could feel it in his chest and in the way he felt weak in his joints. Perhaps his critics were right, perhaps he was too old to be president.

His chief of staff appeared at the door, clipboard in hand.

"Hello, Patty."

"Mr. President."

"How you holding up?"

"I'm holding. I've cleared your original schedule as much as possible so that you can chair the NSC planning meetings, but you're going to need to meet with the president of Ghana at one tomorrow or people are going to get suspicious that something's up."

"Fine."

The chief of staff handed the president a revised schedule for the next twenty-four hours. He was relieved to see that four hours had been blocked off for him to sleep.

"We'll also need to carve out time to work on your address to the nation. Simmons will have a draft ready by three."

"Schedule the meeting with Simmons for eleven tonight and push back the call to Jouanneau," he said, referring to the president of France. "Have you gotten final clearance for the timing of the address from CENTCOM?"

"It was my wakeup call this morning. We're good for three tomorrow afternoon."

61

Tehran, Iran

———————————○———————————

DARIA MADE A FEW QUICK TURNS, ROCKETED DOWN A LONG hill, made another turn, and then parked right behind yet another Paykan, which she and Mark transferred into.

"One of the dogs found me," Mark said, struggling to catch his breath as Daria sped down a narrow alley, brushing within inches of parked cars.

"I saw."

"I had to spray him."

The dog was just another victim, thought Mark. It was stupid to feel that kind of sympathy, he knew, but he liked dogs, and he was sick of watching innocent bystanders, be they dogs or people, being hurt by events they didn't understand and couldn't control.

He turned his attention to Decker's gear bag. It was black and coated with a thin layer of rubber. He placed it on his lap and quickly unzipped it.

Inside was a Canon SLR camera with an enormous telephoto lens, a tin of Skoal Straight chewing tobacco, a Leatherman pocket tool, a digital voice recorder, a tangle of high-gauge wires, a directional microphone, a couple of LED penlights, spare batteries, spare SD memory cards for the recorder and the camera, an RFID reader that looked like it had been modified to expand its range, and a wedge of cheese that stank.

The can of chewing tobacco had a price sticker on it—*Mt. Dustan General Store, $5.59.*

Mark exhaled and closed his eyes for a half second. That store was located in northern New Hampshire—at a place called Wentworth Location, which wasn't even really an actual town, just a name on the map. Decker had a brother who would buy twenty tins of dip at a time at Mt. Dustan's and airmail them to whatever foreign backwater Decker happened to be in.

Mark remembered when Decker had stayed with him in Baku. Beer bottles, left on the counter half-filled with dip spit, had been an issue.

As he tossed the tin of dip to the floor, he wondered whether he was looking at the belongings of a dead person.

"If anyone could survive, it would be John," said Daria, reading his thoughts.

That's what they always said about those super-fit guys who tried to climb Everest, or sail around the world, countered Mark in his head. The rescuers never wanted to give up hope because the people they were searching for were the best of the best. But nine times out of ten, the super-fit guy was still found dead. Everyone had their limits.

"Keep driving while I assess the rest of this," he said. "I'll be quick."

The digital camera had over five hundred high-resolution still pictures, chronicling every step of Decker and Alty's journey as they followed the marked money from downtown Ashgabat to Tehran. Mark speed-clicked through them. There were several of Li Zemin handing a briefcase to Amir Bayat in Mashhad. A series of what Mark believed to be Amir Bayat's house in Tehran followed, then of Ayatollah Bayat's gated estate in northern Tehran. Decker had taken close-up shots of street signs and house numbers along the way, pinning down exact locations.

Some were photos that Alty—a slender, baby-faced kid with a bowl-shaped haircut—and Decker had taken of themselves: there they were in front of the gates of the Imam Reza shrine complex, then in front of the Azadi Tower in downtown

Tehran, then in front of the gates of Tehran University, looking like tourists…

It was as though the pair had been on a low-budget back-packing excursion, yukking it up the whole way.

"Jesus, Deck."

Daria turned onto a highway, slowed down to the speed limit, and picked up the digital recorder. "There's a decent amount of voice data on this thing," she said, after giving it a cursory look.

She played the earliest file. At the start of it, Decker explained that the recording was made in Mashhad, at the Ali Qapu Hotel. Apparently he'd bugged Amir Bayat's room.

Deck's voice was cool and professional.

There were extended phone conversations, primarily Amir Bayat speaking with his news department back in Tehran and calls to room service…Daria translated the Farsi to English as she drove. Mark kept studying the cache of digital photos.

The final batch of digital recordings, according to Decker's voice-over, was from Ayatollah Bayat's mansion in northern Tehran.

"That's what the wires holding Decker's gear bag in the chimney were for," said Mark. "They were microphone wires. Decker was bugging the place through the chimneys."

The very last recording consisted of a short conversation between a man who Mark and Daria decided must have been Ayatollah Bayat and a woman they guessed was his wife. The two spoke formally about what meal the wife should prepare for dinner the following evening, when guests were expected.

The breakthrough came after a lull in the conversation, when Ayatollah Bayat's wife announced, "Amir has arrived."

Ayatollah Bayat and his brother greeted each other, and for over a half hour they talked politics, mostly deliberating over how a young ayatollah seeking an appointment to the Guardian Council could be thwarted. Then a door closed. After an extended silence, they finally got down to business.

Khorasani suspects something.

Why do you say this?

The intelligence ministry is investigating Hashemi.

For what?

He purchased a new car. A Peugeot 405, and he paid in cash.

The fool.

He was told to wait to use the payments.

This is the problem with involving men like Hashemi.

But I had no choice. He was my only link to the Damascus katsa.

Can the payments be traced to you?

I never communicated with him directly.

Shirazi can stall the investigation until the Americans act.

I received word that matériel was moved from Natanz and Fordo yesterday. And I confirmed that Khorasani's daughter will remain hidden until she completes her religious studies. It will not matter how many spies the Americans and the Israelis send to Kish. They will learn nothing.

Khorasani will be in your debt.

Yes, but he must never—

Ayatollah Bayat's wife returned, and the conversation between the brothers ended.

Mark hadn't understood much of what was said. He didn't know who Hashemi was, nor Shirazi. He knew the mention of Natanz and Fordo were likely references to the nuclear facilities associated with those towns, but he didn't know what it meant that matériel had been moved. He knew that a *katsa* probably referred to an Israeli intelligence officer, but had no idea what kind of link the Bayat brothers were talking about.

As a station chief, though, he'd rarely been able to see the whole picture—there were usually too many people, too many moving pieces, too many motives—and he'd grown used to operating with fragments of information. Men and governments were always plotting and scheming. Trying to understand it all was pointless.

To get anything done, he'd had to set aside all that he didn't understand and focus on the tiny sliver that he did.

And what he now knew was that Ayatollah Bayat and his brother Amir were taking money from the Guoanbu in Turkmenistan and giving money to some Iranian named Hashemi, and that these actions were part of some larger scheme that was going on behind the back of their supreme leader—Ayatollah Khorasani.

In Iran, scheming behind the back of a man like Khorasani could lead to being shot by a firing squad and having your body dumped in an unmarked grave.

Or it could leave you vulnerable to blackmail.

"Turn around," said Mark.

"Where are we going?"

They were going to find out once and for all whether Decker was alive, thought Mark. He doubted it—Decker wouldn't have abandoned all his equipment if he hadn't been in a hell of a pinch—but they'd come this far. Mark would see it through to the end.

"Ayatollah Bayat's estate is going to be in lockdown mode," he said. "So let's go see if his brother Amir is home."

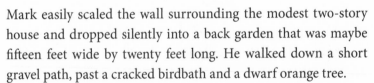

Mark easily scaled the wall surrounding the modest two-story house and dropped silently into a back garden that was maybe fifteen feet wide by twenty feet long. He walked down a short gravel path, past a cracked birdbath and a dwarf orange tree.

In the back of the house was a sliding glass door. As he crowbarred it open, the wood frame snapped with a single loud crack. No alarm sounded.

"Going in." He spoke to Daria over the cell phone connection they'd established; he wore an earpiece and had his phone in his pocket.

Stepping into the living room, he used a penlight to illuminate children's toys scattered around a Persian carpet. There was a fuzzy rocking horse, a sit-and-spin baby minder, a foam soccer ball, little dolls of Muslim women wearing black headscarves, a plastic scimitar…

To his left was a modern kitchen, with stainless steel appliances arranged neatly on a white tile countertop. A tile mosaic depicting the martyrdom of Hussein—the prophet Muhammad's grandson—hung on a far wall.

He placed Decker's gear bag on the countertop and pulled out the digital recorder. Then he turned up the volume as high as it would go and pushed Play.

The voices of the Bayat brothers boomed out.

Khorasani suspects something.

Why do you say this?

The intelligence ministry is investigating Hashemi.

For what?

He purchased a new car. A Peugeot 405, and he paid in cash.

The fool.

He was told to wait to use the payments.

This is the problem with involving men like Hashemi.

But I had no choice. He was my only link to the Damascus—

Mark heard noises upstairs—a young boy calling out for his mother, and then Amir Bayat, whose voice Mark recognized because it was also playing on the digital recorder.

Shirazi can stall the investigation until the Americans act.

I received word that matériel was moved from Natanz and Fordo yesterday. And I confirmed that Khorasani's daughter—

"Who is this! Who dares to violate my home!"

The words were spoken in Farsi, but loud enough for Daria to hear them over the cell phone connection. She translated them for Mark.

A flurry of footsteps sounded, as though the whole family were gathering at the top of the steps.

A woman, sounding confused, called down with a question that Mark couldn't understand and Daria couldn't hear.

Mark's eyes had adjusted to the darkness by then, and he recognized Amir Bayat the second he saw the Iranian bounding down the stairs. He was of average height but considerable girth. In all of Decker's photos, Amir had had been wearing his black turban. Now his stringy hair flopped down over his forehead in a tangled mess. His ears were swollen and bulbous, marking him as a former wrestler.

The voices on the tape ended. Mark pushed Play again.

Amir shouted something in Farsi. Daria, translating, said, "If the Ministry of Intelligence has something they wish to speak to me about, have the courage to do it in the light of day."

Mark shined his penlight at Amir Bayat. Speaking slowly in Farsi, he repeated the words Daria had taught him to say. "Do you speak Azeri? Or English?"

"Who are you?" The words, spoken in passable Azeri, came out as a snarl.

Replying in Azeri, Mark said, "I'm not here from the Ministry of Intelligence."

Amir squinted at the light. "I will not stand for this violation. Turn this noise off, this false recording you have concocted, this—"

A woman—Amir's wife, Mark presumed—appeared at the top of the steps in a gown. Her hair was uncovered. She said something in Farsi. The only word Mark understood was *police*.

Amir's response sounded something like *no*.

"What you are hearing are copies of the originals," said Mark. "If something happens to me, these digital recordings will be e-mailed to the Ministry of Intelligence."

One of Bayat's children began to cry. Amir's wife said something about the police again.

To Mark, Amir said, "Who are you?"

"The man you tried to have killed in Baku."

"Sava."

"Yes."

"Khorasani would approve of what we are doing if he knew."

"But he doesn't know, and he hasn't approved it."

Amir Bayat had no answer to that.

Mark said, "I have a demand."

"You have violated my home. You have looked upon my wife. You have brought my children to tears. You will pay for this."

Indeed, all of Amir's children now seemed to be crying. It occurred to Mark that he was a monster to them.

"If you meet my demand, I will instruct my colleagues to destroy the evidence I have against you."

Bayat yelled something to his wife. Moments later, it sounded to Mark as though the kids were being herded into a room upstairs.

Mark pulled out Decker's camera and began to show Bayat the photos on the LCD screen. When he got to the ones that showed Bayat receiving a briefcase from a Chinese man on the streets of Mashhad, he zoomed in on the faces. "You were followed from the moment you took the money. Your hotel rooms and phones were bugged. Everything you said was recorded."

Amir's face was creased with worry.

"The good news for you," said Mark, "is that my only demand is that you release the American you captured three days ago. He's my colleague."

"I know not of whom you speak."

"I think you do. He's almost two meters tall. Short hair, originally blond, dyed brown. Muscular."

"I do not."

"Then I will need to speak with your brother."

"I have several brothers."

Mark clicked through the photos on the digital camera until he came to the one that Decker had taken of Ayatollah Bayat entering the mansion in north Tehran. "This brother. The brother you are speaking to on the tape. The brother who wound up with the money from the Chinese. The brother who lives in the house where you found my colleague. The brother who is scheming behind the back of your supreme leader. That fucking brother."

A long silence passed.

"I can't guarantee he will see you," said Amir.

"Oh, I think he will."

Over his cell phone earpiece, Mark heard Daria say, "The house is being watched. Get out."

"Who is it?"

"I don't know. A car parked opposite the house just started up and drove away. Someone must have been inside it for the whole time I've been here. Thirty seconds later another car pulled into the open spot. No one's gotten out of that car yet."

"Have they seen you?"

"I don't think so. I'm behind them by about a hundred yards."

"Did they see me hop the wall?"

"Maybe."

"They look like they're planning a takedown?"

"No, but—"

"I got you. We're outta here."

62

Tehran, Iran

———○———

MARK AND AMIR BAYAT SPED THROUGH THE GATES OF Ayatollah Bayat's estate in north Tehran, waved through with barely a glance from the guards out front. Amir parked his green Peugeot at the base of the wide marble steps that led to the entrance. By now it was almost dawn.

They'd been followed on the way over. Daria had picked out the car right away and stayed behind it. Mark guessed it was the Iranian intelligence ministry closing in.

There were more guards on duty at the ayatollah's mansion than there had been the night before. Yellow police tape was strung up on the section of fence that Daria had rammed into.

Amir let himself into the front foyer, removed his worn leather loafers, and slipped into a pair of cheap plastic house sandals. Mark didn't like the thought of leaving himself vulnerable, and he didn't care if he insulted anyone, so he left his shoes on.

He was led to a room not far from the front door. It was a shabby place, with cracked plaster walls. Sticks of incense were kept burning in one corner next to photos of a few young soldiers, boys really, who—according the words at the base of the photos—had died in the Iran-Iraq War. After a while, a tiny woman who took baby steps under her black chador set down a bowl of apples and oranges on a nearby coffee table.

Mark sat cross-legged on the floor, across from Amir Bayat.

"He will come."

"When?" said Mark.

"Soon."

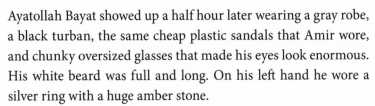

Ayatollah Bayat showed up a half hour later wearing a gray robe, a black turban, the same cheap plastic sandals that Amir wore, and chunky oversized glasses that made his eyes look enormous. His white beard was full and long. On his left hand he wore a silver ring with a huge amber stone.

"Salaam, brother," said Amir. "Praise be to Allah. I am sorry for this disturbance."

The brothers embraced.

"It is no disturbance. A visit from you is always a pleasure. I rely on your wisdom like I rely on the air around me." Ayatollah Bayat gestured with his hands in a theatrical way.

Give me a break, thought Mark.

"I would know nothing at all were it not for your guidance," said Amir. Switching from Farsi to Azeri, he said, "This is the one I spoke of."

Ayatollah Bayat faced Mark and attempted a smile.

Mark had dealt with plenty of people in power over the course of his CIA career. He'd lunched with the vice president of the United States—a nice guy—had downed beers with a billionaire who'd bought an ambassadorship to Armenia—an asshole—and had locked horns with half the political higher-ups in Washington and Azerbaijan countless times. One thing he'd noticed was that the powerful tended to fall into one of two categories: those who still, despite their exalted status, felt the need to puff themselves up with titles and showy displays of wealth, or what they perceived to be knowledge, and those who didn't. He decided to do a little test, to determine which category Ayatollah Bayat fell into.

"Hojjatoleslam Bayat," he said. "Thank you for meeting with me. I have come for information about my colleague."

An awkward silence followed. A hojjatoleslam was a rank below that of an ayatollah.

Ayatollah Bayat cleared his throat.

"Ayatollah Bayat," said Amir. "My brother is an ayatollah."

"Then I apologize. I had been told otherwise."

"My brother is frequently called on to lead Friday prayers."

"I see."

"He is the leader of the Combatant Clergy Association."

"I meant no offense."

Mark's experience had been that the less religious training an ayatollah had, the more sensitive he was about his title. From the deep frown on Ayatollah Bayat's face, Mark figured he'd had little training indeed.

Ayatollah Bayat said, "Is it logical to argue like this while we have serious business to attend to? Please, you must both join me in the library."

The old man walked slowly, gripping the front of his robe with his left hand as he led them to a room ringed by mahogany shelves full of Islamic texts. The ceiling was covered with mirrored tiles, but there was evidence of serious water damage.

"Please, sit." Ayatollah Bayat glanced at Mark and gestured to the nicest chair in the room. "I will call for tea."

Mark was sick of people offering him tea. And of waiting. As station chief, he had listened to hours of intercepted conversations between low-ranking Iranian mullahs. Some were true believers. Some were more interested in politics than religion. Some were fond of sex jokes. But they all knew how to speak quickly and without artifice when they wanted to.

He removed the recorder and camera from Decker's satchel. "I think you'll be interested in these photos and voice recordings. You're on them."

Ayatollah Bayat took a seat in a simple chair that had no seat cushion or armrest. "My brother has told me of the content. I have no need to review the information myself."

"He told you why I'm here?"

"You are searching for your colleague. The one who assembled this information."

"He told you the deal I offered?"

The deal was a straight exchange—Decker for the evidence that Decker had collected.

"He did."

"Your answer?"

"I can tell you this: last week, the dogs that patrol this property at night smelled an intruder. Who would violate this sanctuary, my guards wondered? We have nothing here of value but the work of Allah. Your colleague was discovered on the roof of this house, no doubt engaging in the very spying that led to the information you have in your possession."

Ayatollah Bayat shook his head as though he were a father disappointed in a child. The gesture reminded Mark of the obnoxiously patronizing priests he'd dealt with as an altar boy three decades ago.

"I regret to tell you," said the ayatollah, "that he tried to jump down from the roof in an attempt to escape. In doing so, he hit his head. I can assure you that our doctors tried to save him as an act of mercy, but he will now have to look to Allah for mercy."

Ayatollah Bayat raised his eyes to the ceiling and said, "Oh my servants who have transgressed against your own souls, do not despair of Allah's mercy, for Allah forgives all sins. It is he who is the forgiving, the merciful." Looking back at Mark, he said, "Your colleague died of his injuries before he reached the hospital."

Mark was good at figuring out whether people were lying or not—too much eye contact or not enough, odd pauses, a story that obviously benefitted the teller, forced gesticulations…his intuition in this department had been honed over the course of a long career. And he didn't believe Ayatollah Bayat for a second. "I would like to see the body."

"But how could that be possible? There was no evidence your colleague was a Muslim, and we did not know his name, so the body was buried without Islamic funeral rites, in an unmarked grave, in a cemetery for unbelievers. As is natural."

"Then show me where he jumped, and where his head hit."

Ayatollah Bayat appeared to consider the request, with unease, for a moment. Finally he stood. "Please follow me."

Mark was taken to a courtyard behind the mansion. An eight-foot-high brick wall enclosed the small space. Ayatollah Bayat pointed to the top of the wall about fifteen feet from where it met the building, where a brick had fallen away.

"That is where your colleague hit his head."

Mark eyed the roof, squinting in the bright morning sun. Given that the mansion had three full stories, he estimated that the drop to the wall would have been well over twenty feet. If Decker had been trying to get off the roof the fastest way possible, he probably would have jumped exactly where Ayatollah Bayat said he had.

Assuming that was the case, the distance from the exterior wall of the mansion to the broken brick suggested that Decker hadn't just lowered himself over the edge of the roof and dropped—to get that far away from the building, he would have had to take a giant running leap off the roof. Which, knowing Decker, Mark thought entirely possible.

He gauged the distance again and imagined Decker in midair. For any normal human being, a leap from that height to a brick wall no more than a foot wide would have resulted in a broken leg at the very least. A fatal head injury was a definite possibility, perhaps even a likelihood.

But Decker was no normal human being. Mark figured Deck could have easily made that jump and hit the ground running.

"Was he wounded prior to jumping?"

"No," said Ayatollah Bayat. "It was the fall alone that killed him."

"You're lying."

Ayatollah Bayat stared at him for a while. "Of course death is difficult to accept. As an act of compassion, I am willing to arrange for a *diyya* to be paid to any of his remaining family members. It is not an accepted custom in our country to make such a payment for the death of an intruder, and the rate for a non-Muslim is typically not high, but rational discretion in these matters is often advisable."

Mark took out his cell phone and pushed a series of buttons.

"What are you doing?" said Amir.

Mark pushed a few more buttons on his cell phone and then snapped it shut. "I just sent an authorization code to my colleagues. Unless I revoke it within two hours, it will be too late to stop the release of the digital files that prove you've been conspiring behind Khorasani's back. One of the places the files will be sent is your own intelligence ministry. The only condition under which I will revoke the authorization I just sent is if I am taken to my colleague."

It was technically a lie. His agreement with Daria was that, if he didn't return, she would release the information if and when she saw fit.

Ayatollah Bayat looked as though he'd swallowed something rancid. "What you demand is impossible."

Mark shrugged. "Not my problem."

"Your life is your problem, my son."

The threat was delivered awkwardly, with little conviction—a weak attempt to bully by an old man who was used to others doing his bullying for him. And it was ineffective to boot. Mark had long ago come to accept his own death. He figured his life wasn't so great anyway, and no one was dependent on him. He could afford to gamble.

"You have a choice to make. Either deliver my colleague, or face the consequences."

Ayatollah Bayat turned, as though he were going to walk away. But then, with his back to Mark, he said, "If we were to agree to your terms, how would you propose we conduct the transfer?"

"When I have my colleague alive and in my custody, and we are at a safe distance, a messenger will deliver the original tapes to the guards outside your estate."

"If I bring you to my brother, if we satisfy your demand, how can we be sure that you will honor your commitment to destroy these files? And that you won't tell the Americans of their content?"

"My priority is retrieving my colleague. And I no longer work for the Americans. But the truth is, you can't be sure."

"We have seen your face; my guards have taken your picture. We know you are an American. We are a large group. Even if my brother and I were to be arrested, the group would hunt you down were you to deceive us."

"I know it."

"In or outside of Iran. For days or years, however long it takes."

"Understood."

"I cannot guarantee the condition of your colleague."

"If he's alive and likely to stay that way, you'll have your tapes."

63
Tehran, Iran

M OST OF VALIASR STREET—THE MAIN THOROUGHFARE
that bisected Tehran—had been turned into a one-way
street going north, the better to accommodate shock troops who
might need to speed through the city at a moment's notice to
crush a popular uprising. But up in the far north, the traffic still
flowed both ways. Or trickled, as was the case now.

It was six thirty in the morning. Amir Bayat drove. Mark sat
behind him. Ayatollah Bayat had chosen the passenger seat in
the rear of the car, next to Mark, as though he were used to being
chauffeured around.

Giant sycamore trees, planted over a half century ago, formed
a wall between the road and the trendy cafés that lined Valiasr's
sidewalks. Paralleling the sycamores were *joobs*, deep street gut-
ters that, when they weren't clogged with garbage, brought water
down from the Alborz Mountains. Today the *joobs* were full and
running fast, as the spring heat melted the mountain snows. A
stiff wind had blown off much of the smog that usually blanketed
the city, rendering the mountains visible to the north, and sometimes to the east as well. The mountains were massive, as high as
eighteen thousand feet, their tops shrouded in cloud and snow.

Daria called Mark after a few minutes. "You're being followed again. One lead car, I can't see it now, but it's a gray Saipa.
He was behind you when you pulled into the estate and he pulled
in front of you on Valiasr just after you left."

"I have him," said Mark.

"There's also a guy on a motorcycle, about fifty feet behind you. He showed up just after the Saipa."

Mark glanced in the rearview mirror. "Got him too."

"I'm two cars behind the motorcycle."

Mark told the Bayat brothers the news. "If they're your men, call them off."

Amir and the ayatollah denied that either of them had ordered a tail.

From the worried look on both their faces, Mark was inclined to believe them. "Could they be VEVAK?" Mark asked, referring to the Iranian secret police. "Looking into what you're plotting behind Khorasani's back?"

Amir admitted the possibility.

"Then we'll have to lose them." To Daria, he said, "We'll be able to ditch the lead car, at least momentarily. But we'll need you to help us ditch the tail. I'm looking for a place—a mall, a park, whatever—where we can park out front and meet you on the back side before—"

"Hold up," said Daria.

All traffic had come to a stop. "I'm held up," said Mark.

"The motorcycle is approaching."

Mark wasn't sure whether it was the same sixth sense that had kept him alive all these years, or whether he'd just read too many reports of Iranian nuclear scientists being assassinated by bomb-wielding killers on motorcycles, but the news that the motorcycle was closing in was like a punch in the gut.

At the same time, he realized that the only reason traffic wasn't moving was that the gray Saipa five cars in front of him had stopped in the middle of the road. People were starting to honk.

He looked behind him. The motorcyclist, wearing a yellow helmet with a black-tinted visor, was moving up fast between the concrete barrier in the middle of the road and the line of stalled cars. One hand was on the handlebars, the other inside his leather jacket.

"We've got a bomb."

Mark spoke the warning a second before he actually saw the metal disk in the rider's hand.

He popped open the door to the Peugeot, ran three steps, threw his shoulder into the approaching motorcyclist, and knocked him off his bike.

The metal disk left the rider's hand and sailed high through the air. It landed on the trunk lid of the Peugeot. There was no bounce, just the loud *thunk* of a magnet attaching itself to metal.

Amir Bayat yanked open his door. In the backseat the ayatollah was trying to unlock the rear passenger door, but it was a manual lock and he couldn't get his old fingers around the knob. The motorcyclist sprinted toward the gray Saipa that was blocking traffic. Mark ran after him.

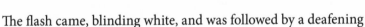

The flash came, blinding white, and was followed by a deafening bang.

Mark's first thought was that the actual blast wave hadn't been that bad. Then he realized he was facedown in the road, several feet away from where he'd last been standing.

The motorcyclist was already climbing into the Saipa at the front of the traffic jam. Mark caught a fleeting glimpse of the driver. He looked Chinese.

Mark turned back to the Peugeot. The windows were shattered, the trunk lid had been blown off, the rear seats were burning—and half of the ayatollah's head was missing.

All around Mark, people were screaming, leaving their cars in the street and running for safety. Mark stood, looking for Amir Bayat, then stumbled back toward the car. Amir Bayat lay facedown in the *joob*. Water and bits of garbage rushed over his head.

Daria ran up and started pulling Amir out of the water. Mark gave her a hand.

The Iranian's right leg was in shreds. Mark saw bits of bone and cartilage.

"Help me get him to my car," said Daria.

Bayat left a slug-like trail of blood in his wake, but halfway to Daria's stolen Paykan, he began to cough. Daria yanked opened the rear door.

Mark heaved Bayat halfway into the car, stuffed his legs in the rest of the way, and jumped in next to him.

Daria threw the car into first and took off as fast as she could.

Mark ripped a manual-window handle off the side of the door, stripped off his shirt, tied it tightly around Bayat's wounded leg, slipped the window handle under the shirt, and began to tighten the tourniquet.

Bayat moaned something about a hospital. He banged on the window of the car with his fist, but in a weak, dazed, halfhearted way. Mark wasn't even sure Bayat knew what was going on with his leg.

After eight twists the bleeding slowed to a trickle. Mark used the knife strapped to his ankle to cut a long strip of fabric from the Paykan's upholstery. He used that strip of fabric, along with another window handle, to fashion an even tighter tourniquet.

"He'll live," Mark said, when finished.

Daria had turned off Valiasr and was rocketing down an empty alley. "I'll get us out of town."

"I need a hospital."

Bayat had passed out after noticing that half his leg was gone. Then Mark had taken a blanket that had been covering holes in the Paykan's upholstery and placed it over Bayat's legs. Bayat was now awake and more lucid than before.

"Who hit us?" asked Mark.

Bayat's turban had washed away in the *joob*. His wet hair was dripping into his eyes.

"VEVAK would never do something like this." Bayat's breathing was labored. "Not to my brother. My brother, is he—"

"He's dead."

"I need a hospital."

"If you don't know who ordered that hit, how do you know you'll be safe at the hospital?"

"I know a doctor—"

"What about your Chinese friends. Could they have turned on you?"

"No."

"You're going to take us to my colleague. Now, as we agreed. After that we can talk about a doctor."

Bayat stared out the window for a while. "There is a house, in the mountains," he whispered, laboring to speak. "Drive first to Karaj, then north toward Dizin. After an hour the road will split. Go west. Soon you will see a private road, down this road is the house. I need a doctor."

"I heard you the first time."

64
Alborz Mountains, Iran

⸺⚬⸺

AFTER HIS BRIEF BURST OF LUCIDITY, BAYAT SLIPPED BACK into a netherworld. His eyes were closed, his head hung limp on the back of the seat, and his face was contorted by pain. Every so often he'd let out a string of whimpers.

They hurtled through Karaj, and then sped north through a series of dumpy little towns with small houses clinging to steep hillsides, through green valleys filled with tall aspen trees, past little concrete roadside mosques where travelers could pray, and across the flanks of several barren hills. A half hour outside of Karaj, they passed a lifeless reservoir. After an hour, Mark smacked Amir on the cheek.

"Where does the road split?"

Amir moaned. "Keep going."

"For how long?"

Amir didn't answer. Mark wondered whether he was dying.

"How long?" Mark repeated.

"Soon."

The Paykan began to struggle as the road became steeper. The air grew colder. Mark saw a little patch of snow tucked into a shady ravine. A few cars with ski racks—headed for Dizin, an aging resort that had been built during the reign of the Shah—sped by them.

They came upon the split in the road and bore off to the west. Five minutes later Amir said, "Here."

To their right was a dirt driveway blocked by ugly steel gates.

"There will be a guard," said Amir, breathless. "I must speak with him."

Mark took out his knife and slipped it under the blanket covering Bayat's legs. He pressed it against the tourniquet. Bayat winced.

"This guard, he doesn't get close to the car," said Mark. "I see him raise a weapon, I cut the tourniquet."

Daria pulled up to the gate. And waited. And waited some more.

"Where's your man?" asked Mark.

Amir lifted his head and strained to see through the front windshield. "I don't know."

"Is this gate always manned?"

"Always."

"Is it locked?"

"Yes."

Mark produced his cell phone. "Call your men."

"The phone won't work here."

Mark checked, and indeed there was no reception. He considered getting out of the car and trying to scope out the situation on foot. But that would take time. Someone might be watching them now.

He leaned across Amir Bayat and used the butt of his knife to smash out the window.

"Sorry," he said to Bayat. "The window handle was broken. Call out to your man."

Bayat sucked in a few quick breaths, then called, "Farid?"

"Louder."

"Farid! Open the gate!"

Mark waited. The road beyond the gate cut through the base of a ravine that was lined with stunted juniper trees and a few larger white pines. Jagged rock-strewn hills walled in the property on three sides, but it was completely open toward the south, letting in plenty of sun. Landslides of black and dun-colored scree had gathered around the base of the ravine. A flock of gray-bellied crows circled overhead.

"Fuck it," Mark said to Daria. "Ram the gate. Get us to the house. We'll improvise."

Daria threw the Paykan into reverse, executed a quick turn, and then slammed into the gate with the rear of the car. The Paykan's trunk crumpled, but the gate popped open. Once through, she turned the car around again and floored it. The Paykan bounced over the pothole-riddled road, and the rear bumper, half of which had fallen off, clattered loudly as it hit rocks in the road.

A two-story house built into the hillside at the end of the ravine came into view. Hidden from the road, it was vaguely reminiscent of a Swiss chalet, albeit a utilitarian one. The green metal roof was rusting in places. A long second-floor balcony with steel guardrails stuck out from the front. Brown paint was peeling off in places on the front of the house, where the sun was the most intense. Tucked behind an overgrown privet hedge, and barely visible from the driveway, was the front door.

"Ram the front door," said Mark.

A man appeared on the second-floor balcony. With a gun. Daria sped up and ducked below the steering wheel.

A few shots hit the roof of the car. Daria kept the Paykan on course. When she was a few feet from the house, she slammed on the brakes. The car skidded into the front door, smashed it open, and came to a stop halfway inside the house.

Mark jumped out. "Stay in the car, low on the floor, with the engine block between you and the house," he said to Daria. "But call out for help, in Farsi, as if you're hurt. It'll confuse them."

"Who's them?"

"Who the hell knows."

"I don't get it."

"Me neither. If things get too hot, take off without me."

Amir Bayat was still upright, but the force of the collision had thrown him forward, so that his chin now rested on the back of the front passenger seat.

Mark leaped over the hood of the Paykan and stepped silently into the house. A stairwell with a chunky wood banister led to an upper floor. Because the house had been built into a hillside, half of the first floor was underground, and there were no windows on the back wall. The lime-green carpet was soiled. The place stank of cigarette smoke and mold.

Now that he was inside, Mark noticed delicate shafts of sunlight streaming in from bullet holes all around him. In the corner lay a dead bearded man. Iranian, Mark guessed. A small trickle of blood, still bright red with oxygen, streamed down his forehead. Whatever fighting had taken place in the house had only ended recently.

Footsteps pounded across the floor upstairs. Judging from the sound, Mark guessed there were at least two men up there.

"Farid!" called Daria in Farsi, from the car. "Help me, I can't move."

Mark crouched behind the stairwell. One set of footsteps drew close to the top of the stairs, and then someone fired down the stairwell. If the shooter made it to the base of the stairs, he'd have a clear shot at the Paykan. He'd see Bayat and hear Daria.

Daria called out for help again.

Someone bounded down the stairs taking three at a time and firing an AK-47. Mark waited until the barrel of the gun was just past the base of the stairs and then he swung his knife deep into the chest of a slender man who looked Chinese. He yanked the gun out of the man's hands, aimed, fired two lethal head shots, and bounded up the stairs.

A voice cried out a question in Chinese from the upper floor. Mark couldn't understand it, but he tried to repeat the question back, hoping to cause confusion even for just a second.

Below, Daria cried out for help again, but this time, she spoke Chinese.

Mark reached the top of the steps and crept down a short hall to a kitchen, stepping over two dead Iranians on the way.

In the kitchen, pots were drying in a rack next to the sink. A bag of rice had been left out on a stained Formica counter. One of the oak cabinets had been left open, revealing an assortment of mismatched glasses inside. He grabbed a glass and hurled it through a set of double doors.

It shattered on the far living room wall, beneath a large framed photo of a glowering Ayatollah Khorasani that hung over a fraying fake-leather couch.

Someone in the living room started shooting at the glass. Mark ducked behind the stove, checked how many bullets he had left—ten or so—then fired eight shots through a thin wall, aiming for where he guessed the shooter was.

Shots pinged the metal stove as the gunman returned fire.

Mark pulled the magazine out of his AK-47 and dry fired the rifle three times, as if it were out of bullets.

The shooter charged. As he did, Mark rolled out from behind the stove, jammed the magazine back into the gun, and fired two quick shots though the double doors that led to the living room. Neither hit the Chinese, even though it was an easy shot. Mark figured a dirty barrel had caused the bullets to keyhole.

The shooter flinched and dove to the ground. Mark charged, kicking over a coffee table that was in his way, scattering an assortment of hammers and wrenches and soiled straps.

The Chinese gripped a compact Heckler & Koch assault rifle and tried to aim as he scurried away on his rear end. He fired a single shot, followed by the click of an empty magazine.

It turned into an ugly, inhuman business as Mark began wielding his knife and the Chinese started using his rifle like a club. After a while, Mark wound up on the floor, writhing as the Chinese kicked him hard in the gut. Mark heard a rib break.

The fight only turned in Mark's favor when he managed to stab the Chinese man's shin so hard that the knife quivered in his hand, as if he'd connected with a solid oak butcher block.

When it was over, the Chinese was on the floor with two pools of blood creeping outward from either side of his chest, growing in size on the parquet floor until they looked like wings.

65

M ARK RAN BACK DOWN TO THE CAR.
"What happened?" asked Daria.

He paused to catch his breath and push the pain from his broken rib out of his mind. "Two Chinese were in the house."

"Guoanbu?"

"Probably." Mark handed her a Heckler & Koch with a new magazine in it, taken from the Chinese in the living room. The AK-47 he'd been using was slung across his back. That had a new magazine in it too, lifted off one of the dead Iranians in the hall.

"Where are they now?"

"Dead."

"Are there more?"

"I don't think so. Maybe." He turned to Amir Bayat, who was glassy-eyed in the backseat, staring out the broken window.

"Where's my colleague?" He slapped Bayat's face. "I'm talking to you, Amir! This is why we're here."

Amir turned to face him. His eyes focused.

"You want your doctor?" said Mark. "Now's the time to keep your end of the deal."

"The basement," whispered Amir.

Mark turned.

"Wait," said Amir. "Below the basement...a safe. You must lift the carpet."

"What are you saying?"

"When my brother..." Bayat's face convulsed as if a jolt of pain had just hit him. "...bought the house, after the revolution, it was too heavy, too heavy to move." He paused, clearly exhausted.

"What was too heavy to move? The safe?"

Bayat's breath was shallow and fast. "I said I could not guarantee his condition. After he tried to escape, the Chinese interrogators—"

"He's in the safe?"

"It was where one of the Shah's generals...stored money... that he stole from the people."

"How do I open it?"

"The year of our revolution. My brother had it reset."

"You're saying that's the combination?"

Bayat gave a slight, pained nod.

Mark turned to Daria. "Stay here." He gestured to Bayat. "Guard this asshole. I'll be right back."

The steps leading to the basement had fresh mud on them, and the stairwell walls were grimy. Halfway down, an Iranian lay dead, still clutching a pistol. Mark flipped a light switch. A bare bulb near the base of the steps flickered on.

The basement floor was made of rough concrete. Half of it was covered with a stained and threadbare Persian carpet. Chains hung from the exposed ceiling beams. A pile of rope, a pair of handcuffs, a wooden ladder, electrical wire, and a metal bed frame had been shoved into a corner. Cans of paint had been piled on a workbench that stood in another corner.

Mark pulled back the carpet, revealing a hinged trapdoor that had been topped with concrete to match the floor. The underside of the carpet stank of mold.

He crouched down and found the recessed handle of the heavy trapdoor. When he pulled up, the trapdoor opened with the sound of metal grinding on metal. A sudden and overwhelming smell of shit made him gag.

Mark stepped back a few feet so that he could let some light in and better see down the hole. At the far range of his vision, he saw what looked like the corner of an enormous block of metal. He grabbed the ladder from the corner of the basement, lowered it into the hole, and climbed down.

Groundwater from the spring snowmelt had seeped into the hole, turning the dirt floor into a bog. Mark placed the AK-47 on the top of the safe and allowed his eyes to adjust for a moment. The safe was at least five feet tall and almost as wide and deep. A thin film of rust covered every inch of it, and its legs had sunk into the mud.

Mark's hand trembled as he put it upon the first of four dials that lined the upper right side of the safe.

He set the dials to 1-9-7-9 and, without pausing to think, pushed down hard on the safe handle. It remained closed. He pulled up. Nothing gave.

"Dammit," he muttered.

He wiped his forehead with his rust-covered hand and inspected the dials again.

It was 1979 when the Shah left and Ayatollah Khomeini took over. But the demonstrations had started a year earlier.

Mark tried 1978. The lever didn't budge. He considered dragging Amir Bayat down into the hole and making him open the safe himself. Then he remembered that Iranians didn't use the same calendar as the West. Instead of counting from the birth of Christ, they counted from the year that Muhammad had fled from Mecca to Medina. To convert the Western calendar to the Iranian calendar, you needed to subtract 622 or 621 from the Western calendar, depending on what time of year it was...

Mark subtracted 622 from 1979, entered the numbers 1-3-5-7, and pulled on the handle.

The safe opened. Inside sat a naked man, a broken giant, huddled up with knees pressed into his chest and his mouth pressed against the wall.

Mark hesitated before touching the body, not completely sure that it was even Decker's.

The arms and legs were purple with bruises, the face swollen and caked with dried blood. The ammonia smell of piss made him dizzy.

Mark knew that Decker had always gone out of his way to operate anonymously when behind enemy lines. Which meant there were no SEAL trident symbols or other tattoos on his body that could identify him as an American.

But before he'd joined the SEALs, Mark knew that Decker *had* gotten a tattoo—a bad approximation of the Millennium Falcon—while in high school. He'd had it removed years ago, leaving only a slight discoloration on his left calf, which had grown less and less noticeable with each passing year.

Mark gently touched the left calf of the body in the safe, intending to scrape away some of the dirt and blood so he could look for the little bleached patch of skin. He noted, almost with surprise, that the body was still warm.

Mark didn't have time to react to the onslaught.

One second he was crouched in front of Decker and the next he was rocketing backward, out of the safe and into the mud. Two hands were clenched around his throat. He tried to cry out but produced nothing but choking sounds.

Decker drove him through the mud like a plow, all the way across the dirt floor and into the corner.

Mark tried to cry out again, but couldn't. Decker's choke hold was blocking the blood flow to his brain while simultaneously crushing his esophagus. In a few more seconds, he'd pass out.

Despite the ferocity of his initial onslaught, however, Decker was weak. Mark felt a momentary slackening around his neck and used the respite to suck in a quick breath, throw a knee to Decker's groin, and yell, "It's Mark!"

Decker's hands tightened again around his neck. But this time, Mark didn't resist. Instead he allowed his head to sink back into the mud and with his right hand gave Decker two taps on the back—the martial arts signal that you've given up.

Decker continued to squeeze, but only for a second longer. Then he went completely slack and slipped to the side onto his back.

For a moment they were both silent, hyperventilating in the weak light. Mark looked over at what passed for Decker's face. Both eyes appeared to be swollen shut—Decker was operating blind.

"Who are you?" asked Decker.

"It's Mark. Your friend, Deck. Your friend."

66

DECKER WAS SHIVERING AND HAD TROUBLE STANDING—HIS left ankle appeared to be broken, and the untreated bullet wounds on his left thigh and shin were oozing.

Mark helped him find the rickety ladder that led out of the hole to the basement floor. Decker pulled himself up it, but then collapsed in a fetal position on the dirty Persian rug.

Mark inspected his friend's eyes. They were like a boxer's after losing a brutal fight. "Can you see anything?"

Decker was still on the floor and seemed completely dazed by the turn of events. Mark repeated the question.

"A little bit." He stopped to catch his breath. "Out of my right eye."

"Can you fire a gun?"

"Fuck yeah."

Mark took a Makarov pistol from the dead Iranian on the steps. "Careful, it's off safety."

"Will I need it?"

"I don't know. I think the house is clear but I haven't done a sweep."

He heaved Decker up to a standing position again and together they navigated the steps up to the ground floor.

Decker blinked at the bright natural light spilling in from the windows.

"Daria!" called Mark. "I got him."

They stumbled into the front foyer. The Paykan was still lodged in the entrance door.

"Back it up," said Mark. "We're getting out of here."

Daria, who'd been concealed behind an overturned table in an adjacent room, showed herself.

"John, God…" She looked horrified. "What did they do to you?"

Decker was filthy, leaning to one side as he favored his good leg, and barely recognizable. He was also buck naked, and the dirt couldn't hide his massive torso and tree-trunk thighs.

"Back up the car, we're getting out of here," Mark repeated.

Daria kept her eyes fixed on Decker.

"Daria, let's go," said Mark.

She climbed over the hood of the car and slipped into the driver's seat. The hood was smashed in, but the car started. She pulled back a few feet. Mark helped Decker to the rear door, intending to seat him opposite Amir Bayat.

Decker took one quick look at Bayat, raised his Makarov, and—without even seeming to think—shot Bayat in the temple.

"I promised him I'd let him live," said Mark.

"I didn't," said Decker.

67

Northern Iran

———————○———————

THE CABIN WAS TINY, PARTIALLY HIDDEN BY A GROVE OF DATE palms, and one of twenty in a largely vacant vacation camp that was nestled on the shores of the Caspian Sea. Its roof was covered with quaint-looking thatch that had been put there for show, but the rusted corrugated metal beneath it was visible.

Daria stood in front of the cabin and looked out toward the bright horizon on the sea. The waves lapped gently on the beach. It was a pretty but deceptive picture, she knew. The Caspian was a dumping ground for all of Central Asia. Filth from the Volga, oil spillage from the international rigs, sewage from all over…

Decker lay on a bed inside the cabin. She and Mark had cleaned and tried to disinfect the wounds on his leg, made him drink a liter of juice and eat some rice, and then given him lots of painkillers and several amoxicillin pills, an antibiotic that Daria had bought over the counter at a pharmacy.

Daria looked around for Mark and eventually noticed him sitting in the shadow of a nearby tree, where the scrub grass ended and the beach began. They'd checked in as a married couple from Turkey, on their way back from a pilgrimage to Mashhad, and had smuggled Decker into the cabin after the woman who ran the place had gone back to the office.

Daria strolled up to Mark, sat down next to him, and dipped the tips of her shoes into the gray sand. Their shoulders touched.

"Hey," she said, pretending not to be nervous. She'd been doing a lot of thinking on the drive down from the mountains, and she'd come to the conclusion that she needed to leave—the sooner the better. There were two reasons for that, neither of which she wanted to share with Mark.

"Hey."

Daria waited for Mark to say more. When he didn't, she said, "Listen, I'm thinking the intel Deck collected should be seen by Washington soon. All that talk of Natanz and Fordo…"

"Yeah. But we can't send the files from here."

Daria had figured Mark would say that. The Iranian government monitored Internet traffic and overseas telephone calls. It was too risky to try to transfer the information while they were still in Iran.

Mark added, "And we can't move Deck yet. In a day or two, maybe."

"Yeah, but I can be at the Azeri border in a couple hours. And I can cross it no problem with my Iranian passport."

Mark appeared to consider her proposition for a moment. "And I stay here with Deck?"

"You don't need me for the extraction." They'd talked about what he planned to do. He'd be fine without her. "And we should copy and split the files anyway, in case one of us gets caught."

Even though what she was saying made perfect sense, Daria knew she was being manipulative, which made her feel guilty.

Mark wiggled his bare toes in the sand. "OK. Just promise me you'll contact the Agency as soon as you cross." Without waiting for her to answer, he said he'd give her the number of Ted Kaufman, his former boss and the chief of the Agency's Central Eurasia Division, along with a letter code that would allow her to bypass the usual security barriers so that she'd be able to speak to him directly. "Give him a summary of what we found out and then send him the final voice recording ASAP. The photo files might take longer to transfer, but—what's wrong?"

Daria had let her head dip. She really didn't want to deceive Mark. Not after all they'd been through. But she worried that he was dead set on just giving the intel to his old buddies at Langley. For free. He talked a big game about being sick of the CIA and all, and making money off of people like Holtz, but she knew him better than that.

"Nothing. I'll call Kaufman."

"But?"

Daria chewed her lower lip, then looked at him and said, "But I told you back in Almaty I was trying to get intel on the Chinese. For the purpose of selling it."

"Oh, come on."

"I told you, Mark. I told you that's what I was doing."

That was reason one why she needed to leave now—so that she could sell the intel before Mark gave it away.

"I thought we were helping Decker."

"We were. But now…"

"Hey, if you're pissed at the Agency, then pass the intel to someone at State. I don't have great contacts with State, though."

"There's been a serious fracture in the Iranian leadership. Ayatollah Bayat, the head of the Guardian Council, was plotting behind Supreme Leader Khorasani's back and taking money from the Chinese. And now we think the Chinese might have killed Ayatollah Bayat. And the Bayat brothers were talking about moving stuff from known nuclear sites. How many billions does the US spend each year on intelligence? The intel we collected is worth a lot of money."

Mark just shook his head.

Daria didn't want things to end badly. She turned toward him, almost touching his cheek with her hand before pulling back. "Listen, I've got a project going on. Something I care a lot about. But I need to fund it. That's why I was spying on the Chinese in the first place."

"What project?"

"I…" Daria didn't want to tell him; she was afraid he might try to talk her out of what she was doing, and she didn't want to be talked out of it.

"I, what?"

"I'd rather not say."

Mark sighed. "Well, how much *funding* are we talking about?"

"A lot. As much as I can get." She thought about offering him a cut, but didn't think he'd respond well.

"Well, fuck it. I guess I don't care if you sell the intel. But I can tell you that under a million Kaufman can authorize immediately. More than that and you're talking about an approval process that could take days. And as soon as I get out I'll give it to him for free because something tells me there's a lot more going on than either of us know. So you're not going to have long to bargain."

Daria shrugged, but she was smiling inside.

Mark said, "Also, Washington is going to demand exclusivity."

"I'll offer exclusivity. But I won't honor it."

"Oh, that's a great plan."

He sounded more resigned than angry, she thought.

"I didn't think you'd like it. But it's the Great Game, remember? People have been killing each other over here for centuries. It doesn't really matter what either of us does. Since we can't shut it down, we might as well make some money off it."

"That doesn't sound like you talking."

Daria said, "It's not. Those are your words from eight months ago."

"I don't remember saying that."

"Well, I added the part about money. The rest was you."

"Huh. Who knew?"

They sat looking at the sea for a while. She enjoyed talking to Mark, and just being next to him. It reminded her of when they'd been together in Baku.

Stop it.

She had a sudden urge to ask him what he planned on doing with his life now that he'd been thrown out of Azerbaijan and had lost his job and his book. And whether she could help him, the way he had once helped her. To be there for him, in his hour of need.

Don't do this to yourself. He doesn't need, or want, your help. Because he doesn't—

Don't think it.

Because he doesn't love you.

That's what it came down to. The best thing she could do for Mark was to let him be. She'd realized that when they last parted. And she'd accepted it. But being together again...

She had to get out of here, she thought. Now. Before she made a fool out of herself.

"I should be going." She stood up.

"What...now?

"Yeah."

"Why don't we get something to eat first, talk about—"

"I'm not hungry."

Mark looked a little puzzled. "Hey, hold on. After you get to the border—"

"I'll call Kaufman."

Daria started walking away.

"Yeah, but how will I know you made it?"

She refused to turn back to look at him because she knew what her face would reveal. "When you talk to Kaufman on the other side," she called over her shoulder.

"How will you know that *I* made it?"

"Oh, you'll make it," said Daria. Of that she had no doubt.

68

Washington, DC

———————○———————

THE PRESIDENT SAT BEHIND HIS DESK IN THE OVAL OFFICE, listening to an audio file that had cost the US government $990,000—wired to an account in the Seychelles—to obtain. Seated before him, in wingback chairs, were the director of national intelligence, the secretary of defense, and Melissa Bates, the head of the CIA's Persia House. As the tape played, Bates translated the Farsi to English.

It was one o'clock in the afternoon. The attack was scheduled to start within the hour. The file they were listening to had been e-mailed to the CIA a half hour earlier.

Khorasani suspects something.

Why do you say this?

The intelligence ministry is investigating Hashemi.

Melissa Bates hit Pause and said, "Hashemi is a top general in the Revolutionary Guard. He controls security for the nuclear facility at Natanz, and the Mossad has had a plant in his office for over a year now." She started the tape again.

For what?

He purchased a new car. A Peugeot 405, and he paid in cash.

The fool.

He was told to wait to use the payments.

This is the problem with involving men like Hashemi.

But I had no choice. He was my only link to the Damascus katsa.

Bates said, "Here it gets complicated—a *katsa* is a Mossad operations officer, an Israeli spy. The one man the Mossad has in Damascus is legendary. He's been operating undercover for over ten years there and was also the point man for collecting Israeli intelligence coming out of Iran, including intelligence that was coming out of Hashemi's office. Bottom line, this appears to be evidence that the Iranians knew about the spy in Hashemi's office and were using her to feed intelligence to the Mossad's point man in Damascus."

"Did the intel about Khorasani's daughter and the Hezbollah connection come out of Hashemi's office?" asked the president.

"It did."

"So the Iranians were playing us. They uncovered the Mossad's spy in Hashemi's office, and rather than expose her they used her to feed us whatever intelligence they wanted."

Instead of answering, Melissa Bates started the recorder up again.

Can the payments be traced to you?

I never communicated with him directly.

Shirazi—

"Deputy minister of intelligence," interjected Melissa Bates. "And a top hard-liner."

—can stall the investigation until the Americans act.

I received word that matériel was moved from Natanz and Fordo yesterday. And I confirmed that Khorasani's daughter will remain hidden until she completes her religious studies. It will not matter how many spies the Americans and the Israelis send to Kish. They will learn nothing.

Khorasani will be in your debt.

Yes, but he must never—

The tape clicked off.

"We've long thought that Ayatollah Muhammad Bayat was the intellectual leader of the hard-line conservatives in Iran, and that he would welcome a confrontation with us," said Melissa

Bates. "If you listen closely to his sermons and read through the lines on some NSA intercepts, it's not hard to conclude that he thinks Iran needs better external enemies so that Iran's internal enemies can be silenced without fear of sparking a revolution. And he's well aware of the fact that nuclear power is pretty popular with all Iranians, even those who hate the regime. My guess is that he was hoping that an attack on the nuclear program would rally people around the flag and breathe new life into the regime."

"So he set about finding a way to provoke us," said the president.

"What I think we're learning right now is that Ayatollah Bayat and the Chinese teamed up to feed us false intelligence about Khorasani's daughter being raped by the Israelis, and about Khorasani taking his revenge by giving a nuclear weapon to Hezbollah. And that Khorasani himself is clueless about it all."

"You trust the source of these tapes?" asked the president.

"Not entirely," said Bates. "They come from a woman who left the Agency eight months ago, and it wasn't an amicable parting. But she claims, and we can confirm, that she's been working with one of our former station chiefs, a guy named Mark Sava—and we do trust him. Three days ago he survived an assassination attempt in Baku, so the two of them are knee-deep in something."

"You've spoken with Sava about the intel?"

"No. We haven't been able to contact him. Our understanding is that he's still in Iran. Apparently he gave her classified contact information for our Central Eurasian division chief, which is why we were able to get the intel so quickly. The other thing we can confirm is that one of the voices you just heard on that tape is without a doubt Ayatollah Bayat himself. He frequently delivers the Friday prayer service at Tehran University, so we know his voice. It's a perfect match."

The president considered the matter, but only for a moment. "Get me CENTCOM and the Israelis on the phone. We'll stand down. For now."

69
Two Days Later

M ARK AND DECKER SAILED OUT IN THE LATE AFTERNOON from an Iranian fishing town not far from the Azeri border. The boat was only a few meters long, with a single sail. A strong south wind was blowing.

Plenty of other boats were out on the water, eager to catch what fish they could before the predicted rain really started coming down. Most of them were motorized, though, especially the ones that ventured far out into the sea. At ten miles out, Mark's sail was an anomaly. But everyone would just think he was a crazy caviar poacher, he knew, driven by greed to take risks. And nobody bothered the poachers.

The wind had only started up in earnest a few hours earlier, not long enough to really whip the waves up into a frenzy, and they made good progress gliding over the relatively calm waters. Mark was at the stern, with the tiller in one hand and the mainsheet in the other. Decker sat on a damp cushion a few feet in front of him, wearing a baseball cap and a white dress shirt. He'd rolled the sleeves up on the shirt because it was several sizes too small for him.

When the land behind them disappeared from view, Mark changed his tack so that now they were sailing almost on a full run, doing six or seven knots, he estimated. With the wind at their back, everything became quiet except for the creak of the wooden mast as the boat yawed back and forth. The gray sail, stained over the years by spatters of grease and fish guts, appeared as one with the dark sky.

"Stop for dinner in Lenkoran?" said Decker.

Mark was still amazed at Decker's powers of recuperation. He was like one of those gag birthday candles whose flame kept relighting itself, no matter how many times you blew it out. The morning after Daria left, Mark had woken up to find Decker wrapping his ankle with long strips of ripped bedsheets. All the food in the cabin had been eaten. Decker had taken more antibiotics and painkillers on his own and had changed the dressing on his gunshot leg. After sleeping for another day, he'd been ready to move.

Mark knew that, to some extent, Decker had to be faking it—no one could bounce back that fast from that kind of abuse. But the fact that he was able to fake it at all was impressive.

"So is that a yes?" asked Decker. "Because I could use some food."

"No." Mark had called Orkhan just before setting sail and then throwing away his cell phone. In exchange for immediate safe passage from the coast to the US embassy in Baku, he'd agreed to give the Azeris a copy of Decker's surveillance files. And to continue Heydar's SAT tutoring via videoconference. For free. Mark had also tried to get his persona non grata status lifted as part of the exchange, but Orkhan had refused. After one day at the embassy, he'd need to leave again. "The Azeris are going to pick us up at sea before we get there." Mark pointed to a boat on the horizon that looked a little bigger than the rest. "I'm hoping that's our ride there."

"No kidding?" said Decker.

"No kidding."

"You're full of secrets, huh?" Decker let one of his swollen hands drag in the cool water and pretended not to wince as he adjusted his wounded leg. He was looking out toward the bow of the boat. After a couple of minutes, he said, "So you probably heard I had a thing for Daria."

"Oh?"

"She didn't tell you?"

Mark didn't feel like talking about it, so he lied. "No."

"We went to dinner a couple times in Ashgabat."

"Sounds fun."

"Thing is, every time, we'd wind up talking about you. About your surveillance techniques, your recruitment techniques, your damn book, your tomato plants, I mean, I'm not kidding—we'd go to dinner and they'd serve something with tomatoes in it and before long we're talking about your damn tomatoes—"

"The tomatoes are gone. Everything in Baku is gone."

Decker continued as though he hadn't heard Mark, "You know how my mom and dad met?" Without waiting for an answer, he said, "Through AA. They'd both already been through the twelve-step program, the whole works. So before they even started dating, they understood each other in a way other people couldn't."

Mark could guess where Decker was going with that. "Come on, Deck. Give it a rest."

"I'm just saying. You and Daria are the only two people I know who could spend so much time together and never really talk. You guys are wired to protect secrets. About yourselves, about other people, about everything. It comes naturally to you. Anyone outside the CIA would think you're freaks, but you two, if you ever did talk, might really understand each other. Just something to think about. So what happened to your tomato plants?"

Mark hadn't told Decker about the extent of the destruction. Mainly because he hadn't wanted Decker to feel bad about having initiated it.

"The e-mail you sent me was intercepted. So your Chinese Guoanbu buddies in Ashgabat arranged for someone to kill me. My place got completely trashed and I got tossed out of Azerbaijan. It was a disaster. I lost my job, my book, and my home all in the span of a few hours."

"Sorry about that."

"Me too."

"Hey, I tried to ditch Alty's iPhone after I sent the e-mail, but I fucked up. It was kind of a tight situation."

Mark thought about Alty's brother Nuriyev and all the pain that would result from Alty's death. "I'll bet."

"No hard feelings?" asked Deck.

"We're good."

A break in the clouds allowed a few slivers of sunlight to penetrate the dark sky. The light sparkled as it hit the blue water, and then a burst of wind stretched the sail taut, so that the water rushing off the bow bubbled like a fountain.

Mark began to think of all that had happened since leaving Baku, and how little he still knew about what had really been going on. The situation was too fluid, too layered, too complex. There were limits to what one washed-up spy—or for that matter, an old ayatollah or a Chinese Guoanbu chief, or even a supreme leader—could understand. Why kill yourself trying?

He exhaled deeply, and instead began to think again of Daria, and of what Decker had just said about her.

That was another situation that he'd thought was insurmountably complicated. But for a moment he allowed himself to consider the possibility that things had changed.

When he'd first met Daria, she'd been a young, naive idealist. And he'd been a cynical, burned-out spy. But since then, a leveling of sorts had taken place between them. The hunt for Decker had made that clear. So maybe now it was as simple as two people liking each other.

He began to wonder where she had gone, and what she was doing with all that money she'd undoubtedly made, and whether he'd even be able to find her if he tried.

The latter question was the only one he was able to answer with certainty.

Of course he'd be able to find her. It had taken him—what?— three days to find Decker? Finding Daria would be a piece of cake.

Epilogue
Bishkek, Kyrgyzstan

───────○───────

THE OLD WOMAN SHOOK HER HEAD AND CLUCKED WITH DIS-approval as she drew the long muslin curtains closed. They had been washed the previous month but had already grown dirty again from little hands tugging on them. She'd have to wash them again tomorrow.

Even with the curtains shut tight, the afternoon light filtered into the room, making strange patterns on the worn red carpet. Although the children were supposed to be sleeping, one little boy's eyes were open, staring at the patterns. The old woman gave him a look, and he quickly turned his head.

The children were all in identical pine toddler beds. One had a harelip, another the short neck and small ears of a Down syndrome child. The rest appeared normal. Because of a lice infestation the week before, the boys and girls alike all had their hair cut tight to their scalps.

The woman enjoyed the stillness for a moment, lulled by the sibilant rhythms of the children breathing. Until she heard the sound of gravel crunching under car wheels, that is.

She froze up, hoping it wasn't that government inspector from Bishkek who'd come by last month. She walked back to the curtains and pulled one open a few inches.

A black Volga idled in the driveway. The checkerboard symbol on the car marked it as one of the city's expensive official taxis, and she could see the silhouette of a single passenger in the backseat. *A single passenger*, she thought to herself, shaking her

285

head with disapproval at the extravagance of it, especially when there was a bus stop just down the road.

But the old woman's displeasure abated when she saw who stepped out of the taxi. The foreigner had dark hair and carried a briefcase in her right hand. Her green dress stood out next to the bright blue bench at the end of the driveway.

Every year there were new ones, thought the old woman. She didn't trust the do-gooders. She didn't believe in their ability to perform miracles. Still, she remembered liking this one more than the rest. Instead of saying what her organization was prepared to give, this foreigner had first asked what was needed.

What was needed? What was needed were parents! Someone to read a story to a child, to make him a favorite meal, to buy him a favorite toy. No one here had anything of his or her own. It wore on the children. Their minds didn't grow. They were starved for individual love.

The old woman recalled with some embarrassment how she had opened up to this foreigner, one of the few that actually spoke Kyrgyz. They'd talked just five days ago in the main room, with the children milling all around them.

The foreigner hadn't promised any miracles, and she'd made it clear that she was visiting many orphanages in the region. But with several children squirming on her lap, she'd asked questions. Would money to hire an assistant help? Legal help to speed the adoption process? Modern medicine wasn't a substitute for love, but did the children at least have access to adequate health care?

The old woman remembered how pretty the foreigner had been, despite the scarring on her face. Even the two-year-olds had fought to sit on her lap.

Daria, that was her name. The old woman was pleased with herself for remembering.

Just then, another official taxi appeared in the driveway. The old woman peered out with incredulity. Two in one day?

A man with tousled hair and a face peppered with stubble stepped out of the second taxi. He wore an ill-fitting suit. It only took the old woman about half a second to decide that she didn't like this new visitor. He was older than the woman in the green dress, and the cynical, dispassionate look in his eyes made her think of mean-spirited government inspectors.

So she was disappointed by the outrageous display of intimacy between them. Some women, she thought, turning away in disgust, just had lousy taste when it came to men.

Acknowledgments

———o———

I AM DEEPLY INDEBTED TO MY AGENT, RICHARD CURTIS, AND the team at Amazon Publishing—particularly Jacque Ben-Zekry and Andy Bartlett.

Christina Henry de Tessan deserves a special thank-you. The story would be incomplete, and in places incomprehensible, were it not for her efforts. She's an extraordinary editor.

I'm also grateful to David Mayland, my brother and friend, for pitching in as an editor, promoter, and lawyer; to Marine Corps aviator Captain Gavin Miranda, and other members of the US Armed Forces, for their time and expertise; to the people in Azerbaijan, Iran, and Turkmenistan who helped bring this story to life; to my uncle, Tim Gifford, who helped copy edit this book; and to my wife, Corinne, and my two children, for their support and love.

I would also like to thank the many reporters, scholars, and ex-CIA officers who, through their books, lent insight to this novel. An annotated bibliography can be found at DanMayland.com.

About the Author

Photograph by Corinne Mayland, 2012

DAN MAYLAND HAS BEEN detained by soldiers in Soviet Czechoslovakia, lived in France, explored Iran, Azerbaijan, Turkmenistan, and Kyrgyzstan, and gone mountaineering in Colombia and Bolivia. He is a graduate of Dartmouth College and has written articles for the Iranian.com. Mayland's first book, *The Colonel's Mistake*, was the inaugural novel of the Mark Sava series.